DARK ANGEL

DAVID KLASS

DARK ANGEL

FRANCES FOSTER BOOKS
Farrar, Straus and Giroux
New York

Distributed in Canada by Douglas & McIntyre Publishing Group
Printed in the United States of America
Designed by Barbara Grzeslo
First edition, 2005
10 9 8 7 6 5 4 3 2 1

www.fsgkidsbooks.com

Library of Congress Cataloging-in-Publication Data
Klass, David.
      Dark angel / David Klass.— 1st ed.
         p.   cm.
      Summary: When his older brother is released from prison, seventeen-year-old
Jeff's family secret is revealed, causing upheaval in his home, school, and love life.
      ISBN-13: 978-0-374-39950-4
      ISBN-10: 0-374-39950-6
      [1. Brothers—Fiction.   2. Ex-convicts—Fiction.   3. Secrets—Fiction.
4. High schools—Fiction.   5. Schools—Fiction.]   I. Title.

PZ7.K67813Dar 2005
[Fic]—dc22

                                                        2004053340

For Perri

DARK ANGEL

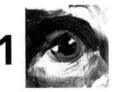

1

On a Saturday evening in late September, a pretty girl in a red bikini ran along the edge of the surf. Behind her, the Seaside Heights amusement pier jutted into the Atlantic. The roller coaster plummeted, and kids' high-pitched screams skittered wildly through the salty air. Joy and fear. We're scared and we love it. Stop! Keep going!

A purple sunset bridged sky and sea. The girl was tall and athletic, and she ran in smooth strides that ate up big bites of toasty sand. Her long brown hair trailed behind and seemed to float magically out over the line of surf. Beth was her name, and the good news was that she was running to me.

Yet even as I sat there watching her speed toward me, surrounded by my friends from school, with a radio thumping music and a cooler full of drinks planted in the sand, I knew that real trouble was also headed my way. It was racing toward me faster and faster, step by ominous step.

This would all fall apart. The bliss, the magical Indian summer, Beth, all of it. And not only couldn't I stop it, but I had to start it.

Soon. I had already waited too long.

I don't know if you've ever held a secret so powerful that it could make someone you love stop caring for you in the blink of an eye.

If you ever find yourself in possession of such a secret, you might be braver or more honest than I was. You might come right out with it at the first opportunity. Here it is. I think you have the right to know this. Now I've told you everything. Do you still love me?

But with all due respect, I don't think you'll act that nobly. I bet you'll do what I did: keep it to yourself in the safest hiding place there is—your own mind. Tuck it away for as long as possible and try to pretend it isn't there. Pull it out and examine it in the dark of night, when you're all alone, and then shove it back quickly.

The strange thing is that no one will be able to guess you own such a secret. Not your sharpest teacher. Not even your dearest friend. So you'll feed off the false hope that maybe if you just wait, the secret will vanish into the swirl of sand as the wind kicks up along the beach. Perhaps it will float off like driftwood with the night tide, or circle away like a knot of gulls into the purple sunset.

Don't be fooled. It won't disappear. Eventually it will catch up with you, and you'll have to confront it.

Near me, a bunch of my buddies played a violent game of sand soccer. The ball got half-buried in a dune. Smitty and Charley Hu, Junior Martinez and Kerry Vaughn kicked sand into each other's faces and pushed and elbowed and shouted. One player was better than the rest, faster and more skillful.

Tommy Fraser dug the ball out, dribbled around Charley, and blistered a shot through Smitty's legs.

Goal! Cheering. Whooping. Insults back and forth.

And then she was there. Breathing hard. "How come you're not playing?"

"I decided to sit this one out."

"Good," Beth said, "then you can go for a walk with me. It's a gorgeous sunset."

Normally I wouldn't need much convincing. She saw me hesitate. "What's wrong?"

"Nothing."

She looked down at me. Hands on hips. "Jeff?"

I stood up. "Okay. Let's go."

"You don't sound enthusiastic."

"Do you want me to turn a cartwheel?"

"Bet you couldn't," she said, and then she turned one of her own. I watched her spin, hands splayed wide in the sand, lithe legs whirling. Then she was standing again, smiling in triumph, hazel eyes flashing. "Your turn."

"Forget it. I can't compete with that. Anyway, guys don't turn cartwheels. We're not built for it."

"Chicken," she teased softly.

We started off across the sand toward the pier. Packs of kids still roamed the boardwalk, flirting and fighting and playing video games. Cotton candy and balloons. Arcade games of Ring Toss and Frogger, and pyramids of milk bottles that never completely toppled. Here on the beach, the air was tangy with salt. Beth took my hand.

5

A few minutes from now, when we walked back this way on our return trip, she would know. I couldn't *not* tell her about Troy and what was about to happen. Kids would be talking about it at school. It might even make the newspapers. Better she hear it from me.

"So come on, what's the big mystery?" she asked. "You've been acting weird all day. Make that all week."

"There's no mystery," I told her, which of course wasn't true. "I just don't feel comfortable talking about it when there are other people around."

"Talking about what? Jeff, there's nobody else here."

A tall guy jogged by, grooving to headphones. I nodded at him as he ran past. "Almost nobody." The wind had picked up, and waves crashed against the steep bank.

"Did you do something wrong?"

"No," I said too quickly.

"You did, didn't you?" Beth sounded a little gleeful. I guess I don't do enough things wrong.

"I said no!"

"Wow," she whispered, "this is really serious."

She nestled close, and I put my arm around her. We could hear music from the pier now. Springsteen from a boogie box, cranked to ten thousand decibels. Circus music from rides jingled merrily. On the end of the pier couples smooched. We could see them silhouetted by the sunset, pressed close.

The pier normally closes on Labor Day, but the rides and game booths had stayed open for a few extra weekends to milk a little bonus money out of the unseasonably warm weather. This was the final Saturday night. By Monday everything would be closed and shuttered. One last perfect summerlike evening on the Jersey shore. I held Beth tighter.

She was my first girlfriend. I had asked her out on the last day of school, and we had spent the summer together. It was the best thing that had ever happened to me in my entire life. Nothing even close. I would have done just about anything in the world not to tell her what I knew I had to. "Warm enough?" I asked.

"Yes. But curious. What's wrong?"

"Wait till we get off by ourselves."

"We could find a boat and row out to sea," Beth mocked gently. "Then there wouldn't be anyone around but fish, and they probably don't care about your secret."

"It's not my secret," I muttered, looking down. With each step our sneakers pressed twin prints into the sand.

"Then whose is it?"

"My family's."

That surprised her. "You mean you guys have a real family secret . . . like a mad aunt in the attic?"

"Worse."

"A mummy's curse?"

"Worse."

"Jeff, don't tease me. Your parents are the nicest people I've ever met. It's hard to believe they have a secret worse than a mummy's curse following them around."

"Yeah," I grunted. "But I think if you gave them the choice, they'd take the mummy any old day."

We reached the old amusement pier and walked beneath it. It was gloomy and noticeably cooler. There was a feeling of danger—anyone might be lurking down here. It was also a well-known make-out spot. Beth and I had been taking things one step at a time, getting to know each other slowly. I was surprised when she stopped walking, rested her back against a wooden support, and pulled me close. "Now we have a little privacy," she said. "We don't need to talk at all." She kissed me on the lips.

I kissed her back. She put her hands around my neck. Pressed her body against me. But it was the wrong time for this. I had to tell her tonight. Beth felt me tense up and pulled away. "Okay, full confession. What is it?" she asked. "Did you find someone cuter?"

"No, because there is no one," I told her.

"Right answer," she said. "Then what?"

I led her deeper under the pier, to where silver-black water splashed against the supports. Music filtered down from overhead. It was a cool, shadowy, and mysterious spot.

Beth looked at me. No one should have such pretty eyes. Sometimes I swear I can hear them speak in a soft, musical voice that has no need of words.

"I'm not hiding anything," I said back to her eyes.

She looked surprised. "I never said you were."

My hands fell to my side. "Enough," I said. "Here goes."

But before I could get the words out, she took my right hand and squeezed it. "Wait. Jeff. Listen, seriously. If you're so uncomfortable talking about this, you really don't have to. I mean, if it's a family secret and it's private, then maybe I shouldn't hear it."

"No, you should. I want you to know me. I want you to know my family."

"I already do. Your parents are great."

"There's more," I said.

"More what?"

"More family."

"What are you talking about."

"I have a brother."

She looked back at me, and I got the feeling that she might have laughed out loud, if something in the expression on my face hadn't convinced her that I was serious. So she said, "No you don't. I mean—I would know. Your parents would've talked about him. And there are no pictures of him in your house. I've seen your family photo albums."

"Yup, you have. And you're right, it's just like he doesn't exist. Like he's been wiped clean. Like he was put in a transporter and beamed out into space and the atoms of his body are floating through the galaxy." For a long moment we were both silent. "But he's rematerializing. His name's Troy. He's coming home."

"Home from where?"

"Far away."

"You mean he was in another country?"

"Further than that."

"Jeff, will you stop it. There's nothing farther than another country. Just tell me the truth."

So I held her loosely by the wrists, and looked right into her bright hazel eyes. "He's been pardoned," I told her.

"I don't understand."

"My brother's coming home from prison, which is a lot farther away than any foreign country. He's been doing hard time since he was sixteen—about five and a half years. He was tried and sentenced as an adult, but some court in New York just decided he should have been tried as a minor, and other things happened at his trial that shouldn't have happened. So they're letting him out. And he has nowhere else to go, so he's coming here."

She was silent for maybe ten seconds. "How long was his sentence, before they changed it?"

"Life."

"Life?"

"Life," I said again. "And now some court of appeals is setting him free. Poof. Just like that."

"Jeff, what did your brother do?" she asked. But those pretty hazel eyes were speaking much more truthfully in their language without words. "Tell me he didn't do anything awful," they were saying. "Tell me he didn't hurt anyone."

The wind made a whistling sound through the pier supports, and it sounded like breath being sucked in over sharp teeth. "He killed a kid," I told her. "A boy from our old school near Buffalo. Stabbed him in the stomach with a knife. The kid's name was Billy Shea, and he went into cardiac arrest on the way to the hospital."

Beth shivered. "It was an accident? Or self-defense?"

"No," I said. "He meant to do it. It was intentional, premeditated murder." I heard my voice getting louder, and the words tumbling out angrily, but I couldn't stop myself. "He'd gotten into lots of trouble before that—serious trouble—he was like a ticking time bomb. It was only a matter of time before he took a human life." And now I was way out of control, angry and loud, and Beth was looking at me a little scared. "And they should have made Troy pay for it," I told her. "An eye for an eye, a life for a life, that's the only fair way—but instead they're letting him go after less than six years. And he's coming here. Next week. To live with his family and start over again."

She looked back at me, unmoving, unblinking, and I understood exactly what those pretty hazel eyes were saying, so I held her tighter and whispered in her ear, "There isn't anything I can do about it. I'm his brother. My parents are his parents. We have to take him in."

2

*S*tar *Trek* to the contrary, space is not the final frontier." So said Mr. Tsuyuki, our advanced-biology teacher. He shot us one of his strange smiles that seemed to indicate we now all shared a secret, except that as usual no one had the slightest idea what he was talking about.

Mr. Tsuyuki is a genius. I don't use the term lightly, but he graduated from Columbia University with a degree in physics-philosophy, and he seems equally at home teaching biology, chemistry, or physics. I bet he could also teach math, and probably a lot of other subjects, too. He's rail-thin, with wire-rimmed glasses that are always slightly tilted. It's odd that a guy who can understand Einstein's Theory of Relativity can't figure out how to make his glasses sit on his nose correctly.

"Space is boring," Mr. Tsuyuki told us. "Way overrated. Space is old, cold, and lifeless. We can peer far into it, and we're not finding anything all that interesting. A black hole here, a dwarf star there, but nothing to make us want to build a space-ship, develop warp drive, and leave our own green, wonderful planet."

"What about walking on the moon?" Tom Fraser asked.

Fraser was the Golden Boy. He got good grades without trying, was the captain of our soccer team in his junior year, was our only All-League player, and looked like he belonged in a Nike commercial. He worked evenings at the Surfside Diner, and even though his family didn't have much money and lived in a converted mobile home out near the railroad tracks, Fraser somehow saved enough from his part-time job to dress well and to drive a really cool van.

We called him Franchise Fraser, because the only games our team won were the ones he scored two or three goals in. He was tall, with long black hair that hung down almost to his broad shoulders, and an infectious Irish sense of humor that went with a winning smile. Girls loved him, which concerned me a bit because Mr. Tsuyuki seated the class alphabetically, so Tommy Fraser sat next to Beth Doyle . . . my Beth.

Today Fraser was wearing black jeans and a tight blue T-shirt that showed off his biceps and triceps. Beth was wearing a short white skirt and a green halter top; her legs and arms were bare. Their desks were about ten inches apart, and I watched Mr. Tsuyuki through the gap between their shoulders.

"What was so great about walking on the moon?" Mr. Tsuyuki asked Fraser. "What did we find there? Moon dust. Can't be eaten. Can't be used. You wouldn't want to sprinkle it on your eggs." There were some laughs. "Or put it in your shoes to kill athlete's foot." More laughs. Besides being brilliant, Mr. Tsuyuki could be quite funny.

"Yeah," Franchise Fraser responded, "but we got there. Wasn't that a pretty good achievement?"

I saw Beth nod. Don't get me wrong—it's not that I was even a little bit nervous or jealous, but I was very happy that Tom Fraser had a steady girlfriend. Her name was Lisa Sullivan, and she was as pretty as he was handsome. Lisa and Tom had been a couple since the eighth grade, and they were perfect together. You could tell that next year they were going to be homecoming king and queen.

"In my humble opinion, the Apollo missions were pointless achievements," Mr. Tsuyuki said. "All that money, good Lord—it could have been spent on curing hunger and disease here on Earth. The exploration of space is a false step for us, a mistake born of our hubris." He paused for just a second, and his voice got a little serious, and even a bit sad. Maybe it was just my imagination, but it occurred to me that he might now be speaking about more than just the Apollo missions. He might be talking about himself, and how someone with such a brilliant mind and education ended up teaching science at a mediocre New Jersey public high school. "We must know our limits," he told us. "We were not meant to explore the stars. As a species, we're not up to it. We don't live long enough. We're not smart enough. We barely made it to the moon."

He shot a look at Junior Martinez, our class clown, notorious for sleeping through lectures. Junior had his head down on his desk, cradled in his arm. "Some of us barely make it to school on time, right, Mr. Martinez?"

Martinez stirred, nodded, and gave a loud yawn.

Mr. Tsuyuki waited for the laughter to die down. "Any other ideas what the last frontier might be? Smitty?"

Smitty was my best friend, a big, soft-spoken lug of a guy with an open, friendly face and striking rust-colored hair that his father, who was a deacon of the church and owned the big grocery in town, cut short for him. Smitty played goalie on our team and was warmhearted and good-natured, except that he was a pessimist. He helped out at the local marine animal refuge and subscribed to half a dozen nature magazines, and he worried about stuff that nobody else my age worried about.

Smitty knew that the rest of us found his opinions a little far-fetched. So even though he'd raised his hand, he hesitated that day, and Mr. Tsuyuki had to prod him. "Go ahead, Smitty."

"The final frontier is how we destroy ourselves by polluting our planet and using up all of our natural resources till the earth can't support human life anymore, so we commit mass suicide as a species, and the cockroaches take over the earth?" Smitty guessed. He said it in a perfectly reasonable tone, as if he was discussing whether it would rain tomorrow, and then he looked around quickly. "Why are you laughing?"

"It's only Monday, Smitty," Mr. Tsuyuki pointed out. "Try not to depress us too much. We have to get through the rest of the week."

"You don't think it could happen?"

"Cockroaches might take over our school's cafeteria, but I don't think they'll conquer the planet anytime soon." Mr. Tsuyuki paused for more laughs at his mention of our cafeteria's problem with humongous cockroaches, and he glanced around at us. "Anybody else? I'll give you a hint. The last frontier is not an event. It's a place, a thing, right here on Earth. Do any of you know what I'm talking about?"

There was a long silence. Nobody had a clue.

For a moment I flashed to a date. Saturday. This coming Saturday. My own last frontier. A definite day. A place—my house. A dreaded thing, crawling closer by every slow minute that ticked off our classroom's clock. The impending certainty of it was all around me as I sat there, trying not to think about it. A final frontier in my own life where the comfortable would end and the new and dangerous would begin. It seemed absurdly soon, perilously close. My parents had written the date on our kitchen calendar in big red hopeful letters. TROY'S HOMECOMING! In less than a week Troy would be getting out. Five nights from now he would be under my roof.

Beth broke the silence. She raised her hand and called out, "The oceans?" It was a smart guess because Mr. Tsuyuki had his own sailboat and spent most of his spare time out on the water. Beth was a straight-A student, and when she spoke in class she almost always came up with the right answer, but she didn't this time.

"A few flounder and fluke do not the final frontier make in my book," Mr. Tsuyuki told her. "Anybody else?"

His eyes swept the room. I felt them pause on me. The truth is I'm not great at English or history or most other subjects, but I've always liked science. Sometimes I think I could be one of the top science students at our high school if I tried a little harder. But it's better to coast along a little above average than to draw attention to yourself. I let his eyes pass over me.

Mr. Tsuyuki shook his head, sadly. "Okay, I'll tell you," he said. "Or even better, I'll show you." He opened a drawer behind his desk and took out what looked like several big, curved pieces of plastic. "Here," he said, "is the final frontier. See how neatly they fit together. Anybody know what these are?"

"The Eastern Seaboard?" Junior Martinez guessed, his voice sleepy as if he had just woken from a nap.

That shut Mr. Tsuyuki up for a moment. "What?"

"You know, the Eastern Seaboard. Like . . . Massachusetts, New York, New Jersey, Maryland . . . ?"

"How could the Eastern Seaboard be the final frontier?"

Martinez shrugged. "That's what those pieces of plastic look like to me."

Mr. Tsuyuki stared down at Martinez for a long moment. "It's not surprising that you don't recognize what these are, Mr. Martinez," he said. To the rest of us he explained, "What we have here is the final frontier, which we will be studying in our next unit. It's the most exciting frontier of all, the key to human behavior, consciousness, thought, and even perhaps to good and evil." His voice got a little softer, as if for dramatic effect. "It is the human brain. Cerebellum. Cerebral cortex. Brain stem. Thalamus. Hypothalamus."

The bell rang. As we got up, Junior Martinez muttered, "Still looks to me like the Eastern Seaboard."

Beth and I usually walk out together, but on this day she seemed to be in a hurry. She had already gathered up her books and taken several quick steps. I caught up with her by the door. "Hey," I said.

"Hey."

"What's the rush?"

She looked a little nervous. "Trig test from hell next period. I gotta look over some things."

"Don't sweat it. You'll ace it," I told her. And then, because I could see how nervous she looked, and that she was in a hurry to do a little last-minute cramming, "I'll see you after school."

Beth had already started to walk away. "Umm . . . sure . . . I guess . . . See you later," she mumbled.

"Yeah, good luck on the test. When in doubt, smudge. I'll come down to the orchestra room after soccer practice, same as usual."

"Bye, Jeff," she said. There was a tremor in her voice that I had never heard before.

3

We crested the hill and rounded the corner by Shore View Road, and suddenly we were in the stretch run toward the school soccer field. I could see Coach Wallace standing by the goalposts, watching us, stopwatch in hand.

The members of our soccer team were strung out over about a hundred yards, with Franchise Fraser, our fleet captain, in the lead, and big Smitty, our lumbering goalie, bringing up the rear.

I was near the front. Running easily. Arms pumping. Neck and neck with the two starting wingers. Charley Hu, the world's most serious guy and our team's starting left wing, was on one side of me. He was the top student in the senior class, the vice president of the Student Council, and he even ran with a serious look on his face, as if he was carefully pondering the exact moment to pick up one foot and the perfect spot to put down the next.

On my other side was Junior Martinez, our starting right winger and the clown who thought a human brain looked like the Eastern Seaboard. Junior was the exact opposite of

Charley—he was loose as a runaway goose—and he never seemed to worry about anything, including hurting other people's feelings. The world could be about to come to an end, and Junior would still be laughing.

He was our team's practical joker, and the favorite butt for Junior's jokes was Charley Hu. Junior had done everything from tying Charley's shoelaces together at the beginning of a soccer game so that Charley's first step when the whistle blew led to one of the great stumbling and falling acts of all time, to getting the combination to Charley's locker and substituting girls' red lace panties for Charley's Fruit of the Loom briefs.

I can still see Charley standing there, holding up the frilly red lace panties with a look of bewilderment on his face till Junior shouted out, "Hey, Charley, cute lingerie!"

And then Charley looked up and saw us all staring at him, and he shouted out, "Damn it, Martinez, that's not funny. Where are my undershorts?" The embarrassed look on his face, and the way he said "undershorts," was so comical that we cracked up laughing as Charley began chasing Junior around and around the locker room.

They were both good wingers, though, Charley and Junior, or at least they were better than me. I was the first sub—I went in for them when they got tired, which gave me about fifteen minutes' playing time per game. And now I was running between them as we came to the home stretch.

"Sayonara, Charley," Junior said, picking up the pace.

" 'Sayonara' is Japanese, moron. I'm Chinese," Charley

told him, gasping a bit but staying right with him. "And it's sayonara for you."

They were halfway between a jog and a sprint now, and even though they were both a little faster than me, I managed to keep up.

"Hey, Jeff, you got some extra energy today?" Martinez shouted. "Better save some of that for Beth. She was looking very foxy in study hall. And she was being very friendly with Franchise Fraser."

"Don't try to make him jealous, Martinez," Charley Hu grunted. "What do you know about having a pretty girlfriend?"

"I know you'll never get one, Hu."

"I'll get one before you will," Charley told him.

"How do you figure?"

"No girl wants to go out with a clown."

"Wrong again, Hu. The only reason I don't have a pretty girlfriend now is because I can't choose between them all."

"You can't choose because there aren't any to choose from."

"You don't have a clue, Hu." And Junior picked up the pace even more. "Sayonara."

Charley matched him stride for stride and shot back, "*Hasta la vista*, Martinez."

We were two hundred yards from the soccer field, and I could see the white net blowing around the back of the goal like a giant spiderweb and Coach Wallace standing in front of it, watching us sprint in, chewing on his red mustache like it was a stick of gum. I fell back a step, and then another step. I couldn't match this pace.

But the truth is, I didn't care. The truth is, I wasn't soccer crazy or incredibly competitive and dying to make the first string like some of the other subs. For me it was enough to be running with them, listening to their stupid banter, surrounded by my other teammates, just one of the pack, accepted by all, friends with many, jogging through ankle-high grass.

You see, I've known worse. And it came back to me as I ran, without warning. So that for a moment I wasn't in south Jersey anymore, surrounded by teammates.

I'm in a very different place.

I am twelve years old, in the corner of a snow-covered playground in a town just outside of Buffalo, on a freezing afternoon, and I am surrounded.

It's a ring of faces, elbows, knees—boys older, bigger, shouting, taunting, with a big kid named Mickey in the middle, facing me, fists clenched. "Come on, jerkoff," he says. "Come on."

"I don't want to fight you," I say, looking him in the eye, trying to hold my ground without pissing him off any more, which is a delicate balance to strike. "I don't want to fight anybody." I turn to the circle of faces. Many of them are faces I know. Even former friends. "I just wanna go home."

"You're not going anywhere," Mickey says, pushing me in the chest so hard I almost fall down.

My own arms come up in self-defense. With an effort, I keep my fingers from clenching into fists. Even at twelve I'm smart enough to know that a fight at this moment is a no-win proposition. But I also can't be a coward. So I say, "Just let me go." And I try to walk through the circle.

Hands grab me. Throw me back.

Mickey trips me. I go down hard. Cut my lip. Taste blood. Get back up quickly. And now my fingers are clenched into fists.

This delights the circle. There are whistles.

"You gonna fight me?" Mickey asks, loud enough for everyone to hear. "Maybe you're gonna try to kill me?"

Faces around the circle shout advice to Mickey.

"He's a killer. Like his brother."

"Runs in the family."

"Watch out, Mick."

"Yeah, but *he* doesn't have a knife."

"Just don't turn your back on him, Mick. *Go on, stomp him. Break his face!*"

"I hate what my brother did as much as any of you," I say. "Just let me go home. That's all I wanna do."

"No way, jerkoff. You can't duck this. Your brother ain't around anymore," Mickey tells me. "So you got to pay for what he did." Mickey swings. A whistling punch. It's a funny description, but punches do whistle toward you. And then they stop with a CRACK.

This punch breaks my nose. One clean shot. CRACK.

At the CRACK when the fist hits my face, there's a flash of light. Then I realize that I'm on the ground, on my back, and there's a roaring in my ears. The sickening, sweet taste and smell of my own blood is in my mouth, damp and thick and cottony. Mickey's on top of me, trying to rub my face in the snow. I can't get him off.

Voices float in, as if from far away:

"Kill him, Mick."

"*Yeah!* Bust him up good."

"Make him eat snow!"

"*Lookit him cry!*"

And I am eating snow, and crying, and the roaring in my ears is thunder, and the pain has come now, such intense pain that I am almost blacking out, and thank God someone else has come, it's the assistant principal of our school, a man named Mr. Olemeyer, who I never liked much, but now he's saving my life, wading through the circle, pushing kids out of the way.

"You are savages," he is saying. "Get out of my way." And he reaches me. Picks me up like a baby. Cradles me in his arms. I'm still crying.

And tears welled in my eyes five years later as I sprinted the final twenty yards through the brush grass to the soccer net where Coach Wallace waited, his stopwatch in his hand and a look of amazement on his face. Because I had somehow passed Junior Martinez. I had passed Charley Hu. I had run down three or four other guys. And as I raced in with tears on my cheeks I was two strides ahead of Franchise Fraser, and nobody ever beat Fraser in a race.

Nobody. Ever. He was the fastest distance runner in our whole school. Faster even than the cross-country guys. But I had just smoked him.

"Way to turn on the jets, Hastings," Coach Wallace shouted, and then, as I passed him and he saw my face closer, "Hey, you okay?"

"Yeah," I gasped, sinking down in the grass by the goal, "I'm fine, Coach."

Beth wasn't waiting for me in her usual spot outside the orchestra room. And she wasn't inside, either.

"She left practice early," Pam Spencer, Beth's best friend, told me. "She didn't look well."

That surprised me. Beth had looked fine in bio class. "What do you mean? Is she sick?"

"I don't know. Is she?" Pam studied my face. Hesitated. "Did you guys have a fight or something?"

"No. Why? Did she say we did?"

"She didn't say anything," Pam said. "She just didn't look well. You'd better call her."

So when I got home, I called her. The phone rang twice. Her dad finally answered. He's a serious man, and I'd always been just a little intimidated by him. He owned his own construction business, and while he'd always been perfectly nice to me, I got the feeling that he would be a bad man to have as an enemy. I could never figure out where such a hard man got such a sweet, sensitive daughter.

"Oh, hi, Mr. Doyle," I began. "This is Jeff. Is Beth—"

"Yes, she's in," he said, cutting me off. "But she can't come to the phone."

"Is she sick?" I asked.

"No," he said. "But she told her mother and me yesterday

about your conversation. About your brother. And how he's coming home to live with you."

I gripped the phone a little harder. "Yes, sir. I know you'd want me to tell her the truth."

"Oh, absolutely. And I know you'd like me to tell you the truth. So the truth is, we'll keep your little family secret to ourselves, but Beth's mother and I have decided that until we know more about the situation, you two shouldn't spend time together."

"Mr. Doyle, that's not fair. I didn't do anything wrong."

"Sometimes life isn't fair," he said. "But I'm sure you can appreciate that we don't want our Beth to be around a convicted murderer."

"I would never let anything happen to her," I began to say, and then he cut me off again.

"That makes two of us, Jeff. And I'm sorry to have to say this, but as for your not doing anything wrong, don't you think that you and your parents had a responsibility to tell my daughter about your brother when she was getting to know you? Then maybe we all wouldn't be facing such a situation now."

I didn't like his implication that my parents and I had done something wrong. "No one expected this to happen," I replied. "We handled things the best way we could."

"And Beth's mother and I are doing the same. This isn't easy for any of us." For a minute I thought I heard Beth's voice in the background, but I couldn't be sure. "Look, Jeff," her dad said, "you're a nice kid. I've got nothing against you. And Beth is very fond of you. But I've lived in this town all my life, and I care what people here think of me. And I care what people think of Beth. And I won't allow her to be in any situation where either her reputation or her very life is in danger. No way I'll stand for that. So you and she are just gonna have to cool it."

I took a few deep breaths. Tried to think. "And what does she think about all this?" I finally asked.

"She's pretty confused," he said. "She's made it plain to her mom and me how much she cares about you. But she also respects the wishes and wisdom of her parents. She knows we want what's best for her. And we don't want the two of you hanging out together anymore, at least till we see how this all shakes down. Got me?"

There was a long pause. "I hear what you're saying, Mr. Doyle."

"That's not what I'm asking, Jeff. Are you going to back off, or are we going to have a problem?"

And now I was gripping the phone receiver so hard I was probably leaving my fingerprints in it. "I respect you, sir, but you're not my father and you don't tell me how to behave. Beth and I are seventeen years old, and we can make some decisions for ourselves."

Mr. Doyle spoke quickly, his voice louder and his tone noticeably harsher. I could picture him on the other end of the line, a big man with enormous shoulders and thick arms, used to barking out orders to his construction crews. He didn't appreciate back talk. "You leave her alone," he commanded.

"Don't speak to her, don't spend time with her." I heard him draw in a breath, and then each word came out short and hard and angry. "Don't you dare cross me."

Then he hung up.

I put the phone down and stood there, remembering suddenly and with great clarity all the reasons, big and small, why my parents and I had sold our old house and moved four hundred miles from Buffalo to south Jersey.

It had started all over again.

4

My parents went to get Troy in our SUV. It was a Saturday and they left early in the morning. It would take them till about noon to make it to the prison, and I figured they would be home with Troy before nightfall.

I didn't go. I didn't need to make an excuse or offer an explanation—I just said that I wasn't going, and they didn't press me.

I figured I would see him soon enough.

From our front porch, I watched my parents walk across our front lawn toward our blue SUV. My mom was all decked out for the reunion in a yellow dress, pumps, and carefully applied makeup. I wondered if while she had been applying her eyeliner and lipstick, she had been conscious of the fact that she was on her way to a state penitentiary.

My poor mother. When she reached the SUV's door, she turned and waved to me once, and there was such tension in the simple gesture that I wanted to go give her a hug and beg her to stay here with me, and not subject herself to this ordeal. My mom is a tall woman, just an inch or two shorter than my dad.

She's had a problem with nervous tension over the past few years, and she's on medication to help her stay calm.

I could tell by looking at her eyes that she hadn't slept a wink the previous night. I wondered how many pills she had taken that morning.

Mom got into the SUV, and the first thing she did was take a map out of the glove compartment and unfold it. I used to think she followed maps to help my dad navigate, but I came to realize that driving makes her nervous, so she likes to have something in her hands, to distract her.

My dad doesn't need navigation help. He's an electrical engineer, a very quiet, methodical man, and if he doesn't know how to get to a place, he'll probably go online and print out the easiest route the night before making the trip. He was wearing a white shirt and a green sports jacket that he took off, folded, and placed on the backseat before getting into the SUV and carefully buckling his seat belt. I watched him adjust the rearview mirror, and wondered what memories were going through his mind.

My dad and Troy had never gotten along. My father can drive all day without breaking the speed limit even once. How could he begin to understand a son who had broken every rule there was to break since he had been in kindergarten, including, eventually, the most serious rule of them all? My dad is the sweetest, gentlest, most decent man I've ever met. I don't know if it comes from a faith in God, or a love of his fellow man, or if it's just the way he is, but he seems to live by a very selfless and simple moral code: he tries to do the right thing in any situation, and he is trusting of others, even complete strangers.

Once in a while someone takes advantage of him for this and makes him seem naïve or even stupid, but mostly people seem to repay his trust with warmth and respect. In the five years since we moved to New Jersey, my dad had made dozens of good friends.

I don't think Troy ever had a good friend in his entire life. The only law I ever saw him follow was the law of self-gain. If something seemed good for him, or exciting, he would do it, and damn the consequences. He was stealing from stores before he was ten, and getting into bloody fights on an almost weekly basis. I followed along four grades behind him in school, and I couldn't believe the number of enemies he had made. Boys his own age hated him, girls feared him and whispered about him, and even some of the nicest teachers stared at me when they read my last name off their attendance sheets. "Any relation to Troy Hastings?" they asked, and when I nodded, they looked at me darkly.

When Troy became a teenager his fights grew more serious, his brushes with the law more severe. And then, one dark winter night, he committed murder. He was tried, found guilty, and sent away for life. I thought we would never see him again.

But blood is blood. Part of my dad's moral code entailed taking responsibility. He had raised Troy and he was going to take responsibility for the result, no matter the consequences. He let the SUV warm up for a minute or two, and then he steered out the narrow driveway.

I had that day to myself. It was a day of waiting.

I thought of calling Beth, but she didn't have a phone in

her room, and I knew if I called her family number, her father wouldn't let me talk to her. He'd probably slam the phone down.

I thought of going for a run, or to the public dock for some fishing or crabbing, but for some reason I didn't feel like going outside. I guess I didn't want my friends and neighbors to see me. I didn't want to have to exchange polite conversation with people like Mr. Baines, who was raking leaves in his backyard.

"Oh, hello, Jeff, how are you on this fine day? And where did your parents drive off to so early?"

"I'm fine, thank you, and my parents went off to a New York State penitentiary to pick up my older brother, the murderer, and your tomato plants are looking very good."

No, I didn't want that. Nor did I want to look through the family photo albums, where pictures of my brother had miraculously reappeared in the past few weeks. I had thought that my mother had thrown them all out. But I guess she had just hidden them away, and now they were back, and I found myself flipping through the albums despite myself.

Troy's baby picture. My grandma used to say that every baby is a little angel of God, and there Troy was in diapers, balancing on my mother's knee, laughing, fat, and happy, lacking only a halo.

It was so strange to see him there, mixed in with pictures of my mother and father as a happy young couple. My father had a full head of hair and a mustache, and my mother looked so young and beautiful. There they were on vacation at a park near Niagara Falls, with three-year-old Troy posing proudly between them, a shovel in his hand and a sand castle visible in the background.

I hadn't yet made an appearance in the family albums—turning the pages, I was struck by the fact that Troy had been a member of our family before I had. He had known my parents before I had. They had lavished their full love on him for four years before I had entered the world.

A few pages later, there he was again at age six or seven, a Wiffle ball bat in his hands, already something intense and unnerving in his gray eyes.

How do little angels of God grow into terrors? At what moment does the change begin? How and when does the darkness take hold?

I snapped the album shut and put it back on the shelf.

Eleven-thirty.

My parents would be nearing the prison.

I tried to do some homework in our dining room, but my mind kept flashing back to the family meeting we had held there two weeks ago. Three of us around a table with four chairs.

"We can move the fold-out couch down to the basement," my dad suggested.

"No child of mine will sleep in the basement," my mom said. "He can have my studio." My mom has a small printing press set up in a back room of our house. She uses it to make her own Christmas cards and occasionally does small printing jobs for friends and neighbors. For a year after we moved to New Jersey she worked as a graphic artist, but as the year went on, she seemed drained of more and more energy, and deadlines and a boss who shouted at her gave her panic attacks, so that she finally decided to quit.

"You sure, Linda?"

"I haven't been able to get much work done anyway, lately."

"Okay, then," my dad said. Then he felt my glance and realized that I hadn't said anything yet. "What do you think, Jeff?"

I looked from one of them to the other. "What do I think?" I repeated. "I'm thinking you two have lost your minds. You must be deluding yourselves. I'm thinking you can't have forgotten who he is or what he did or how it nearly ruined all of our lives. We've moved on. Made a new start. We're sitting here in our new home in our new town. And now you're taking him back?"

"He may have changed," my mother began. "We have to give him a chance."

"Leopards don't change their spots," I muttered.

"He's not a leopard," she said. "He's your brother."

"I'd prefer a leopard."

"Jeff, we're a Christian family—" my father said.

"Yeah? Then what about 'Thou shalt not kill'?"

The skin around my father's eyes tightened, and when he spoke his voice came out so low it almost sounded fragile. "He made a mistake . . . when he was still a relatively young man . . . and he's paid for it . . ."

We were looking into each other's eyes. I thought I saw weakness and delusion, and I guess my dad thought he saw intransigence and selfishness. I heard my own voice get louder.

34

"No, he didn't make a mistake. Remember, the jury held that his crime was premeditated. Troy did exactly what he intended to do. *And he didn't pay for it. No way he paid for it. He got off—*"

My mom cut in quickly, playing peacemaker. "Jeff, I promise we won't let his coming home ruin our lives here."

I took several quick breaths. Tried to calm down. "How do you plan to stop that from happening?"

She must have thought about this before. She answered quickly, speaking words she no doubt hoped were true. "There's nothing for Troy in a little town like Pineville. He'll want to get on and start his life in a big city, where there are lots of opportunities. He just needs a place to get on his feet, and some warmth and family love . . . and then he'll move on, to New York or Philadelphia. You'll see, it will all work out for the best."

I looked at her, and then at my father. They were not stupid people. Could they really believe what they were saying? Was I wrong? Was I that hard-hearted or mean-spirited or selfish? Or was I right and could they not handle the truth?

My father's hands clasped tightly together on our oak table. "Jeff, I ask you to reconsider one thing you said. That Troy hasn't paid for what he did. I believe that's not true. Your brother has paid a steep price." The hands on the oak clenched tightly—I couldn't tell whether in prayer or in nervousness. "And when people spend years in penance, I believe they can and do change."

"Not Troy."

"Yes, Troy. He's not the way you remember him."

"How do you know?"

My father hesitated. "Because I've talked to him . . . and I've seen him with my own eyes."

This was news to me. My dad had never mentioned it. I watched him and waited.

"We've exchanged letters . . ." my father continued. "And we've talked on the phone. And in the last year I've visited your brother several times."

"In prison. You've gone there to see him?"

"Yes."

Family secrets. When they get revealed, they always zing you into silence for a few heartbeats. And if you've been left out, you feel a little betrayed, even if you've been left out for a good reason. So my dad had been to the prison, and had talked to Troy face-to-face. "Why didn't you tell me?" I asked.

"I'm telling you now," he said. "Your brother has had a lot of time to reflect. Twenty-four hours a day for more than five years. No matter what a person's done, it's no fun being locked up like an animal. But he hasn't let it break him." My father suddenly sounded almost proud. "He's read hundreds—probably thousands of books from the prison library. He got a high school equivalency diploma."

"I never said he wasn't smart."

"I've talked to the prison administrators, and to a psychologist who's worked with Troy. They all say he's been a good worker. He's become a skilled carpenter. He's got a clean record. He's been attending church. We've prayed together." My dad paused, and the two hands on the oak separated into tight fists

36

that gently pounded the tabletop every few seconds. "Jeff, he's flesh and blood to you. Let's give him a chance."

What could I answer to my father's soft voice, to his gentle gray eyes that pleaded with me to search my own soul and find kindness and generosity to match his own? "Okay," I finally said. "I'll try. But I want a lock on my door. Not a flimsy chain but a real lock." I saw the looks on their faces. We're not the kind of family that locks doors. "I'm sorry, and I'll try to trust him, but I need to know that I have my own space."

Now I sat at that same table, watching the seconds tick away, knowing that Troy was out of the prison gate by now, with my parents, rolling home in our blue SUV, probably sitting in the front seat next to my father as my mom sat in the back and fumbled with her maps.

Three o'clock came and went. Their trip home would take them near Manhattan. I imagined Troy staring out the window of the SUV at the skyscrapers, drinking in all the excitement, wealth, and power of the grandest city on earth after his long captivity. Maybe my mom was right—maybe he would just rest up here for a time, and then be drawn to a city as a moth flies to a bright light. Here in Pineville, afternoon shadows of trees began to lengthen across lawns and backyards. I felt myself tensing up minute by minute.

They would be on the parkway now, speeding south at sixty-five miles an hour, passing the turnoffs to the busy beach towns of Point Pleasant and Seaside Heights. That's all most people know about the Jersey shore—the parkway and the few exits that lead to the bridges over the Intracoastal Waterway to the long barrier islands with their famous boardwalks and beaches, immortalized by Bruce Springsteen.

I wandered to the back of the house and opened the door of what used to be my mom's studio. It was a small room that faced our backyard, in some ways the prettiest room in our house. Its two windows looked out on the pitted trunk and gnarled branches of an old crab apple tree whose ripe fruit swung from its branches in the afternoon breeze.

The welcome-home committee had done its job. Mom's printing press had been tucked away in a corner. Our spare fold-out couch had been moved in and converted into a bed, and made up with clean sheets and a blue woolen blanket identical to the one on my own bed. Freshly cut flowers from my mom's garden stood in a vase on a table. Next to the flowers my mother had put a brand-new, blank sketchbook and some pencils.

Above the table, a framed pencil sketch hung on the wall. I hadn't known that they had kept any of his artwork. It was a sketch of a raven, every detail of sharp beak and ebony feather rendered perfectly, except that the bird had human eyes. Troy's eyes. Perceptive and mocking—the sight of them in the pencil sketch triggered memories that made me shiver.

They would have turned off the parkway now, for the final stretch. They'd be rolling through the Pine Barrens that few people know much about, but that cover a quarter of New Jersey. They would soon reach the old bay towns that lie on the eastern edge of the Barrens, hamlets like Pineville and Forked

River and Waretown that were forgotten in the fifties and sixties when tourism boomed at the Jersey shore.

I always thought it wasn't just a coincidence that my parents had chosen such a quiet, out-of-the-way town. I suspected they had selected Pineville for the same reason that I almost never volunteer in science class, even when I know the answer. As a family we had been trying to run away, to hide from our own past, and thereby start a new future. The irony was that the person who had driven us into seclusion was speeding through the Pine Barrens toward our new town and the new lives that we had spent five years constructing to get out of the dark shadow of what he had done.

Had Troy really changed? Do bad people become good through penance and reflection? I sat there on a corner of the bed and watched the afternoon give way to evening, as the branches from the crab apple tree seemed to twist longer and longer in the fading light, and I couldn't help doubting it. I knew Troy. For years he was my big brother, my closest friend, my teacher. I had learned from him, and then, even as a young child, I had sensed that there was something wrong with him, something missing in him, and I had gradually turned against him. By the time he was arrested for murder, I had become very afraid of him.

Leopards don't change their spots. Crab apple trees don't suddenly grow cherries. Troy would never change.

The SUV pulled into our driveway at about five-thirty. I watched through the window as the three doors opened at almost the same second. My mom got out of the back. My dad got out of the driver's side. And a short, muscular young man got out of the passenger side and headed for the trunk. He hoisted up a big green duffel bag on his shoulder as if it didn't weigh anything at all, and then the three of them came up the path to our front door.

I left the house and waited for them on the front porch. Troy was wearing a New York Giants cap, the visor hiding his features as he climbed the steps. And then he reached the top step and he was looking right at me. It was amazing how much he had grown to look like my father. I resemble my mom, but Troy had my dad's thin, serious face, the same cleft chin, the same small mouth, the same sharp, intelligent gray eyes. He held out a hand. "Hey, brother."

I looked back at him, and a cold wave of such conflicting emotions washed over me that for a moment I was frozen in space and time. It was so strange to see him standing there, in our town, on our front porch, flanked by my parents, his gray eyes, which I remembered looking up to, now slightly lower than my own.

I didn't take his hand. For a moment I flashed to Beth— I had no desire to touch him with the hand I used to stroke her hair.

"Come on," he said. "I don't bite."

My mom and dad stood on either side of him, waiting for me to take his hand. I found myself reaching out slowly. He met me halfway. His fingers were strong and callused, his palm surprisingly warm. I heard myself saying, "Welcome home, Troy."

"Thank you, brother." His sharp eyes studied me. They had a mocking quality. "You've grown a bit."

"Yeah, well . . . it's been more than five years."

"Don't I know it," Troy said with a little laugh that was hard to read. "More than one thousand eight hundred days. And now I'm home again. Who would've thought?"

No one had an answer for that, so we walked inside our house, and ended up all standing in the living room. There was an awkward silence, which Troy soon broke. "Hey, hey, real nice place." His gaze roamed over the living room furniture, resting for a second on our couch, settling into our armchair, crossing the stone mantel above our fireplace with quick, silent steps, like a cat. "Tons of room."

Our house had never struck me as particularly large before. I found myself thinking that it must have seemed huge to Troy compared to a prison cell. I guess maybe my parents were thinking similar thoughts, because there was another awkward silence.

"And nice town," Troy went on. "Quiet. Lots of trees and lawns and stuff. Nice being so close to the water. First-rate."

I stepped forward. "As a matter of fact, it's a boring place," I told him. "Boring people. Not many jobs, even in summer. No place to go." I looked right into his gray eyes. "There's really nothing here for you, Troy."

He grinned, and that was when I saw that he was missing two upper teeth, and he had a thin scar across his right temple that disappeared into his hairline. "Is that right?"

"Yeah," I told him. "That's right."

41

"You have grown up a bit," he said.

"What's that supposed to mean?"

"Troy," my mother cut in, "why don't I show you where your room is?"

"Sure thing," he said. "I can't wait to get settled in. And then I would love that home-cooked dinner you promised me." He hoisted up his duffel bag on his shoulder and gave me a last long look. "Oh, and, little brother, to tell you the truth, boring sounds pretty good to me right now. After what I've been through, a place with some peace and quiet is what I crave above all else." The gray eyes sparkled. "To me this seems like paradise. I think I might just settle in for a nice long stay."

5

I saw right away that it wasn't a normal police car.

It was parked right in front of our school, and it had no identifying writing on it like *Pineville Police* or *State Police* or even *F. B. I.* The car was a gleaming new black Ford sedan with an impressive blue flasher instead of the usual red police flasher, and tinted windows so that I couldn't see inside. It was parked next to one of our town police cars. Normally I wouldn't have even noticed the two cars as I walked to school. But now I was on high alert.

Even though there were a million reasons why two police cars might be parked outside our school early on a Monday morning, I jumped to the worst conclusion. They were there because of Troy. Our town police had found out about him and they were warning our principal, who would no doubt call me in to question me and demand more information.

I had come to school early that Monday morning to ask my own questions. Beth's locker was on our school's second floor. I took up a position near her locker about fifteen minutes before she would arrive. I didn't want to look like I was staked out waiting for her, so I took occasional trips to the water fountain or peered out a nearby window.

On one trip to the window, I saw our white-haired principal, Dr. Baker, walk two men out the school's front door all the way to their cars. One of the men was broad-shouldered and in uniform, and even from this distance I had no trouble recognizing him as Carl Mayweather. He was the first African American police chief our town had ever had, and there were always articles about him in the local papers, most of them very positive. The other man was shorter and dressed in khaki pants, an open-necked white shirt, and a blue jacket. He was speaking and Principal Baker and Chief Mayweather were listening intently. They reached the police cars and the short man shook their hands, got into the black sedan, and drove away.

I didn't have time to worry about what information he might have been delivering because the corridor was filling up with kids. The trickle of early students soon became a river of hurrying teenagers, and as I watched them yawning into their hands, and opening and slamming their locker doors, and telling their friends about their weekends, I envied how normal and even boring their lives were. Their most serious problem was trying to stay awake on a Monday morning. I kept my eyes glued to locker number 223.

It was a green locker with a black dial. I knew that Scotch-taped to the inside of the door, along with photos of Beth's family and her cat, there were two pictures of me. One photograph caught me in mid-stride in a soccer game, looking intense as I sprinted for a loose ball. The other picture had been taken at the town pier on July the Fourth. In it, Beth and I were shoulder to shoulder and cheek to cheek, as fireworks exploded overhead.

Okay, hit the PAUSE button. Let me tell you about Beth.

I had had a crush on her ever since my family moved to Pineville when I was twelve years old. Literally the first day I arrived, I was walking to the corner to mail a letter, and I saw her ride by on her red ten-speed bike. She was wearing tan shorts and white sneakers, and as she pedaled, her legs flashed in the sun.

I didn't see her again till school started, when I found out her full name—Bethany Anne Caroline Doyle. I had never encountered anyone with four names before. For some reason I had trouble talking to her. I wasn't terribly shy with other girls, but I could barely find the words to say good morning to Beth. Just looking at her knocked the breath out of me, like a solid kick to the stomach, only in a pleasant way, if you can fathom such a thing.

For three years I admired her from afar. I found out where she lived. I learned that she was in the orchestra, and her instrument was the cello. We went to the same school and were in some of the same classes, we spent summers swimming at the same town beaches, and she even learned my name. In three years I think we exchanged less than a dozen words.

Fast forward to the last day of my sophomore year. It was a gorgeous spring afternoon—a dazzling preview of the summer to come. I decided to skip lunch in the crowded and smelly cafeteria, and I slipped out through a side door. Technically, we're not supposed to leave school without permission, but I figured on the last day, two periods before the final bell, nobody would mind. There's a grove of trees near the school, with some nice grassy patches. I took a few quick steps toward the trees when a stern voice from behind me demanded, "And just where do you think you're going, young man?"

I spun around, starting to babble a silly excuse. "Sorry, but I was feeling sick, so I . . ."

It wasn't a hall monitor or a teacher. It was Beth. Grinning at me. "You don't look sick," she observed.

"Very funny."

"It was kind of amusing," she said. "Were you sneaking off to catch some sun?"

"That was kind of my plan."

"Mine, too," she said. "Want company?"

A few minutes later we were lying in the spring grass side by side, on our backs. And we talked. For three years we hadn't had a conversation about anything, and in one fifty-minute period we talked about everything. Soccer. Orchestra. Families. Summer plans. You name it. We covered it.

We lay eight inches apart, and I could see her hazel eyes through a forest of green grass. They were sparkling eyes. Sometimes they looked up at the blue sky. But most of the time they stayed focused on me.

Then the fifty minutes were over. "We'd better get back for

last period," she said. We started walking back toward the school. Neither of us said anything till we were about thirty yards from the side door. "Well, I had a good time talking to you," she said. "Have a great summer."

"You too." I nodded. "I'll see you around."

Fifteen yards from the door. Ten. I took a breath. For some reason this was incredibly hard to do. "Beth? Would you like to go to a movie sometime?"

"Sure," she said. "That would be great." And then she seemed to realize something, and her face fell. "Oh, you mean go with you? Like on a date?"

"Forget it," I mumbled. "Have a great summer."

She burst into laughter. "I was just teasing, silly. I'd love to go see a movie with you. Here, Jeff. Call me." She took my hand in her own. It was the first time we had ever touched. Her fingers were soft and warm. She turned my palm over and wrote her phone number in blue pen on the back of my hand. "Just so you don't forget," she said.

"I'll never wash it again."

"Don't say that. I like guys who bathe regularly. Bye, Jeff. Don't wait too long to call me. Summers can be boring."

I called her the next day, and we went to a movie that very evening. The following day we went to the beach and hung out for hours. Two days after that we rode our bikes to Pine Point Park and went for a walk along the bluffs at sunset. There, among the shallow-rooted pitch pines that clung to the bay rocks, we held hands and kissed for the first time. She closed her eyes. I kept mine open. I remember how her lids lifted very slowly and she looked at me with a slight smile and whispered, "I think it's going to be a good summer."

And it was. The best of my life. We saw each other nearly every day. I got to know her friends. She hung out with my buddies. I listened to her play the cello. She came to the beach and watched endless games of sand soccer. When school started back up, it was great to have such a sweet girlfriend to see during the day and walk home with every afternoon.

Okay, hit the PLAY button.

Just before the homeroom bell was supposed to ring, I spotted her, about fifty feet down the corridor and walking fast, with her head down. She was wearing jeans with a patch on her right knee, and a white shirt with thin pink stripes, and she carried a small knapsack with her weekend books and homework in it. She lifted her head when she got near her locker, and when she spotted me her pace slowed.

Usually when Beth first sees me, she smiles. On this day I couldn't decipher the expression on her face, but it certainly wasn't unmitigated joy. I'd say it was closest to a kind of wariness. She looked nervous and unsure of herself, which is rare for Beth.

I waved and she gave a little wave back. "Hey," I said.

"Hi," she said back. Her eyes moved away from me, down to her fingers on the locker dial, moving it to the right, then the left, then the right again. Those hands that could produce magic on the cello had no trouble dialing the locker combination on the first shot, even when she was this nervous.

She opened her locker door and began rooting around inside it, while I stood there with my arms at my side. I felt I had to say something. I am the master of idiotic questions, and sure enough I came up with a real zinger. "So . . . did you have a good weekend?"

"No," she said quickly. "Of course not."

"Good," I told her. "I mean, I'm sorry you had a bad weekend, but I'm glad that you missed me. If that's what you mean—" I heard myself babbling and stopped talking in mid-sentence—I just shut off the flow of words like water from a garden hose. That's one of the most valuable things I've learned from being in a relationship—listen to yourself talk, and if necessary, just shut up.

Beth turned to look at me for a moment. She was wearing silver hoop earrings and they swung back and forth as she turned her head. "Jeff, I can't talk to you now."

"I didn't do anything wrong."

"I never said you did." She turned back to her open locker. The hallway was emptying out. There was nobody on either side of us. In a second the homeroom bell would ring. I watched her take a thick trig book out of her knapsack and transfer it to the top shelf of her locker.

"Math homework on weekends sucks, doesn't it?" I said.

"At least it gave me something to work on," she replied. "Please, I can't talk to you."

"I love you," I said. It was the first time I had ever said it. To anyone. In my whole life. I never would have thought I could come out with it in the middle of Pineville High, with dozens of kids all around. But there it was. Loud and clear. And nobody heard or stopped or reacted.

Except for Beth. Her right hand froze in the middle of moving books. She looked right at me, and her hazel eyes softened, and then she said my name, once, in a low voice that was between a whisper and a kiss. "Jeff."

I could feel tears in my eyes, and I wiped them off with my right hand. "Sorry, but I do."

Her own eyes weren't exactly dry at that point either. "You don't have to be sorry."

"I'm not really sorry," I assured her. My voice got a little stronger. "As a matter of fact, I'm not sorry about anything. Because I've done nothing wrong. I thought about it all weekend, and I have nothing to feel guilty about. The thing is . . . We have to work this out . . ."

KA-CLANG. KA-CLANG. The homeroom bell rang like a series of small brass bombs exploding overhead. Vibrations rattled down the row of metal lockers. We had one minute to get to homeroom or we would be marked late. "I'm really sorry, but I can't talk to you today," she said.

"Sure you can. We're in the middle of a conversation."

"No. The bell rang. We'll get detention."

"I don't care about detention."

She hesitated. "Jeff, I promised my father I wouldn't talk to you. Otherwise he wouldn't let me come to school."

"That's ridiculous. He *has* to let you come to school." I paused long enough to control my anger. "And I know you well enough to know that you're not afraid of your father. Or anybody else. You make your own rules. That's something I always liked about you." I stepped closer to her. "One of the many things." I put my hand on her shoulder. "Beth, what can I do?" I whispered. "What is it?"

I watched her eyes. I was seeing something in them that I had never seen before. "You're wrong," she whispered back. "I am afraid of somebody." Her hazel eyes seemed to tremble slightly. "I'm afraid of your brother. I'm afraid of what you told me he's done. I've never met anyone who's killed someone. And I don't know if I ever want to." She took a few breaths. "I can't talk about it now."

"Then let's talk after school."

"No," she said quickly. "My father's coming to pick me up."

"Here? He's coming to school to get you?"

She nodded. I couldn't tell whether she was angry, or embarrassed, or both at once. "He made me swear I wouldn't talk to you."

"How did he do that?"

"We got into a shouting fight. I've never had a fight like that with him before. It was awful." She broke off for a moment and took a couple of quick breaths. Now, watching her face, I believed her when she said she hadn't had such a terrific weekend. "Jeff, I really have to go. Look, I need some space for a while to work this out with my dad. Please, give me a little time. Goodbye." She turned away from me, and began hurrying to get to her homeroom before the late bell.

 **6**

Smitty came up to me as soon as I entered the cafeteria. He had already been through the food line, and his tray was loaded with enough meatless lasagna and apples and oranges for three people. Smitty was a vegetarian, but somehow he combined the food preferences of a giraffe with the appetite of a lion. He wasn't fat, he was just big—one of our team jokes was that he didn't need to play goalie; he could just stand in front of the goal and cover up the whole goal mouth. "Hey, Jeffsky," he said in his deep voice that sounded like it was coming out of a cave, "what's the prob between you and Bethsky?"

"No problem," I told him.

"I haven't seen you guys even talk to each other for like a week. You don't walk home together. What's going on?"

"Nothing. We're fine. Lay off."

"A word to the wise," he told me, keeping his voice down. "Before we join those other clowns." He nodded toward a far corner of the room where a few of our teammates had gathered around Junior Martinez. "Patch things up with her, pronto."

"Why? What are you talking about?"

Smitty hesitated. "Look, the last thing I wanna do is make

trouble between teammates. But I heard that Franchise Fraser broke up with Lisa last night."

That shook me. "No way," I said. "They've been going out for years."

"Yeah, well, not anymore. It's over. Which means he's a free man. And I think he has a thing for Beth. So your picking this time to quarrel with her might not be too smart. Of course, it's none of my business. Just thought I'd give a heads-up to my best buddy."

"Thanks for the tip," I muttered as we reached the circle of our teammates.

There were four of them, including Franchise Fraser, standing around Junior Martinez, who was holding something in his hand. "This will be the practical joke to end all practical jokes," Martinez promised, showing us a small tinfoil package.

They were all grinning. Junior was famous for his practical jokes. I watched Fraser standing completely at ease. He was at least two inches taller than the rest of us except for Smitty, but whereas Smitty was stocky, Fraser was lean and muscular. His jet black hair was thick and blow-dried—every strand looked perfectly in place.

"What do you have there?" Smitty asked.

"Keep your voices down," Martinez cautioned, looking around warily. "We gotta keep this top secret."

He needn't have worried. The bedlam of lunchtime in our cafeteria was revving up and would soon camouflage any actions and mask any conversation. All around us, kids were staking out tables for groups of their friends. The first people through the food line were already complaining about today's hot meal—the vegetarian lasagna. "It's not hot, and it doesn't look to me like lasagna," one girl griped as she passed me.

"I see spaghetti in it," her friend agreed. "What kind of lasagna is made with spaghetti?"

There was the rattle of trays and the clinking of silverware, and then the hip-hop that our Student Council had won the right to pump into the lunchroom began to pound through the overhead speakers.

As the music came on, Fraser's whole body began to move to the rhythm. He didn't look to me like a guy who had just broken up with his longtime girlfriend. He wasn't exactly mourning the relationship. Instead, he looked loose and happy and ready for new adventures. I told myself that he had the right to break up with his girlfriend, and to look happy and relaxed the next day. Surely he would never hit on my Beth. Fraser and I weren't exactly friends, but we were teammates. There is a code of honor unwritten but well known: "Hit not on thy teammate's girlfriend."

"Careful, Junior, if it's the kind of secret that could get you in trouble," Fraser cautioned him. "There've been cops at our school a lot lately. I don't know why they're poking around. Does anybody?"

Nobody did. Junior Martinez was unfazed. "This is just a harmless practical joke." He unwrapped the tinfoil and spilled two small bright blue pellets onto his palm. "Blue tracer dye," he told us. "Tasteless. Odorless. Completely harmless. Used in medical tests to track the progress of liquids through the body. I kind of borrowed them from my dad's pharmacy."

"What do they do to you?" Smitty asked.

"Nothing . . . really," Martinez replied in a way that let us know that they did something very serious to you indeed. "You swallow two of these, and for the next few days you'll look normal, and you'll feel absolutely fine. Except for one small thing."

"You'll turn blue?" Fraser guessed.

"No." Martinez closed his palm around the pellets. "But your urine will."

"No way," Smitty said. "You'll piss blue?"

"Bright blue." Martinez nodded. "And if you don't know why number one is coming out blue, as our friend Mr. Hu won't, can you imagine how it would freak you out? It's gonna be the best joke ever. Shhh. Here he comes."

Charley Hu walked into the lunchroom and headed into the food line. He looked serious as always.

I saw the guys whispering together, and knew they were planning how to carry out their practical joke. On a normal day I would have listened in. I might even have tried to talk them out of it, because a practical joke was one thing but slipping somebody pills from a pharmacy, even if the pills were harmless, sounded like a really bad idea.

But on this particular day I wasn't thinking very straight. I was watching Franchise Fraser as he nodded to Martinez, and then the two of them headed over to Charley, who had just emerged with lasagna and his usual container of milk on an orange plastic tray.

Charley sat by himself at a table near a window and took out a book to study. He opened his milk container and took a sip. Junior Martinez and Fraser sat down on either side of him. I watched Fraser strike up a conversation with Charley. Fraser made some kind of joke, gave his infectious laugh, and soon Charley was laughing, too. While Charley was looking at Fraser, Martinez deftly reached over and dropped the two blue dye pellets in Charley's milk container.

"He's gonna notice," Smitty said. "He'll notice the color. Or the taste."

"Yeah," I agreed. "He'll notice when he drinks."

But Charley didn't notice anything. He sat there joking with Fraser, nibbling on his lasagna, and washing the bites down with big gulps of milk from his container.

I felt sorry for him, but I also felt kind of fearful. Because if Tommy Fraser could set his teammate Charley Hu up for such a cruel practical joke without a moment's hesitation, would he even hesitate before going after my girlfriend?

Beth's desk in advanced bio was about four feet in front of mine, and a little to one side. She gave me a quick glance as we walked into class. I smiled back, and then sat down and tried not to stare at her.

At the front of the room, Mr. Tsuyuki appeared excited as he began to talk about the human brain. Normally I would have been interested because he works hard to make his lectures exciting and funny, but all I could do was try not to let Beth catch me glancing at her, try not to inhale the smell of her hair, try not to get jealous of Franchise Fraser, who seemed to be sitting closer to her than usual.

"The human brain is about the size of this Nerf ball," Mr. Tsuyuki began, holding a yellow sponge football up in his right hand. "Hopefully, your brains are a little bit more complex." He let his eyes run down the rows of desks, and people shifted and laughed nervously.

"If I were holding one of your brains in my hand, I could cup it easily in my palm." His fingers tightened around the Nerf ball. "It would be cream-colored—about this Nerf-like consistency. Squeezably soft." He squeezed the Nerf ball, and there were nervous giggles. "As you can see, Nerf balls and brains have a lot in common. But there is at least one important difference." He paused. "I don't think I could throw a spiral with one of your brains."

Fraser called out, "I don't think you could throw a spiral with a Nerf ball either, Mr. T."

More laughter. Mr. Tsuyuki looked pointedly at Fraser, accepting the challenge. Then he tossed the Nerf ball across the room, right at me. I won't say it was a tight spiral, but it was definitely a spiral. I caught it. Everyone clapped.

"Let that be a lesson to you—biology teachers can also play quarterback," Mr. Tsuyuki said. I tossed him the ball back, and he caught it with barely a bobble, transferred it to his right hand, and went on with his lecture. "A human brain weighs a little more than one kilogram, as much as a small melon," he said. "Your brain is constantly working. Sensing things. Picking up signals and hints and messages."

I glanced at Beth. Her right leg was so close to Tommy Fraser's left leg that their knees brushed. Or maybe not. Maybe there was a sliver of daylight in between.

"Right now, as you listen to me, and watch me, and think about what I'm saying, and feel the breeze from the window on your skin," Mr. Tsuyuki told us, "you are using different parts of your brain."

I don't know what part I was using, but I swear I could smell Beth's hair. It smelled sweet—she used a shampoo scented with lilac. The window was cracked open, and that lilac smell drifted across two rows of desks, mixed with the autumn smells of sodden earth and burning leaves from outside.

"The ancient Greeks observed that the brain was separated from the rest of the body, shielded by a formidable wall of skull." Mr. Tsuyuki rapped his knuckles against his forehead to make his point. "They assumed that a place so well protected must clearly be the home of the human soul. So they assigned the thinking and sensory functions that we now associate with the brain to other parts of the body. These days we know a little better..."

As he droned on about the brain, I glanced at Beth. She had her notebook open, and she was writing quickly and neatly. I looked down at my own notebook and realized I hadn't even opened it. I did so. Wrote the date. Smitty was right. A week had passed. She had asked me to give her space, so I had done that. I figured her father would chill out. She would come to me one morning with a big smile and things would be wonderful again. Every day I waited for a thaw, and every day she acted like the universe would come to an end if we had a conversation.

Tommy Fraser leaned over and whispered something in Beth's ear. His lips grazed strands of her hair. She tilted her head toward him, and seemed to be surprised by what he was saying, and then whispered something back. Was he telling her that the police had come to our school that morning? Was she telling him that she already knew all about Troy? Did other people know, too? Would there be a knock on our classroom door any second, and would I be yanked out for interrogation, leaving them alone together?

This was all Troy's fault. His return had caused my problems with Beth. But so far Troy had done nothing I could directly blame him for. He seemed a model of rehabilitation. He read in his room during the day. He borrowed my dad's fishing rod and went to the pier, but he never caught anything. He circled help-wanted ads in local papers. He went to church with us. And every night he ate dinner opposite me, smiling and for the most part keeping silent, but occasionally asking me the most innocent questions in the world about my life and school day.

I had to be polite, but I tried to give him as little information as possible. I locked my bedroom door behind me in the morning when I went off to school. I figured the less he knew, the less damage he could do. I was positive that it wouldn't be long before the snake would venture out of his hole. Troy was a time bomb, waiting to go off. And when he did explode, I was certain he would blow what remained of my happy life in Pineville sky-high.

I was starting to lose it. There was a humming sound that I couldn't get rid of. It was like a headache, except it wasn't just in my head. Even Mr. Tsuyuki, with all his knowledge of human anatomy, would have had a hard time pinpointing it. Maybe it was nervous tension, maybe it was jealousy. I felt it in the soles of my feet. I felt it in my fingertips.

I zoned out for a while. When I snapped back, everyone was laughing at a joke Mr. Tsuyuki had just made. When Beth laughed and her head moved, her little silver hoop earrings caught the light and seemed to dance.

"We're almost out of time," Mr. Tsuyuki said, "so let me ask you a few key questions to keep in mind, while we study your minds. Let's assume for a moment that your brains are not Nerf balls but highly complex machines. Those machines are composed of tissue and blood and, on a smaller level, cells and, on an even smaller level, atoms that all interact according to physical and chemical laws."

I glanced at the clock. Less than a minute left. In front of the room, Mr. Tsuyuki spoke faster.

"Can human thought in all its wonder and diversity, in all its beauty and ugliness, be reduced to purely chemical processes? If the brain can be controlled chemically, what does that say about the way we have traditionally viewed things like moral and immoral behavior, and emotions like love and hate, fear and jealousy?"

He was silent for a few seconds, trying to pull it all together. "So I guess what I'm asking you to keep in mind is: Were the Greeks entirely wrong? Where does our growing knowledge of the chemical nature of the brain leave us in terms of what I'll call, for lack of a better term, the human soul? When we think, are we really making choices or just following chemical pathways? If our behavior can be reduced to chemical reactions, can we hold people to blame for what they do, or don't do? Is there really such a thing as good and evil?"

He stopped talking and grinned, as the bell rang. "That should be enough to think about for one night."

As everybody got up, I remained seated for a few seconds. I saw Beth leave. She didn't look back at me, but to tell you the truth I wasn't thinking about her. I was thinking of Troy, in my house, in the room just beneath mine. Troy who had killed a kid. Troy who faced me every evening across the dinner table and smiled.

Mr. Tsuyuki had asked a good question, but he had left it too vague, too distant. Evil didn't just exist—it had taken up residence in our guest room, one floor beneath where I slept.

61

7

It was as if Troy had won the Nobel Prize.

My mother cooked a special steak dinner with mashed potatoes and asparagus, and she baked a chocolate cake for dessert. My father told the story in an excited, almost triumphant voice, his face glowing with pride. "We got down there just after Walt opened up, when the place wasn't too busy. He took us into his office in the basement, and said our timing was good—he's gonna need some extra help soon. He said it won't be anything too exciting—just bagging at the front and stacking in the stockroom. Said he couldn't pay more than minimum wage to start, but if that was okay, any son of mine was good enough for him."

"I knew we could count on Walter as a good friend," my mother said, half an asparagus spear quivering on her fork.

I sat there thinking that maybe we were the ones not to be counted on by our good friends. But I said nothing. This wasn't a dinner in my honor, after all.

"He sure is," my dad agreed. "Solid as a rock. I didn't feel right keeping back information from him. So I told him to just hold on for a minute, because it was more complicated than that. And I started telling him . . . what I felt he needed to know." My father paused. "Then Troy stopped me."

As if on cue, Troy cut in. "I was the one he was hiring, so I figured he should hear it from my mouth."

"And Troy didn't hold back," Dad proclaimed, as if not holding back was some kind of victory. "He gave Walt an earful. When it was over, Walt thought about it for a while. 'Twenty-one years in the business,' he finally said, 'and I've never been in a situation like this before. But he's your son, Frank, and you and Linda are good people. And I appreciate how he looks me in the eye and tells me the truth about himself. So, Troy, why don't you show up a week from Monday at 7 a.m. sharp, at the back door, and we'll get you started, son. It'll be hard work, but it'll be clean and I'll treat you fair. And we'll forget about what happened in the past, and start you off with a clean slate.' "

"That's all anybody could ask," my mom said. "Congratulations, Troy."

Troy gave her an aw-shucks look. "Thanks, but I mean, it's just bagging groceries."

"He opened a door for you," she told him. Then she looked at me. "Jeff, don't you want to congratulate your brother?"

Troy was watching me keenly from across the table.

"Sure," I said. "Way to go." Normally I wouldn't have had the nerve to say how I really felt. But the last couple of weeks in school had been so awful—from my conversation with Beth at her locker, to the chill between us and my increasing jealousy of Tommy Fraser—that my simmering anger suddenly bubbled up.

"But I'd like to know how his having a job right in the middle of our town, working for the father of my best friend, is going to affect the rest of us."

"Why . . . it won't affect us at all," my mom said. "Except maybe we'll get better service at the grocery now."

She was trying to joke her way through it, but I didn't even smile. "The thing is," I said, "I thought we agreed that Troy was only going to be staying here for a little while. Remember? We were going to give him a place to get on his feet, but then he'd push off and make a life for himself somewhere else. He wasn't going to screw things up for the rest of us. That was the deal, wasn't it?"

My parents looked stunned—as if I'd just said something terribly offensive, to ruin this celebratory dinner. Troy didn't say a word. He just went on eating. But as he chewed steak, I swear I saw a slight smile flicker for half a second at the corners of his mouth.

He has them, and he knows it, I thought to myself.

My mother only calls me by my full name when she's angry. "Jeffrey Hastings, I won't hear one family member speaking that way about another at my dinner table," she told me.

"Then maybe I should leave the table," I suggested. "I'm pretty much finished anyway."

"You haven't been excused," my dad said, and even though he spoke in his usual soft voice, he was unmistakably delivering a command. He paused, and there was a long and uncomfortable silence. "However hard it is, it's best if we all speak the truth," Dad finally said. "And there's some truth in what you said, Jeff. Ultimately it will be best for all of us, including Troy, if he builds his own life. I'm sure he would agree with that, too."

"Oh, absolutely," Troy said, dabbing up some gravy on a sourdough biscuit.

"But he has to start somewhere," my dad continued. "I'm not just talking about clothes and money. I'm talking about a first job. Establishing an employment history. References. Opening a bank account. A credit history. All of these things require a starting point. Do you see that?"

"I see a lot of things," I said. "I see that this is a small town. We have our lives here. That counts for something, too."

"Do you see," my mother asked, "that coming out of where he's come . . ."

"A state penitentiary." I supplied the exact words. Troy cocked an eyebrow and looked over at me. He was still chewing steak. A little blood from the steak spilled out from his lips, and he wiped it away with his napkin.

"Yes," my mother said, hearing the words but in some way not really hearing them; "do you see that, coming out of there, he needs another kind of a starting point, too? A sense of belonging—of people willing to trust him? And that's a starting point that only his family can give him."

"Jeff, I know this is a potentially awkward situation for you," my dad added.

"Everyone shops there," I said. "It's the biggest business in our town. And it's the gossip hub. All my soccer teammates hang out there 'cause Walt gives 'em free sodas and stuff. Everyone's going to know everything—"

"Walt promised a clean slate. He's gonna keep this to himself," my father said.

"Sure he will," I muttered.

Dad didn't appreciate my sarcasm. "You do him an injustice," he said sharply. "He's the kind of man who doesn't tell someone's private business to the world."

"How about to his own son?" I shot back. "Who just happens to be my best friend, and a member of my team." I took a few seconds and tried to calm down. "I'm not saying Troy shouldn't get a job, but why does it have to be there?"

Before Dad or Mom could answer, Troy swallowed a last bite of steak, and looked right at me. "If my own family doesn't believe in me, how can I believe in myself?" he asked in a low voice that seemed to tremble just a bit. And then, in a fragile near whisper, he added, "If my own brother doesn't believe in me, maybe I should just go find a hole to crawl in."

I wanted to say, "Maybe you should," but I figured I had said enough. I looked from his eyes to my mother's and then to my father's. Yes, he had them. Smart as they both were, experienced in the world as they both were, they were good people and they desperately wanted to believe in him. And I couldn't really blame them. My mother wanted the baby she had carried in her womb to turn out nice and normal and to be a source of joy rather than shame. My father wanted to believe that the young man who had grown up in his image, who shared his height and his weight and the very features of his face and shade of his gray eyes, would share his basic decency and morality.

"I wish you all the best," I told Troy. "And I'll do what I can to help."

"Thank you, brother," he said. "That's all I can ask for." And then he turned to my mother. "Ma, I'm so crammed, I hope I can finish a little piece of that cake you were kind enough to bake."

After dinner was done, I went to my room. Closed the door. Locked it. Turned on my stereo. I didn't want classical music tonight—it would make me think too much about Beth. So I put on some rock. Tried to concentrate on social studies homework. I read the same paragraph about the Constitutional Convention about a dozen times. But all I could hear was the rhythm of the music, the pounding of the drums, and they became an insistent knocking, and when I couldn't ignore it anymore I put down my pen, walked over, and opened the door.

"Didn't you hear me knocking?" Troy asked.

"I was listening to music."

"Yeah?" he said. "You shouldn't listen to it that loud. It can hurt your ears." He looked over me and past me, his gaze sweeping around my room. He checked out my stereo with several dozen CDs on a rack. My golf clubs. My telescope. The two antique maps on my wall, one of China and one of the Ottoman Empire. I swear I could see his eyes flick to my clothes closet and gauge the number of pants and shirts hanging there. He said, "That's a nice lock on your door. Looks new."

"Yes, it is."

"You always keep your door locked when you study?"

"Just when I feel like it." I was standing in the doorway, blocking his entry, and also his view of the far corner of the room where my desk sat, with a framed photo of Beth on it.

"Just when you're scared of something?"

"I like privacy."

"Not me," Troy said, and without even asking permission he stepped around me, into my room, and closed the door behind him so that we were both alone together inside. "I had enough of being shut in."

"I can imagine."

"No, I don't think you can," he said. "Now I like open doors. I like wide windows." He looked at the bank of windows that faced out at the backyard. A tree branch ran close to one of them, and it was possible to climb from that branch through my bedroom window. I saw him notice it with his quick eyes, as if making a checklist of all entrances and exits. Next he looked up through my skylight, at the moon and the stars. "I like sky. You got a nice room here, little brother."

"It's okay."

"I'm not going to hurt you," he said.

"I'm not afraid of you."

"Then you'd be a fool, and I never saw you that way." He walked over and peered through my antique brass telescope, which sits on a stand near the window. "How much did this cost?"

"I don't know. It was a Christmas present three years ago. Troy, I'm in the middle of some homework."

"Yeah, let me see what you're studying these days." He

walked over to my desk. But of course he wasn't really interested in my open textbook. Instead he took a good long look at what I didn't want him to look at. His eyes crawled over Beth's photograph. "She's pretty," he said.

"I don't want to talk about her with you."

"Dad said you have a nice girlfriend."

"We're not going to talk about her, Troy."

"Yes, brother Jeff, I can see that you're comfortably set up here. You've got it all working real sweet. I hear you're on the school soccer team, too. It's not a sport I know or care much about, but I might come and check out one of your games. Just to be brotherly."

I turned off my stereo. We faced each other in silence. "What do you want here, Troy?"

"To clear the air. Things were getting a little testy at dinner."

"I mean, what do you want in Pineville?"

"To bag groceries at the supermarket, and ease my way back into civilized society." The eyes mocked me. They jumped again to the photograph of Beth. "She's more than pretty. Frankly, she's hot. Did you ever—"

"Get the hell out of my room."

"I'd like to draw her. Do you think she would pose for me?"

I took a step toward him. "No, I don't. Right now, Beth's not even speaking to me because she heard about you, and what you did, and that you were coming to live with us. So that's what you've done to wreck my life so far."

69

Again he smiled with just the corners of his mouth. "No, that's what Beth did to you. But if it's any consolation, she couldn't have really cared about you very much if she let herself be scared away so easily. As for me, Jeff, I just want to get to know you again. I'd like to be friends. I think we could be great friends. We've had such different life experiences that I bet we have lots to teach each other."

He was still smiling, but his voice dropped a bit, and suddenly there was a dangerous look in his eyes that I remembered from years ago. "On the other hand, if you persist in making my life difficult here, I'll eventually have no choice but to fight back. And I'm tougher than you are, and I've always been smarter and meaner than you are, so if you're dumb enough to make this a war, it's going to be a war you're bound to lose in a big way. You might want to read Sun Tzu and Machiavelli and learn from them the stupidity and pointlessness of picking a fight with an enemy who's stronger than you are. Sleep on it, why don't ya. Sweet dreams, brother."

8

The warm weather gave way to a succession of cold and rainy October days, one danker and chillier than the next. Despite its bleak name, the Pine Barrens can be a cheerful place in the summer, green and vivid with life. But there comes a time every fall when the weather turns, and suddenly the endless miles of stunted pine trees with their jagged branches and bristly needles become a grim presence. They were in our backyard, on the way to school, rimming the soccer field—a crowd of darkly dressed onlookers watching everything I did, whispering in the wind, sharing ominous secrets.

Beth and I had two more brief conversations at school, but no matter how I started our talks, she always finished them by saying the same thing: she needed time to figure things out, so would I please just not push too hard. I could tell that she still cared for me but she was afraid, and her dad was laying down the law at home in no uncertain terms.

So, hard as it was for me, I backed off. As I gave Beth the space she asked for, Fraser moved in. Every time I turned around in school, he seemed to be walking with her down a hallway, or standing near her locker, telling her one of his silly jokes and smiling his infectious smile. I couldn't gauge her reaction except that she smiled and laughed, and I knew that Fraser's jokes weren't that funny.

I had a lot of trouble sleeping. I normally fall sound asleep the second my head hits the pillow, but suddenly I couldn't find the magic switch that would release me from daytime worries to nighttime oblivion. So I lay awake hour after hour, listening to the rain beating on the skylight and thinking about the source of all my frustration.

Troy's bedroom was directly beneath mine, and his words of warning echoed up through my sleepless hours. The more I thought about what he had said, the more I had to admit that he had been speaking the truth. If I tried to fight back against him, I would lose. He was older and tougher and had survived many battles in an infinitely more dangerous place.

I took *The Prince* and *The Art of War* out of the library and read them on those sleepless nights. Troy had been right: Machiavelli and Sun Tzu would have advised me not to take on a stronger enemy. In their own way, they were as cold as he was. They wrote about what worked, what was pragmatic, and most of all about how to win. They didn't seem to care at all about the innocent people who lost, or suffered pain, or whose lives were destroyed.

When I left the house I was careful to lock my door, but I had the strong feeling that Troy was spending time in my room. I couldn't prove it, but when I came home I felt his lingering presence. Books jumped from shelf to shelf. Drawers in my desk that I kept shut were left open a crack. And my photo of Beth seemed to dance around my desk, as if someone was picking it up in my absence and holding it to the light, and then putting it down in a slightly different spot.

It was a relief when Troy started work at the grocery. He put in long days right from the start, so I didn't see that much of him. Walt was testing him with a hellish work schedule. When I came down for breakfast at seven, Troy would be gone, and he wouldn't return home till after the rest of us had finished dinner. My mom would fix him some leftovers, which he ate in front of the TV set. Then, late, as I finished my homework, I would look out my window and see him standing on our tiny second-floor balcony, smoking a cigarette and looking out to sea.

He would stand very still, holding his cigarette loosely in his right hand. From that balcony there's a view of Barnegat Bay, and I could tell he was following the lights of the boats as he smoked. He would turn his head to watch them cross the inky black water as if imagining himself sailing away from this town, from this house, and from his new and tedious job.

Every so often he would raise his cigarette to his lips, tilt his head back slightly, and inhale as if drinking. From my side view I could see the tip of his cigarette glow red as he drew on it, and then white smoke would come curling out of his mouth and nostrils. I figured smoking that way was a habit he had picked up in prison, and I wondered what harsh memories his late-night cigarettes ignited. He never talked about his experiences during five years at a state penitentiary, but as I watched him stand motionless, I sensed that he had seen things and done things that had marked him as permanently as that long scar on his forehead.

As the cold dark days dragged by, there was one small bit of cruel but fascinating comic relief. Poor Charley Hu looked worse every day, his eyes red, his movements jerky and nervous. I guess the blue dye was passing through his body, and it clearly was scaring him.

What he didn't know was that word of the practical joke had spread through our school. Everyone seemed to be watching him in the cafeteria, and whispering about him as he sat alone doing his homework.

"He'll tell his parents," Smitty said. "Or he'll tell the school nurse."

"No way," Junior Martinez answered with a laugh. "He's too embarrassed. Have you ever seen Mr. and Mrs. Hu? Do you know how dignified and conservative they are? They would think Charley was nuts. And can you imagine him telling old Edmunds such a weird thing?" Our school nurse, Mrs. Edmunds, was seventy, and when she had to talk about sex in our health ed class she found ways to do it without directly mentioning any sexual organs or any recognizable sexual acts. "No," Junior said with a confident laugh, "Charley'll keep his lips zipped and hope his mysterious case of the 'blues' clears up by itself. When he looks like he's really going nuts, I'll tell him myself."

You could tell in soccer practice that Charley was off his game. We were getting ready for our big game against archrival Lakewood. As the game approached, Coach Wallace put us through longer and longer practices, and poor Charley was just a shadow of the aggressive and confident left winger we were used to seeing. He screwed up in ball control drills. He was hesitant in intrateam scrimmages. He was the first one into our locker room after laps, and he didn't even change clothes with the rest of us, as if there was something very private that he was ashamed of.

I kind of felt for him. I, too, was hiding something from my teammates and my friends at school. No one had found out about Troy. Beth and her parents had kept my secret to themselves, Walt had apparently been as good as his word, and not even the whisper of a rumor floated around our high school. Every day I expected someone to say, "Hey, I heard something about your brother?" or "Did you see today's paper? There's a story about your family." Every time a messenger came to the door of a classroom I was in, I expected to be summoned to the principal's office, where a panel of school officials and local law enforcement would grill me about the murderer in their midst.

I agonized over what, if anything, I should tell Smitty. We had been best friends for several years, and surely I owed it to him to let him know what was going on at his dad's store. But each time I resolved to tell him, I found a reason to avoid him at school, and when I couldn't avoid him I just plain chickened out. Smitty was a great guy, but he liked to talk. If I told him, the whole town would soon know about Troy. I finally decided that if Smitty's father knew the truth and didn't think it was necessary to tell him, it wasn't my responsibility.

Sun Tzu and Machiavelli would have agreed. I could almost hear their voices as I tossed and turned in bed. "Look after number one and let other people worry about themselves. Protect yourself, Jeff. Safeguard your own interests."

It sounded sensible, but in those long hours when I waited for dawn I wondered whether it wouldn't be better just to tell everyone the truth. He's my brother. He's a murderer. I keep my door locked. You'd better lock your own.

"No, Jeff," the voices whispered. "You haven't done anything wrong. Maybe Troy will fit in at the grocery. Maybe you're wrong about him. Maybe he'll stay out of trouble. This secret can destroy your life. Why wreck everything when there may, in fact, be no need?"

9

Our school orchestra played its fall concert on a cold and rainy Thursday night. I wasn't sure whether I should go, since Beth had asked me to give her space. But I figured the concert was open to the general public, so at eight o'clock I headed over to the school and joined the small crowd filing into our old gymnasium.

We sat on wooden bleachers, facing the basketball court, on which a band shell had been set up. There were fewer than a hundred people there, mostly the relatives of performers. They all seemed to know each other, a small community of classical music lovers. I sat by myself—it reminded me of when Beth had come to my soccer games to lend her support and express her affection, even though she didn't know or care anything about soccer.

When the orchestra first came out and took their seats, I followed Beth with my eyes. She was wearing a long blue skirt and a white blouse, and even from a distance of fifty feet she seemed to feel my glance and looked up into the stands. Our eyes met for a heartbeat and then she looked down quickly, and the music on her stand must have been fascinating because she didn't look at me again all night.

Her father, on the other hand, never stopped glancing at me. He was sitting two rows beneath me and twenty feet to my right, and if Beth could feel my eyes on her, I could feel her dad glowering in my direction. Mr. Doyle kept his thick arms crossed over his chest during the concert. The beautiful music apparently wasn't soothing to him, because he had a nervous habit of rubbing the points of his elbows into his cupped palms, as if grinding an invisible object to dust.

Beth looked beautiful, and there was something sensuous about the way she played. The post of the instrument rested against her cheek, while her knees gripped the round body of the cello like it was a live and wild thing that she needed to tame with pressure from her thighs. Her eyes were half-shut, and her whole body seemed to sway as her right hand drew the bow back and forth over the strings.

I closed my eyes and listened for the cello parts. Beth had once told me that the cello is the instrument whose tone most closely resembles human speech, and several times I fancied I could hear her speaking to me through her instrument. "I love you but why did you put me in this position?" the voice seemed to ask. "Jeff, it's not my fault what I do, it's your fault. And if I do something that hurts you, you can't blame me, but only yourself."

Thirty minutes after the concert started, as if answering some cue designed to torture me, Tommy Fraser entered the gym through a side door. He was a guy who was usually comfortable with his surroundings, but as he stood by himself on the side stairs, scanning the rows of bleachers for a familiar face, I could see that this was a world he didn't know at all. He spotted me and headed right over in my direction. "Hey," he said, plopping down next to me and slapping me on the back like I was his best friend. "How ya doin', Jeff?" He was dressed a little fancier than usual in a nice green flannel shirt, the sleeves rolled up above his elbows, and he smelled slightly of aftershave.

"Hey," I said back.

He put his feet up on the empty bleacher in front of him, and began tapping the toe of his right track shoe to a Haydn concerto. "Nice stuff," he said. "A little slow, though, huh? Needs some ba-ba-bam."

"I'll tell Haydn next time I see him," I promised.

"Who?"

A lady in front of us turned her head and shot us a disapproving look. Tommy lowered his voice to a whisper. "People here need to lighten up," he said.

We sat in silence, side by side, and I believe we were both watching the same brown hair sweeping back and forth as the same nimble hand guided a bow over cello strings. The music stopped speaking to me—perhaps Beth's cello was now addressing someone else.

Mr. Doyle seemed to think so. Perhaps it was just my imagination, but after Franchise Fraser arrived, the hostile glances that Beth's dad was throwing our way seemed to double. And once or twice I could have sworn Fraser looked right back at Mr. Doyle and met the big man's cold glare with an unblinking stare of his own.

Intermission finally arrived, and the orchestra members filed out.

"So," Franchise Fraser said to me. "What are you doing here, J-man?"

I looked him right in the eye. "Watching Beth," I said.

"You guys are still together, huh?"

"Why would you think we're not?"

" 'Cause I never see you together anymore," he said. "You're lucky. She's a nice girl. A real honey."

"Yes, she is," I agreed, and there was a warning in my voice that he couldn't have missed. "What brings you here? I didn't know you were a classical music fan."

"To me this is fancy elevator music." He gave me one of his patented grins. "We're thinking on the same wavelength, J-man. I came more for the scenery than the show. There's some real talent in the orchestra, if you catch my drift."

His drift was hard to miss, and I inhaled the scent of his aftershave. "What about Lisa?" I asked. "Isn't it going to take you some time to get over her?"

"Life goes on," he muttered, and anger crept into his voice. "You know who you can trust, J-man? Nobody, that's who. You gotta look out for number one."

I mulled that advice over, wondering who exactly he meant I shouldn't trust. Was he putting me on guard that even though we were teammates, all was fair in love and war? "You and Lisa were together for years," I finally said. "I always figured you'd be homecoming king and queen."

"That's all such garbage," he snorted.

"What is?"

"Those stupid school traditions from the Middle Ages. Like we're gonna marry the first person we go out with, and live happily ever after. Do you buy the first car you take for a test drive?"

"If you like it," I said.

"Well, I intend to test-drive a lot of cars," Franchise Fraser declared. "I'm a free man now. Lots of fish in the sea. You're only young once, you know. We're gonna look back at these years and wish we had taken more chances." Tommy stood up and looked around almost hungrily, as if checking to see if there were any fish he could reel in here and now. "How long is this intermission, anyway?"

"It says fifteen minutes in the program."

"Let's get some air." He headed out the gym through a side door, and I found myself following him, just like when he led laps for the soccer team. We reached a stairwell and he headed up instead of down. He climbed three flights and kicked open a door to the roof. I didn't ask him how he knew the door was open. Tommy Fraser knew things like that. He had probably come up on this roof to make out with Lisa.

The town of Pineville spread out beneath us, a patchwork of lawns and houses, many of them already dark for the evening. The lights of Jeb's Marina glinted off the water in the far distance. Fraser surprised me by taking out a joint and lighting it up. I had never seen him smoke even a cigarette before, and our school has a zero tolerance policy for drugs. Of course, I knew that a lot of kids smoked pot, and that there was a growing problem with Ecstasy and even methamphetamines, but drugs were always taken at private parties or behind closed doors. By smoking on school grounds, Tommy was taking a big risk. If they caught him, they would throw him out. He inhaled, held the smoke in his lungs, exhaled, and offered it to me.

"No, thanks."

"You're not into taking risks, J-man," he observed. "Except when it comes to your dating habits."

"What do you mean?" I asked.

He grinned. "Didn't you see old man Doyle giving the two of us dirty looks? Probably thought one of us was going to deflower his daughter during the intermission. What's he got against you?"

"He's just . . . protecting Beth," I said vaguely.

"From you?" Fraser laughed. "He should be dancing a jig that she's sweet on you. I mean, you're about the safest guy I know for a nice girl to be dating."

"Thanks," I muttered. "What does he have against you?"

"I worked for him one summer, pouring concrete. We didn't get along. The guy's a jerk, and just me being here tonight and watching his daughter play seemed to piss him off. If I were you, I'd be careful. He really looked like he wanted to wring one of our necks." And then he surprised me by asking, "So what's this about you having a brother?"

"What do you mean?"

"This goon bagging groceries at Walt's market said he was your bro. He didn't look anything like you. How could he be your brother and nobody's ever heard of him before?"

So there it was. Walt and Beth had kept my secret, but Troy was letting everyone know that we were brothers. Once that was public knowledge, the rest would no doubt follow.

"You'd better ask him," I said.

"I did," Franchise Fraser revealed.

"What did he say?"

"Told me to mind my own business. Seemed like a true asshole. So who is he and what's he doing here?"

I hesitated. "He was right. You should mind your own business."

Fraser laughed. "Okay, chill," he said. "But I sure wouldn't want him for a brother." He took another long toke from the joint and we stood looking down at Pineville. "Look at this one-horse burg. Lights going off and it's not even ten o'clock," he said. "How can a shore town have nothing going on? You ever think about how small and boring and stupid this place is?"

"I like it here," I said. "I'm surprised you don't."

"Why is that?"

"Well . . . you're kind of what this town is all about." I heard jealousy and bitterness in my own voice as I said, "Captain of the soccer and baseball teams, most popular guy in the school . . . You're 'Franchise' Fraser."

"Thanks, J-man," he said softly, as if I had just paid him a compliment that moved him. "But the only good thing about a town like this is that eventually you leave it behind." He flicked away the joint and glanced at a watch. "I gotta go work the late shift flipping burgers. You go back and watch your honey." The way he said it sounded a bit sarcastic—like he knew we were no longer together, but he was willing to humor me. He paused and gave me a long, strange look. "Jeff, you're a nice guy. Whatever happens, I want you to think of me in a good way. Okay?"

Now at least we were talking about Beth right out in the open. "No way I can promise that," I told him. "I may be a nice guy, but there are some things I won't ever forgive."

"And I can't blame you for it." He glanced at his watch again, and then he was moving for the stairs at a good clip. "Bye, J-man. Enjoy the rest of the concert. Give your little honey a big hello from me." And he disappeared down the stairs into darkness.

10

It happened at ten minutes after the stroke of noon, without warning. I was there to see it, sitting at one of the tables in our cafeteria with Smitty and Franchise Fraser and a couple of other guys from the soccer team. Poor Charley Hu wasn't sitting with us. He chose to sit all alone in a corner, in some kind of self-imposed quarantine. He looked about as stressed out as a guy can be without spontaneously combusting.

I could guess what the redness in the corners of his eyes meant from my own recent struggle with insomnia—Charley Hu hadn't had a good night's sleep in weeks. Halfway through his lunch, poor Charley dropped a can of soda onto the floor. I figured he dropped it because his hand was shaking. He bent down to pick it up and knocked his plate off the table. A few people turned to look at him. He just sat there, taking deep breaths.

"Okay," Junior Martinez told us. "This joke's gone far enough. It's time to be merciful."

"You're gonna tell him?" Fraser asked.

"When the moment is right. Check it out." Martinez circled the big cafeteria, stopping at most of the tables, and I guessed that he was priming the audience for the grand finale of his big joke. It was soon clear that most of the people in the cafeteria were in on it, and were watching him to see what would happen.

Junior chose his moment, waved to everyone, and approached Charley from behind, with a big grin on his face. He tapped Charley on the shoulder. Charley slowly turned to face him. "What?" Charley demanded in an edgy tone, as if angry that his solitude had been disturbed. And then, louder, *"What do you want?"*

Junior spoke in a loud voice, so that everyone in the cafeteria could hear. "CHARLEY HU, DO YOU PISS BLUE?"

Charley's face registered incomprehensible shock, as if his deepest secret had just been flashed out on TV. All around the cafeteria, kids burst into laughter. I have to admit I laughed along with them. It was hilarious to see Charley's face begin to register that he had been set up, and that everyone was in on the joke.

Then everyone stopped laughing because Charley snapped.

Junior Martinez was ready to dodge out of the way, but he never had a chance. Charley Hu didn't so much run after him as fly after him. In a flash he knocked Junior down and was on top of him, punching and kicking him. Junior covered up and rocked from side to side, howling. I initially thought Junior might be laughing, till I walked closer and realized that he was screaming, because Charley had a plastic cafeteria knife in his hand and was jabbing him with it again and again.

Luckily for Junior, the plastic knife wasn't very sharp. It soon broke apart and didn't do much serious damage. But by the time Mr. Morrison, our big American studies teacher who also coached JV wrestling, managed to pull Charley off, Junior was bleeding in several different places. As Mr. Morrison and three other teachers dragged Charley out of the cafeteria, he was still in a mad rage, shouting curses at Junior and trying to get at him.

I was heading to study hall, twenty minutes later, when an ambulance arrived. We gathered by a window and watched as Junior was helped into the ambulance, which sped away with its siren and flasher on, even though I was pretty sure Junior hadn't been seriously hurt.

My study hall buzzed with conversations about the fight. No one could believe that a model student like Charley had completely flipped out. Many of us had been in on the joke, so we all felt a little guilty, and we were curious to see if Charley would be punished.

Beth and I were the first two students in bio class that day. She looked unusually tense—I hoped it wasn't just being alone for a few seconds in a classroom with me that made her look that way. "Hey," I said.

She nodded and sat, and started taking out her notebook and pens.

"You hear about the fight?" I asked, trying to break the ice with a little chitchat. "I was there. It was just a stupid practical joke that got out of control. I never expected Charley to wig out like that."

Beth nodded and fussed with her pens, shuffling them around her desk like it was a matter of tremendous importance whether the blue or black one was closer to her right hand.

I walked over and stood next to her desk. "Beth? Are you just going to nod and move your pens around? I mean, if you're not going to talk to me ever again, maybe we could communicate in Morse code."

She looked up at me. Her hazel eyes had never looked prettier or more scared. "Last time we talked, by my locker . . . my dad found out."

"How? Found out what? We didn't do anything wrong. We just talked."

Beth lowered her voice to a whisper. "He's threatening to send me away."

"Away where? What are you talking about?"

But she shook her head and looked quickly down at her notebook as two or three kids walked into the room. I guess she didn't know who was supplying information to her father, and she wasn't inclined to take risks.

I studied Beth's back as the classroom filled up, watching how tense she was and how she didn't say much to anyone, even to her friends. How could her father send her away without her agreeing to it? Or was she so freaked out about Troy that she would willingly leave her friends and her life here behind? Or was there something else going on?

Mr. Tsuyuki closed the door and looked out at us for a few seconds. His glasses were tilted to the right on his nose, and when he adjusted them, they seemed to tilt slightly to the left.

He kept his hands flat at his sides, and there was something subdued in his expression. He said quietly, "Today we're going to talk about crime and punishment." He was a meticulous man who made his lesson plans months ahead of time, so I figured it was a coincidence he had chosen this topic on the day Charley and Junior had their big fight. His eyes swept the room; they seemed to linger for a second on Junior's empty chair.

Junior had been a lousy bio student. His main class contribution had been poking fun at Mr. Tsuyuki, who had teased him right back, always calling him Mr. Martinez, with exaggerated respect. I was never sure if Mr. Tsuyuki enjoyed the banter, or if he just went along with it. Now I watched Mr. Tsuyuki's eyes move from Junior's empty chair to study the rest of us. "Let's start with a basic question," he said. "Is there such a thing as evil?"

Nobody raised his hand. We were all used to Mr. Tsuyuki's trick questions. After a few seconds he gave up waiting. "Let me be more specific. Do you believe that people can be evil?"

"Child molesters," a girl called out.

"Serial killers," a boy ventured.

"Two extreme examples." Mr. Tsuyuki nodded. "What about two million evil people? That's the number in our prison system. Two million people locked up, spending years at taxpayer expense eating and sleeping and supposedly rehabilitating but also paying for their evil deeds."

I thought about Troy and how my dad said he had paid at least part of his debt. More than five years—one thousand eight hundred days, a lot of it in a maximum-security prison. He had been in his teens when he went in. Had he been beaten? Had he been raped? Had he killed again inside? He must have witnessed and taken part in cruelties that I couldn't even imagine—

Mr. Tsuyuki's voice broke my chain of thought. He was probing and asking questions, linking point to point in a logical chain to lead us where he wanted us to go. "When we find someone guilty of a crime and lock him up, what are we really saying about them?" he asked.

"They broke the law and need to be punished," Pam Spencer guessed.

"Dig deeper," Mr. Tsuyuki prodded. "Suppose a toddler carries a toy out of a store without paying for it. Do we lock him up?"

"No," Beth said. "Because a little kid doesn't know he's breaking a law. He just wants a toy."

"Ignorance of the law is no excuse," Mr. Tsuyuki said.

"Yes, but an infant doesn't know he's doing something wrong," Beth tried again. "It's not like he's choosing to steal something. He's just a kid who wants a toy."

"Bingo!" Mr. Tsuyuki exulted. "He isn't competent to choose. So when we lock up those two million people, we're not only saying they did something wrong but saying that they were competent to choose a good way or an evil way, and they chose the evil way. Do you all agree with that?"

We nodded warily, not knowing where he was going.

"The ability to make a free and competent choice is at the

very heart of our legal system. It's also at the heart of our democratic system. Each citizen gets one vote, and the freedom to make up his own mind. And it's at the heart of Western religion. When God told Moses 'Thou shalt not kill,' what was he really saying?"

I almost never volunteer in class, but that day my arm shot up. For a second I flashed to Billy Shea bleeding to death on the curb of a parking lot, pleading with the kids who found him not to let him die. My tone got sharper, as it always did when I spoke about Troy and what suffering he had inflicted. "You have a choice and you must choose not to kill," I said. "And if you choose wrong, then you have to pay the price, to God and to man."

Something about my tone caught people's attention. Everyone in the class suddenly seemed to be looking at me except Beth, who stared down at her notebook.

"Good," Mr. Tsuyuki said. "And whether the price is an eternity in hell or years in jail, it's all based on the idea that you could have acted differently, but because of some evil in you, you did the Thou Shalt Not, instead of the Thou Shalt." He headed back to the front of the room, and I knew that he had led us to the desired place. "Now," he asked, picking up a stack of printouts, "what does this have to do with science class and the human brain?"

He handed us each a reading list. "There are a lot of articles here by people who aren't so sure you actually have a choice. They're not sure those two million people sitting in

American jail cells had a choice. And they just happen to be some of our most brilliant scientists, including a Nobel laureate."

He finished handing out the packets and put his hands in his pockets. "What they believe," he said, "is that people who appear to us to be evil are really just broken."

"Bleeding-heart liberals," Franchise Fraser grunted. "Everybody's a victim."

"But suppose just for one moment that everybody is a victim," Mr. Tsuyuki said softly but very seriously. "Suppose you're on a jury and the defense lawyer flashes up an image of the defendant's brain and can pinpoint the exact structural reason why he or she committed that crime. Why, in fact, they had to break the law."

"Then they're innocent but insane," Beth said.

"Suppose they're just as sane as you are," Mr. Tsuyuki shot back. "Maybe it's just that a very specific part of their brain is broken. And suppose we can fix that part of their brain. Should we still lock them up?"

Nobody said anything.

"There are psychiatrists and neurologists doing studies on violent lawbreakers, from juvenile delinquents to adult murderers, who are finding that these felons share amazingly similar patterns of abusive childhoods, brain injuries, and psychotic symptoms. If you can show that a very specific combination of genetics, environment, and brain damage will make someone violent, are people who are unlucky enough to possess that combination evil, or are they really victims?"

Again the class was silent. Evil, I thought to myself. Nothing can excuse violent cruelty. Evil does exist, and I had seen it up close, and the only thing to do is to lock it away.

Mr. Tsuyuki was winding up. "Several states have approved chemical castration for sexual offenders. They're given injections that reduce testosterone levels, which reduce sex drives. In the next ten years there'll be hundreds if not thousands of new psychiatric designer drugs that will allow us to treat many different behavioral problems right at the source. Suppose we can stop someone from stealing by giving him a drug. Suppose we can stop a serial killer from killing by giving him a shot every two weeks. Doesn't that mean they weren't evil in the first place, just lacking something on a chemical level?"

Mr. Tsuyuki thumped the packet. "I've included an excerpt from a book by Dr. Francis Crick, who won a Nobel Prize for co-discovering the double helix. In Dr. Crick's book *The Astonishing Hypothesis*, he claims that everything that makes you *you*, from your personal identity to your free will, is really just the behavior of nerve cells and their associated molecules. If he's right, and that's all there is, can nerve cells and molecules be evil?"

The bell rang. "Read the first two articles on the list, and the suggested paper topics," Mr. Tsuyuki said. "Now for the bad news. You're going to each pick one topic and write a fifteen-page paper. Oh, and come back on Monday knowing whether or not you believe in good and evil."

There were loud groans. Franchise Fraser finally piped up

with "Hey, Mr. T., I already made up my mind. Assigning us a fifteen-page paper *is* evil."

"No, it'll be good for you," Mr. Tsuyuki assured us. He was standing by Junior Martinez's empty desk as we filed out of the classroom. He muttered, half to himself, "And, by the way, the kind of evil we're talking about has nothing to do with plain old teenage stupidity. Playing a cruel joke or stabbing someone with a plastic knife doesn't make you evil in my book—it just makes you a normal seventeen-year-old blockhead."

11

Circle up!" Coach Wallace ordered us before practice. From the anger on his face it was obvious that he was more concerned about what had happened to two of his starting players than he was about the big Lakewood game.

Coach is a tall, thin man with a pocked face who played soccer at Rutgers and takes a lot of pride in our team. He can't take too much pride in our victories, because year in and year out we lose more than we win, so he consoles himself that we are, to use his phrase, "well-behaved scholar athletes." On this Friday afternoon, he stood for several seconds looking around at us with his hands on his hips.

"I guess you all heard about what happened in the cafeteria today," he finally said. "Congratulations to all of you who were in on the joke. You really pulled off a great gag." He shook his head. "All the practices we've had, all the road trips we've taken on the team bus, and you still don't have the slightest notion what a *team* is. Frankly, I'm disgusted."

He stood there looking around at us, and didn't say another word. He hawked up some phlegm and spit it out on the grass. The silence stretched longer and longer till somebody had to say something. Franchise Fraser was our captain and he took the plunge. "Coach, we didn't do anything."

"That's right, Captain," Coach Wallace agreed with him. "You did nothing. Nothing to rescue a teammate who was worrying himself sick. And nothing to stop a teammate who we all know is just a good, fun-loving guy from wrecking his high school career over a practical joke he should have been talked out of. You did nothing. And now they're both gone."

"Gone where?" Kerry Vaughn, a senior fullback who was Charley Hu's closest friend, asked worriedly.

"Charley is going to be suspended for using a weapon in a fight. It'll go on his high school transcript, just as he's applying to colleges. I'm sure it will impress the admissions people at Harvard and Yale."

"But it was just a plastic knife, and no one could blame him for going a little crazy . . ." Kerry pointed out.

"There's a board-mandated policy against school violence," Coach Wallace reminded us. "No exceptions. And Junior . . ." Coach Wallace's voice quivered. He was fond of Junior, a fine player who provided most of the laughs on our team. "Junior may be expelled. And all of you did nothing. So, tomorrow we play Lakewood and we should be practicing our butts off. But instead I'm canceling practice. All of you just go home. And tonight why don't you spend a little time thinking about trust and friendship and how you can come through for a teammate, or leave him to his own worst impulses. Whatever you do, get the hell away from me, 'cause I can't stand to look at any of you."

Coach Wallace turned and stalked off the field, and we just stood there.

"Well, that was a real bummer," Franchise Fraser said. There were a few nervous laughs.

"You think what happened is funny?" Kerry snapped.

"In a way," Fraser admitted. "Don't try to get on my case. You knew what was going on, and you didn't tell your best buddy why he was pissing blue, so back off."

Kerry had no answer for that. He just hung his head.

"Everybody be here early tomorrow," Fraser said. "Game starts at one, and we should all be dressed and on the field at twelve-thirty. That's it. Practice is over."

We walked off the field in silence. Nobody felt like talking after what our coach had said, and the way he had looked at us.

Coach Wallace's words kept echoing in my head that afternoon and evening. You have to reach out to your teammates. You owe the truth to your friends. And to teammates who are also best friends, you owe a lot more than I had given to Smitty. I called him up on impulse, even though I was pretty sure such a popular guy would have plans for Friday night. I was wrong.

An hour later, we were biking to the Seagate Mall to see an action movie. We hunched down over our ten-speeds, faces into the wind, and plowed forward side by side. Smitty is usually talkative, but on this Friday night he stayed quiet. I wasn't exactly super-happy either, so we did the long ride mostly in silence. We reached Toms River and crossed Route 44 on the footbridge as cars whizzed beneath us, their headlights an endless glowing snake.

As we walked our bikes across the bridge, a gust of cold wind snapped our jackets back and forth. "So, Jeffsky, do I smell bad or have you just been avoiding me 'cause you got so many better things to do?" Smitty asked.

He was grinning, so I smiled back. For an instant I was tempted to tell him everything. That was why I had called him up, wasn't it? Instead, I heard myself say, "I haven't been avoiding you, big guy. I've just been busy. Remember, I called you tonight."

"Yeah, true," he said, and the wind blew so hard that his teeth chattered. "And thanks for the invite. It's a really great night for a bike ride."

The movie was about as stupid as Hollywood blockbusters can get. Even the fights and car chases irritated me, and I couldn't wait for the lights to come back on.

Smitty had been in a quiet mood, but during the movie he rocked around on his seat and whispered "Yeah!" and "Get him!" and "Kick ass!" as he munched through a tub of buttered popcorn with so much gusto it sounded like a swarm of termites demolishing a wooden cabin.

When Beth and I started dating, we took Smitty along with us several times. Beth offered to fix him up with some of her friends, including Pam Spencer, who I thought Smitty had a secret crush on. But my big friend was terribly shy. He insisted that he didn't want Beth to play matchmaker, and said that he also didn't want to be our third wheel. So as we started spending more time together, he hung out with other guys on our team. Now it was the two of us again, just like it had been in the days before Beth. I sat there missing Beth more and more, till I couldn't wait for the movie to end.

After the movie Smitty and I hung around the mall, riding the escalators, roaming the food court, nodding to kids we knew and checking out groups from other towns. This may not sound all that exciting, but on a Friday night in south Jersey if you don't have a date, it's about as hot as things get. Smitty normally comes up with all sorts of stupid things to do and has lots of dumb jokes to share, but on this night he was as silent as an oyster.

"What's bugging you?" I finally asked, as we split a pizza. I personally like pepperoni, but Smitty is a vegetarian and when you hang out with him you have to settle for mushroom or extra-cheese. You'd better eat quickly, too, or Smitty will vacuum up more than his share of the pie.

"Nothing. Why?"

"You're not exactly a ray of sunshine. Was it the movie?"

"You kidding? The movie was kick-ass!"

"Then why are you moping around?"

Smitty looked back at me. "You'll think I'm crazy."

"No I won't," I promised.

He hesitated. "Swordfish," he finally said.

"What?"

Once he'd taken the leap, he was willing to keep going. "You know, big fish with swords instead of noses," he said quickly. "*The Old Man and the Sea.*"

"I know what swordfish are, but what do they have to do with anything?"

"Long lines are driving them to extinction," Smitty explained. "I read about it in this magazine. Boats go out and lower these unbreakable fishing lines eighty miles long, with thousands of hooks that they just leave down there, baited, floating in the depths of the ocean. Swordfish take the bait and die on the lines, and hang there in darkness till the boats decide to take their lines up. They're such an old species of noble fish, and soon they'll be gone. Someone will eat the last one, grilled medium rare with a little rosemary and lemon butter."

"Okay, I won't eat any more swordfish," I promised him. "Not that it's one of my customary foods. Now lighten up."

"Can't," Smitty said even more glumly.

"Why not?"

"Turtles."

"What about turtles?"

"Leatherback turtles are gentle giants—they can grow more than nine feet long and weigh two tons."

"They sound kind of like you," I told the big guy, trying to lighten the mood.

But Smitty didn't even grin. His mind was fixed on giant sea turtles. "They've been around forever—they outlived the dinosaurs," he said. "They've survived every predator nature has thrown at them for millions of years, but fishermen with long lines will drive them to extinction any day now." Smitty's voice cracked, and he looked like he was in personal pain. "And for absolutely no purpose. They get tangled up in the long lines set for swordfish, and they can't fight their way free, so they suffocate down there, and nobody even eats them or uses them for anything." He broke off, and wiped his eye with his shirt sleeve.

I saw a few kids in the food court glancing at us, no doubt wondering what was wrong. It's strange to see such a big guy tearing up. "Come on, Smitty," I said, "pull yourself together. You're gonna drive yourself nuts."

"I knew you'd say I was crazy."

"I don't think you should worry so much about things you can't prevent. It is kind of nutso."

Smitty looked back at me, and I could tell he didn't appreciate being called nutso. There weren't any more tears on his face. In fact, he looked angry. "At least I know what's bothering me," he said. "And at least I'm not afraid to talk about it, even if it makes people laugh at me and call me names."

"What's that supposed to mean?"

"We used to hang out a lot, right? You used to be my best friend."

"Hey, I still think of you as my best buddy," I said. I knew where he was heading, and I tried to knock him off the path. "But getting back to those turtles for a minute, why can't scientists find some way to save them?"

"So we should tell each other the truth. Isn't that what friends do?"

"Yeah, sure."

"One minute you and Beth are lovey-dovey, and the next minute you're not even talking, and you're calling me up to see movies at the mall on a Friday night. So we go to the mall and you spend the whole night looking like you're in agony, and then you tell me that I'm nutso. So what happened to the loving couple?"

"Beth and I had a fight," I told him. "When you get a girlfriend, big guy, I guarantee you'll argue with her."

"Thanks for the warning. So I guess it must have been a really bad fight."

I shrugged. "It's kind of private."

"But you didn't break up?"

"No," I said, and the tiny word popped out a little too loud, so I said it a second time. "No."

"Good," Smitty said. "I'm glad for you. Because I've heard some things . . . just stupid rumors . . . but if you're still going out with her they can't be true."

"What things?" I asked.

"Not important. Forget it."

"Come on. You can't not tell me now."

His big hands fingered a pizza crust. "Just that Andy Stoltz saw her and Fraser walking together."

"Where?"

"On Maywood Avenue. Just, you know, walking."

"Why would Andy tell you if they were just walking?"

"Well . . ." Smitty's fingers picked the crust apart. "They were all alone together on that part of Maywood near the dunes, where there are no houses. And Andy thought that Fraser had his arm around her. So he asked me if you two were still going out. But he must have just been seeing things."

"Yeah," I muttered, "maybe he needs new glasses."

My best buddy Smitty heard something catch in my voice.

He looked back at me long and hard before he asked, "You okay, Jeff?"

"Absolutely."

"Meaning you don't want to talk about it?"

"What?"

He leaned forward. "Come on."

"Come on where?"

"I might be a little nutso, but I'm not stupid," Smitty said, managing to sound sympathetic and a little pissed off at the same time. "And I agree with what Coach said today. We are responsible for looking out for our friends and teammates. You're my teammate and my best friend. So what's screwing up your life?"

"Nothing."

"So who's this jerk living with you, with the criminal background, who's working at my dad's store? I mean, he says he's your brother, but that can't be true, because I figure you would share it with your best friend if you had a brother."

The food court seemed to whirl around and around, and then righted itself. "Where did you hear about his criminal background?" I asked.

"My dad told us. He said he wasn't going to get into specifics, but he was hiring someone who had made mistakes and paid for them, and I kind of figured what that meant. Who is he?"

"He's my brother," I acknowledged. "I should have told you about him before, but I didn't . . . because I was ashamed of him. Sorry."

"If he did something wrong, why should you be ashamed?" Smitty asked.

"Good question. I don't know the answer. But I am."

"So what's his story?" Smitty asked. "What'd he do?"

"Just some bad stuff," I mumbled. "You know, got into fights."

"You mean like assault?" he pried.

"Yeah."

"Did he hurt someone bad? Did he serve time?"

I stood up. "I don't want to talk about it."

He stayed seated. "I guess not. You didn't tell me he was coming home, you didn't tell me he was living with you, you didn't tell me he was dangerous even though he's working with my family, and now you won't tell me why he's screwing up your life. We must really be best friends, huh?"

I shrugged. "Smitty, turtles and swordfish are problems we can talk about if you want. But besides some stupid rumors that you probably shouldn't be repeating, there's nothing threatening my world right now. So maybe we should head home, because we've got a big game tomorrow."

Smitty remained seated. "It's pretty early," he muttered. "I'm gonna hang here and finish off the pizza."

"Suit yourself," I told him, and left on my own.

12

Hastings, you're starting at right wing," Coach Wallace shouted to me across the locker room, an hour before game time. This wasn't a total surprise, because with Charley and Junior gone, our offense would be severely shorthanded. Still, it was a newsworthy event in the locker room—I didn't start all that often.

"Jesus, we must really be desperate," Franchise Fraser cracked, and a few guys laughed. He saw the look I threw him. "Lighten up, J-man. I was just joking."

"Maybe you could hold up your hand when you're telling a joke to signal us," I suggested.

"What's the matter with you?"

"Nothing," I almost snarled back. "What's the matter with you?"

He shrugged. "Somebody's having his period," he said, and walked away.

What was the matter with me was a night of dreams so bad they made sleeplessness sound inviting. Biking home alone from the mall the previous night in the freezing wind, I had felt the scratchy tickle in the back of my throat that foretells a bad cold. By the time I got into bed I felt a little nauseous and also slightly feverish. I thought insomnia might strike again, but I soon drifted off into a wretched sleep.

Perhaps it was Smitty's talk of swordfish and long lines, but I spent the night swimming through dark depths, battling like a leatherback turtle to escape from a vast and invisible net. Sometimes it was Fraser's voice I heard taunting me as I struggled to get free, other times Troy's mocking gray eyes trailed me as silently as a shark, and occasionally I heard Beth's laugh, ringing forlornly, a lost buoy in the darkness.

The harrowing night finally gave way to a cold and gloomy day. I probably should have stayed home sick, but I knew that with two players out, Coach Wallace was counting on me. After my confrontation with Fraser in the locker room, my teammates sensed my mood and gave me space, so I dressed alone. I pulled on a long-sleeved cotton shirt that would keep me warm for about five minutes, till it soaked through. Then the Pineville soccer jersey, the black shorts, the yellow socks that held my shin pads in place, and the soccer shoes that would soon be so caked in mud they would be unrecognizable.

"This is not gonna be pleasant." Smitty nodded to me as our team gathered by the basement's rear exit. After our argument in the mall the previous night, things felt a little strange between us.

"It's not supposed to be," I muttered back. "Anything fun happen at the mall after I left?"

"Nope. I left soon after you," Smitty said. He looked like he wanted to say more, but Franchise Fraser shouted, "Okay, guys. Let's go for a swim!" and we were swept up in the stream of players and carried out the door.

We jogged out into the cold wetness, elbows nearly touching as we ran side by side, all of us aware that this was a misadventure from the start. Our own coach thought we lacked character, our few fans would probably not come out to support us on such a day, and we would lose by two or three goals to a better team.

I tried to hang tough and disregard the fever and lightheadedness, but the cold drizzle that was falling from the dark clouds overhead also seemed to be seeping up from the sodden grass. A tiny sprinkle of diehard fans, bundled up in sweaters and ponchos and sheltering under umbrellas, had turned out to see us lose. My dad was working that Saturday, and my mom is not a sports fan, so no near and dear one had come to watch my big start, which suited me just fine. I never had any illusions of being a soccer star—to tell the truth, I almost preferred sitting on the bench and coming in for twenty minutes a half.

We could have warmed up indoors, but that would have been an admission of weakness. Instead, we circled up in the wet grass. Franchise Fraser led us through our warm-ups, and he seemed to be enjoying this. "On your backs, raise your heels six inches, and just lie there for a minute. Soak it in, guys. It's not gonna get any drier, so you might as well get baptized! Let's show them we love crappy weather! Okay, now all of you losers up in a sitting position. Groin stretches. Push those knees apart. One day one of you may actually need your groin for something, so stretch it good."

I'd known Fraser long enough to understand that his insults were intended as encouragement, but even so I couldn't forget the rumor that Smitty had repeated to me. Had Fraser really been walking with his arm around Beth? Could my girlfriend and my teammate have betrayed me so quickly?

As I stretched, I couldn't stop myself from throwing repeated glances at our captain. The cold drizzle damped down Fraser's thick black hair and meandered in tiny streams down the slope of his forehead, slid over his sharp nose and smiling lips and dripped off his cleft chin. He seemed to relish the whole experience, insulting us and spitting farther and farther after each exercise, as if going for his own record. "Okay, you clowns," he finally shouted, "let's bring it in to Coach Wallace."

We headed for the bleachers, and I saw that three more fans had joined our little cheering section. On a high bleacher, shoulder to shoulder, Beth and Pam huddled beneath a pink umbrella. I tried to catch Beth's eye, but she wasn't looking at me. Fraser waved at them, and they both waved back.

But someone was watching me that day. Troy didn't have an umbrella, and he wasn't exactly in our home bleachers. Rather, he stood by himself off to one side, clad in a green rain slicker with the hood propped up by the beak of his New York Giants cap. He wasn't making any attempt to mingle with our other fans—he was just standing there watching me as if studying an animal whose behavior he wanted to know more about, perhaps because it would enable him to hunt it down later on.

I walked right over to him. Behind me I heard Coach Wallace call out, "Hastings, get over here," but I ignored him and focused on Troy. It was a shock to see him on school grounds, near my team, only twenty feet from Beth. "What are you doing here?" I asked.

"I came to watch you play soccer, brother."

"I didn't invite you."

"People rarely do," he acknowledged, and flashed me his half-smile. The gray eyes mocked me, just as they had in my nightmares.

"I don't want you here," I told him.

"Hastings!" Coach Wallace called again, more sharply. I was holding up his speech to the team before the game. "Have you gone deaf?"

"I think it's time we got to know each other better," Troy said in a low voice. "I've never been to a soccer game before. Your coach is calling you, Jeff. Better go."

I realized there was no way I could get him to leave if he didn't want to, so I turned and hurried over to the rest of the team. Coach Wallace wasn't in the best of moods. "What the hell were you doing, Hastings? Didn't you hear me?"

"Take it easy on him, Coach. Now that he's a starter, he's got to sign autographs for his fan club," Fraser said, and there were laughs. Maybe Fraser was just defusing the coach's anger with a joke, but when he jostled my shoulder as if we were sharing a laugh, I pushed his arm away.

Coach Wallace looked around at us, and I realized that he wasn't angry anymore—he looked grim, or maybe just plain sad. A raindrop slid down his pocked face, from his eye to the side of his chin, as if in place of a tear. "I just wanted you guys to know that as of eight o'clock last night Charley is officially suspended, a punishment that will go down on his school transcript. And Junior has officially been expelled from Pineville High for his stupid prank. So those of you who knew what Junior was up to and didn't stop him can carry that around with you on the field today."

Suddenly the cold day seemed even colder. We stood there in silence, looking back at him. Minutes passed. "Maybe some of you really didn't know what was going on," Coach finally said, in a softer voice. "Maybe others of you wanted to stop it, but didn't know how or just waited too long. I understand that peer pressure can be a strong force at your age. Still, you're almost men. You'll be able to vote and get married and enlist in the Armed Forces soon. So you should be able to understand that the soccer part of what we do here means nothing. It's the team that's important. The relationships, the friendships, the shared experience and responsibility. Otherwise we're just wasting time kicking a stupid ball around a wet field."

I glanced at Franchise Fraser, who was looking up at Beth. He felt my gaze and turned back to look at me and grinned. The fever and the cold suddenly made me weak at the knees, so that I almost slumped down.

"Now I've said what I had to say, so let's put it behind us," Coach Wallace finished. "Lakewood's out on the field waiting for you. They're a good team, but you can be a better one. Show me something today. I don't care if you win or lose, but play as a team and show me something."

His speech inspired our team. We dominated the first half

from the starting whistle. Kerry Vaughn, our stopper, who was Charley Hu's best friend, translated his guilt at not having warned Charley into defensive ferocity. Every time Lakewood brought the ball over the half line Kerry popped up out of nowhere with a jolting tackle to stop their attack and start one of our own. He fed several wonderful through balls to Franchise Fraser, who wasn't accustomed to getting such gifts, but made the most of them. Twice Fraser got behind their defense with slashing runs up the middle, and both times he finished with blistering shots into the upper corners of their goal.

Our team refused to give back the early lead. Man for man, we played one of our best halves ever. I was the sole exception. I may not be a soccer star, but I'm also not usually that bad. Every time I tried to trap the ball it skittered away on the wet field like a wary otter avoiding a snare. I jumped to contest several fifty-fifty headers, and when their player didn't beat me outright, the ball either sailed over the top of my head or smacked me in the face like a sucker punch.

Most of the time I just ran up and back, feeling useless and totally out of it. I've been in games before where the ball rarely came my way, but on this day it felt like I was playing on a separate field from everyone else. Every now and then I would glance at the sideline and pick out the pink umbrella that seemed to be floating atop the bleachers like a big question mark. Beth was never looking back at me. Meanwhile, Troy paced the sideline, trailing the action, keeping his gray eyes riveted on me.

My fever generated a pounding headache. I kept waiting

for Coach Wallace to take me out, but our team was playing so well that he must have been reluctant to make any changes. Finally, mercifully, the ref blew his whistle three times, ending the first half.

"Great stuff, guys," Coach Wallace told us as we ran in after the whistle. "Vaughn, you're a tiger out there today. Fraser, great finishing."

Fraser wasn't there to hear him. He had strutted up the bleachers and was standing with his hands on his hips, laughing and exchanging small talk with Beth and Pam. I saw him reach up and try to take the pink umbrella from Beth's hand, but she didn't let go, so they both held it as he talked. I tried not to watch them, but I couldn't tear my eyes away. My headache throbbed, and I shivered.

"Are you okay, brother?" Troy asked from nearby.

I wasn't okay. I felt light-headed and grabbed a bleacher railing for support. "Just go away," I hissed.

"You don't look so good," Troy observed.

I turned away and tried to ignore him. On my other side, Coach Wallace was complimenting one player after another. As I turned, he caught my eye. Loud enough for everyone on our sideline to hear, he said, "What's up with you out there, Hastings? You look like you're sleepwalking."

"Rain makes some people doze off," Franchise Fraser said, descending the bleachers. Some of the guys chuckled, and their laughs seemed to encourage him. "Time to wake up, sleeping beauty. We're winning." He grabbed me in a friendly bear hug and ground his knuckles into the side of my head, as in an old Three Stooges routine.

"Get off me," I half shouted.

Fraser seemed to think it was some kind of game, and held me even tighter. "Rise and shine!"

"Get the hell off!" I bucked and rocked, trying to shake him off.

But Fraser had me in an iron grip and wouldn't let go. "Coach, I think he's snapping out of it," he shouted. He ground his knuckles into my scalp one last time, and then he released me and I saw a big grin on his face.

Something in me snapped. Maybe it was the fever, maybe jealousy, maybe stored-up frustration that Troy had moved into my house and was now present at my soccer game and I couldn't do anything to keep him out of my life. Whatever it was, when Fraser let me go, I didn't pull away. Rather, I pushed him hard in the chest. "Keep your hands off me."

He looked shocked and amused at the same time. "Easy, Hastings, you psycho. What are you doing?"

I pushed him even harder, my open palm striking with enough force to knock him back two steps. He almost went down. *"Just keep away from me,"* I shouted at him.

I heard the voices of Coach Wallace and several teammates: "What's going on?" "Hastings is flipping out." "Are they fighting?" "No, they're just fooling around."

"Enough, J-man," Fraser said back. He was still smiling, and his voice managed to imply we were buddies just horsing around, but there was now a dangerous gleam in his eyes. He whispered a warning, "Push me again and I'll punch you right in the nose."

I pushed him again. Actually, it was halfway between a push and a punch. Fraser stepped back to avoid it and I lost my balance. Then he shoved me and I fell backward into the mud. I heard Beth's voice screaming, *Stop. Stop it!* I scrambled to get up, but in a heartbeat Fraser was standing over me, waving a closed fist as if he wanted to shake hands with my face, asking in a very reasonable voice, "You want me to break your nose for you, J-man?"

I never got to answer the question because Franchise Fraser let out a scream. Troy had materialized out of nowhere and yanked Fraser off me by twisting his right hand and wrist backward and to one side in what must have been some kind of aikido or jujitsu grip.

I managed to sit up in the mud and take it all in. Step by step, Troy pulled Fraser away from me. The wrist grip must have hurt a lot, because Fraser was still screaming. Coach Wallace and my teammates watched without moving or saying a word, as if frozen in amazement that such a thing could happen to the captain and star of our team on our sideline.

"Don't touch my brother again," Troy said to Fraser in a flat, emotionless voice and let him go. And then Troy stepped back to me and said, "Get up, Jeff. Let's go home," and he extended a hand.

I looked up into those gray eyes and pushed his hand away. "I told you to get out of here."

But before we could settle the matter, Fraser stepped quickly toward Troy with both fists clenched, saying, "I don't know who the hell you are, Mighty Mouse, but I hope you like pain . . ."

It was very clear what was about to happen. Franchise Fraser was more than a foot taller than Troy and must have outweighed him by fifty pounds. He was the best athlete in our school, and while he wasn't exactly a bully, I had seen him in several fights over the years and there was no question he knew what to do with his fists. He had just been attacked, hurt, and embarrassed in front of his own team, and that kind of thing didn't happen to Franchise Fraser.

He shuffled toward Troy, taking the small, balanced steps of a skilled boxer, and he threw a right hand so fast it was a blur. The punch landed with a loud BAM and broke Troy's jaw, ending the fight before it could even start.

Except it didn't happen that way. It should have, but it didn't. Because Troy slid under Fraser's punch like it had been telegraphed to him a day ahead of time and he had been sitting around waiting for it to arrive. He didn't pull away from Fraser but rather stepped toward him, and brought his knee up into Fraser's groin. Fraser let out a high-pitched yelp of surprise and pain and doubled over. Troy grabbed a clump of Fraser's thick black hair and yanked him forward and down, and as he was falling Troy kicked him in the side. Fraser yelped again and rolled over on the grass, clutching his ribs with one hand and his groin with the other.

The unexpectedness of the fight and the speed and fury of

Troy's victory had frozen my teammates, but they were beginning to react. *"Get away from him!"* Coach Wallace shouted, and several of my bigger and braver teammates stepped toward Troy, who ignored them. All of his attention was focused on Fraser, who was curled up on the muddy ground. "If you touch my brother again, I'll kill you," he said in his emotionless voice. "You understand?"

Fraser must have managed to nod because Troy turned away from him, and faced my four teammates who had edged almost within grabbing distance. "If any of you are stupid enough to touch me, I'll rip your arms out of their sockets," he promised, in the same flat voice. My teammates must have believed him because they stopped moving forward and started backing up warily.

"Are you coming, brother?" Troy asked me.

He read my answer in my face and walked away very quickly across the wet grass.

Fraser made it up to his knees and let out a moan. "Are you okay?" Coach Wallace asked, hurrying over to him.

As if in answer, Fraser vomited.

"Jesus. Do you need an ambulance? Someone call the police," Coach Wallace commanded. "And see which way that guy went..."

But it was too late. Troy had disappeared into the gray afternoon as if he had melted into the rain and fog.

13

I was up in my room, under the covers with a 102 temperature, when I saw the red lights flickering off my wall. The flashing cherry pattern looked cheerful and festive—I tried to convince myself that one of our neighbors was setting out his Christmas display way too early. But even with a fever I was pretty sure what was really going on, so I finally got out of bed, walked unsteadily to the window, and peered out. The police car pulled up right in front of our house, and Chief Mayweather got out with two serious-faced deputies.

I was surprised it had taken them so long to find us. Almost twenty-four hours had passed since Troy had knocked Fraser to the wet turf. I figured they had come to arrest him for assault, and I couldn't figure out why they had let so much time pass, but small-town police departments move at their own pace.

I put on a bathrobe and started down the stairs. Troy and my parents were in our living room with the three policemen. Troy was standing still as a statue, not saying a word, but his eyes flashed combatively. My mother was very agitated. "You're sure I can't get you anything to drink?" she asked as if the three cops were paying a social visit, but her voice was so tense it quivered and nearly snapped apart.

"No, ma'am, thanks, but we're not thirsty," Chief Mayweather answered politely for all of them. I had never seen him up close before. He was a big man with strong features, and a very direct way of looking and talking.

My dad had looped his left arm lightly around my mom for reassurance. With his right hand he motioned the police toward our couch. "Please sit, gentlemen. Tell me how I can help you?" And then, as he studied their faces, he asked, "What's happened?"

"We'll be happy to fill you in later on, Mr. Hastings," Chief Mayweather said, "but first we'd like to talk to your son, alone. This man is your son, yes?"

"I'm his son," Troy answered, "and I'll talk to you, but not alone."

Chief Mayweather wasn't accustomed to being denied or contradicted, and he showed his displeasure by flashing Troy a stare that could have melted granite. "Let me give you some friendly advice," he offered in a voice that was anything but friendly. "Your best bet is to cooperate and not give me any lip."

"Thanks for the advice, pal," Troy said back. "Are you charging me with anything? Are you here to arrest me?"

"Not now."

"Then if you want me to be helpful, here's some friendly advice. Let's play this my way," Troy suggested. "Because I'm pretty sure I could answer more of your questions and be more helpful if I had my family around me."

"Call me Chief, not pal," Chief Mayweather snapped. He and Troy glared at each other. "It would be easier for everyone if you didn't drag your parents into this."

"They're already in this," Troy said. "And I don't trust cops. I want witnesses to everything we say and do, so that you guys don't try to twist anything later on." I could tell that the three cops didn't like the implication that they might do something dishonest. But Troy wasn't done. "And I want my family around me because I've brought trouble into their house and I love them and I trust them and I want them to see and hear the truth."

"That's very sweet of you, to be so considerate of them," Chief Mayweather observed sarcastically.

"Thank you. And that includes my brother," Troy said, "who can back up part of my story. He's got pneumonia, but he's listening on the stairs, so he might as well come down."

Everyone glanced up at me. I must have looked pretty goofy standing there halfway up the stairs, listening in my blue terry-cloth bathrobe. "Jeff, you should be up in bed," my mom said, but I trudged down the stairs and joined the crowd in the living room, and nobody stopped me.

I sat in a leather armchair. The three police parked themselves on our couch. Mom and Dad sat facing them on a love seat. Troy remained standing. He took out a cigarette and lit it. My mom has an absolute rule about no smoking in the house, but nobody said anything to stop him.

"So," Chief Mayweather said, "I'd like to know exactly where you went and what you did after you attacked Tom Fraser on the soccer field yesterday."

119

"I didn't attack him," Troy said. "I was defending my brother. I pulled that guy off Jeff and told him to buzz off."

"That's not the way it was described to me."

"One of us was there, Chief, and one of us wasn't," Troy said. He turned to me. "Jeff, did I pull him off you?"

I felt their eyes on me. "Yes," I said, looking back at Troy. "And then you kneed him in the groin and kicked him in the ribs and threatened his life."

"Here's the way I remember it," Troy said. "First I defended you by pulling him off. Then you and I were talking and he came at me with his fists clenched and promised to give me some pain. So I defended myself, which I have a legal right to do. And he's a bigger guy than me, so when he threw the first punch I had to take him down and make sure he would stay down. Isn't that what happened, brother?"

I didn't want to help Troy, but the truth was the truth. "He's right. That is what happened," I admitted to the police and my parents.

"So if you want to charge me with assault, charge me," Troy said. "I've got at least one witness who saw it my way, and I bet there are a dozen more who will come forward and tell the truth, even if they don't like it."

"This isn't about charging you with assault," Chief Mayweather said.

Troy looked mildly surprised. "Then what's it about?"

"I know who you are," the chief said in a low voice.

"Yahoo for you."

"And I know what you did, and I know how lucky you are to be here."

"I'm a free American citizen," Troy said back to him, "just like you, Chief. We're both lucky to be here, enjoying Sunday morning in this friendly little town."

"Except that one of us is a convicted murderer."

My mom made a sound in her throat. She stood up and walked away quickly. Dad got up and followed her, and in a few seconds we heard her vomiting into the downstairs toilet, and my father talking to her in a very soft voice.

Chief Mayweather sat forward on the couch, and his tone when he spoke was harder and more accusatory. "Where did you go yesterday after you defended your brother on the soccer field?" he asked Troy for the second time.

"I went for a walk," Troy answered.

"Alone?"

"That's right. I was angry at myself for being drawn into a fight. I knew it would screw things up for my family, and they've been very kind to me. So I went for a long walk."

"It was raining," Chief Mayweather reminded him. "And freezing cold. How long did you stay out in that?"

"A long time," Troy replied. "I was wearing a coat, and I wasn't really thinking about the weather. I like cold rain."

A toilet flushed, and I heard my mom walking up the stairs, heading for her bedroom. My dad came back into the living room and stood by the door, grim-faced, listening to what had become an interrogation.

"You were just walking alone?" Chief Mayweather asked Troy.

"Yup."

"Did you see anybody? Talk to any friends?"

"I don't have any friends," Troy said.

"When did you get home?"

"After dark. I let myself in through the back door and went to bed."

"So nobody saw you from midafternoon till this morning?"

"Possibly." Troy half nodded. "Nobody I know, anyway. What's this all about, Chief? You come in here, you say you're not charging me, you upset my family, my mom, and then you grill me. If you think I assaulted that guy, let's cut the crap. Cuff me, bring me in, and put me face-to-face with that Fraser guy in a courtroom. Let's call some witnesses and see who's telling the truth."

"I couldn't do that right now," Chief Mayweather admitted grudgingly, "even if I wanted to."

Troy looked back at him. "Why not?"

"Because Tom Fraser has disappeared," the chief said. He spoke in a low voice, but the words seemed to hang in the room as if stamped on the air.

"What?" I said. "How . . . ?"

Chief Mayweather was focused on Troy. "You don't look surprised."

"Nothing surprises me, Chief, after some of the things I've seen."

"Tom Fraser showered up with the team after the game and drove off in his van at about two yesterday afternoon, and no one has seen him since. He didn't report to work last night. He didn't come home to sleep. His parents have called all his relatives and friends, and none of them have heard anything."

"I'm sure he'll turn up," Troy said. "He probably just needed a little space. 'Cause his pride was hurt."

"Probably," Chief Mayweather agreed, standing up. He flexed his arms as if they had gone to sleep, and muscles bulged like clusters of grapes. "But it is a little worrying. You living here. You getting into a fight with him. You threatening his life. And then him disappearing, and you having no alibi."

"I can see how it would be worrying for you," Troy agreed. "But I'm sure you know that in situations like this where something strange happens, people like me with records and histories are always the first ones to be suspected. It often turns out they had nothing to do with it. A lot of strange coincidences happen."

"When I need your help with police work, I'll ask you," Chief Mayweather said. "Till we get this settled, I want you to keep us advised of your whereabouts. If you move, if you take a trip, let us know."

"I'm not going anywhere," Troy told him. "I like it right here in your safe little town."

Chief Mayweather unexpectedly turned to me. "Jeff, one last question. Your brother says he pulled Tommy Fraser off you. Why were you and Tommy fighting in the first place?"

"It was just a silly personal thing," I muttered.

"It could be important."

"It's not," I said.

"Let me be the judge," the chief said. "It was important enough to get you two fighting each other. What was it?"

I looked back at him and didn't say anything for ten long seconds while I tried desperately to figure out some way to keep Beth out of this. I remembered what her father had said to me over the phone about how important it was to protect her and her reputation in this small town where they had lived all their lives. I also remembered how Mr. Doyle had glared at Fraser the night of the fall concert, and how Tommy had remarked to me, "He looked like he wanted to wring one of our necks." I decided not to mention that.

"Jeff," my dad prompted me. "Just tell the truth."

I looked from face to face and saw that there was no way out, so finally I said, "I thought Tommy was hitting on my girlfriend, and I got jealous."

"And why did you think he was hitting on her?"

"Because some guy said he saw them together. But it was probably nothing."

"And what's your girlfriend's name?" Chief Mayweather asked.

"Beth," I mumbled.

"Beth what?"

"Doyle. Beth Doyle."

"Could you give me her address and phone number?"

I saw that one of the deputies had taken out a pen and pad and was carefully writing down my answer.

14

J eff, we've got a problem," my dad said Monday morning when I came down to breakfast. He was in the kitchen, standing by the breakfast table, hunched over the front page of the local news section of the newspaper. As I approached the table he looked up, and I could almost read the headline in the pain on his face. "This is . . . terrible," he muttered. "Just awful."

There it was in big letters, the lead story in Section B: HIGH SCHOOL STUDENT MISSING FROM PINEVILLE, with a large photo of Tommy Fraser in his soccer uniform. In the picture he was taking a penalty kick, measuring the shot with careful eyes. His long black hair tossed in the wind, there was a serious smile of concentration on his face, and all in all Franchise Fraser had never looked better.

Just beneath the photo of Fraser, the headline of another article caught my eye: CONVICTED MURDERER LIVING IN PINE-VILLE IS A SUSPECT. I held my breath and scanned the first two sentences: "A convicted murderer, now living in Pineville, was questioned by police Sunday morning, a police source revealed. Troy Hastings, convicted five years ago of knifing to death a high school classmate in Buffalo, New York, and now living with his family in Pineville, threatened the life of Tom Fraser, the missing teen, hours before he disappeared."

I looked up at my dad. Worry and even a kind of fear showed clearly in his face, but I also saw a very uncharacteristic red-hot anger. His teeth were clenched so that his jaw muscles stretched the skin taut over his cheekbones, and his normally kind gray eyes flashed with fury. I understood why he looked worried, but his anger baffled me. "How can they print something like that?" Dad demanded. "They're attacking our family. There's no evidence. No one's been charged."

"How often do kids like Tommy Fraser disappear from our town?" I shot back, my eyes scanning the rest of the article about Troy. They had pieced together much of his criminal and prison past. The article described the fight at the Lakewood game, and detailed my role in it without naming me. Still, all my teammates and everyone at school would know. "This is big news," I muttered numbly, my whole body going into cold shock as I finished reading. It was taking a few seconds to sink in, but I was already aware on some level that I had reached a break point in my teenage life, and that things for me, in Pineville, would never be the same again. "We're big news."

"Well, we shouldn't be," Dad said. "It's not fair." He glanced at the newspaper a final time and then stood up straight, his hands on his hips, his eyes sweeping the kitchen as if searching for a referee to appeal to so that a bad call could be rectified. I didn't feel sorry for him, even though he was a good man who was clearly troubled and in pain. I felt furious at him.

The quality I liked best in my father—his core decency and almost childlike trust in his fellow man—suddenly seemed like stupid naïveté that had gotten us all in this mess.

"Dad, stop it!" I said so sharply that he lowered his hands from his hips and stared back at me. *"Wake up!* They're a newspaper, right? It's their job to report breaking news. We're front-page news now. We have to figure out what to do, because this is only going to get worse."

"You don't know that—" he began.

"I do know that," I shouted at him, and my hand knocked a glass of orange juice off the table. My dad and I are both neat by nature, but neither of us made the slightest move to clean up the shards of broken glass or the orange puddle that slowly spilled out, following the cracks across the wooden floor. "You brought this down on us when you allowed Troy to come live here. *God damn it! I told you this would happen!"*

"Don't you take the Lord's name in vain or raise your voice to me in my house—" Dad started to say.

"How can you even care about that now?" I cut him off. "Listen to what I'm saying instead of the way I'm saying it. *We're screwed.* We as a family are screwed. I've been trying to tell you and Mom—"

"And we have heard you," Dad replied, his own voice getting loud. "We did take your fears into account. But we tried to do the right thing in bringing Troy home. Faced with the same circumstances, I would do the same thing again. He's innocent until proven guilty, just as you or I would be. This is a time when we have to believe in Troy more than ever, and rally

round him. You, his brother, have to believe in him. He says he had no hand in this—"

"Where is he?" I asked.

"He left for work already, same as always," my dad said. "I talked to him about this and he swore again he had nothing to do with it. Didn't know the boy who disappeared. Didn't see him after your game. Would never risk going back to prison for such a stupid, meaningless argument with somebody he didn't even know. Jeff, I watched him drink his coffee and eat his corn-flakes and look me in the eye, and I believed him. Do you really think he could have killed someone in cold blood and be lying to us and acting so normally? Do you really think that of your own brother?"

"Here's what I really think," I answered him. "Don't let him come home. Pack his stuff up and throw it into the street. Cut all ties publicly and permanently. Do it now or you'll regret it."

"I'm ashamed to hear those words come out of your mouth—" Dad began, and then he broke off as music sounded loudly and incongruously nearby, and my mom walked into the kitchen, humming loudly to herself.

There was something wrong with her. Mom must have known what was in the paper, and she couldn't possibly not have heard us shouting at each other, but she was humming "Oh, When the Saints Go Marching In" and smiling with a terrible forced brightness. She stopped humming to say, "Good morning, Jeff," as if nothing was amiss. "How's your cold? You look better. Oh, I see there was an accident." She pulled some paper towels off a roller and knelt to soak up the orange juice.

Dad and I exchanged worried glances over her bent back. My mom's medication sometimes made her appear woozy, but never completely out of touch with reality. Whatever was going on with her now, it was more worrying in its way than the article in the morning newspaper.

"Morning, Mom," I said. "You don't have to clean that up. I'll take care of it."

"Too late," she said, on her knees, her elbow moving back and forth as she mopped. "Take some cereal. There are raisins in the cupboard." She started singing the words to herself in her delicate soprano voice:

> *"Oh, when the saints go marching in,*
> *Oh, when the saints go marching in . . .*
> *Oh Lord I want to be in that number . . ."*

"I'm not hungry," I muttered.

"You have to have something for breakfast. There are some bananas in the tray . . ."

I didn't want to argue with her; suddenly I just wanted to get out of there. I needed to escape from that kitchen in a hurry—from my father, who was still defending and apologizing for Troy, and from my mom, who was humming along happily in her own little world while our real world sizzled and burned in the headlines on the front page of our daily newspaper.

I grabbed a banana from the fruit tray, bent down, and gave her a kiss on the cheek. "Gotta go."

"Bye, Jeff," she said.

My father followed me out. "Let's talk later . . ."

"Want some advice?" I asked him. "Hire a lawyer." The suggestion surprised him, but before he could respond I said, "Gotta go. Bye." And then I was out of that house, running down our street and away from it all. I sped up and jogged past the houses I had grown up near over the past years. I knew them by heart—the Baineses' brick ranch house, the Alts' white colonial with the big windows that needed to be cleaned, the Warricks' old Victorian with its grape arbor out back.

As I ran I imagined a montage of our neighbors clustered around their breakfast tables passing their morning newspapers around. They wouldn't be making any accusations yet, but in my mind I saw and heard them cocking eyebrows and exchanging suggestively guarded comments like "They always seemed to be such a nice family," and "Did you ever have a clue that something like this might be going on over there?"

I surprised myself by veering off suddenly onto Quarterdeck Lane. This was a tree-lined dead-end street that led away from school toward the shore. It also happened to be the direction that offered me the greatest chance of not bumping into anyone I knew.

I picked up my pace till I was nearly sprinting. It felt good to push myself forward faster and faster, to pump my arms and suck in deep breaths of cold air. I crossed a narrow bridge over a brackish stream, and soon the deep blue of Barnegat Bay appeared behind the row of expensive beach houses lining the rocky shore.

There was a tiny park at the end of Quarterdeck, built directly at the water's edge. It wasn't much of a park really—just a gazebo with sweeping views of the bay and a tiny playground with swings and a slide for little kids. A pretty young woman with long blond hair was pushing her little daughter on a swing. They were wearing matching pink winter coats and playing a silly game. Each time the girl swung forward the woman shouted "Boo" and they both burst into laughter. The woman gave me a quick look as I jogged up, and then as I headed to the gazebo she turned back to her daughter and shouted "Boo" again.

I saw a red Lexus with New York plates in the parking lot, and figured the woman must be visiting someone in Pineville. This park is a community secret, and there was no way she could have found it if she was just passing through. She was probably a houseguest in one of the expensive beachfront homes. Some of those homes cost nearly a million dollars and are owned by New Yorkers or Philadelphians who drive out on weekends and holidays. It says a lot about Pineville that the nicest houses in our town are owned by people who are rarely here.

I reached the gazebo and sat on a bench looking out at the water. I watched an old fishing boat chugging across the bay toward the lighthouse on its lonely way to the fishing grounds that lie miles offshore. A single gull trailed it, cawing shrilly as if complaining about the morning chill.

I propped my feet up on the bench, stuffed my hands into my jacket pockets, and thought of the one family member I hadn't encountered that morning. My father's question rang in my mind: did I really think my brother could be responsible for Franchise Fraser having gone missing?

On the one hand, it seemed incredible to think that Troy, still a relative stranger in Pineville, had tracked Fraser down after the soccer game, hurt him, driven him away, or even killed him, concealed what had happened, and was now acting so normally. Also, my father's argument about a lack of motive was compelling. Why would Troy, having just been freed after five years in prison, risk everything to take action against someone he had only just met?

Because he was Troy. My mind answered the question loud and clear. Sure he could have done it, and faced down our town police chief, and eaten cornflakes with a steady hand. It made no sense because he made no sense.

The more I thought about it, the harder it was for me to believe that Troy wasn't in some way involved. Things in our little town had been chugging along normally year after year. The routines of teenage life here—with interrelated circles of school, sports, friendship, and dating—were as familiar and regular as the tides that raised and lowered the waters of Barnegat Bay. One day Troy arrived with his Giants cap and his duffel bag, and soon everything was completely out of whack. The most popular kid in school had vanished off the face of the earth. The exact nature of the cause and effect might be unclear, but the link seemed obvious and undeniable. Chief Mayweather saw it, I saw it, and I couldn't believe that my father didn't also see it.

It occurred to me that maybe that was the real reason Dad looked so angry. Maybe he saw it clearly but was just in denial.

I heard a patter of footsteps. The little girl had left the

playground and run toward the gazebo. She looked like she was three or four, with blond hair that matched her mother's peeking out from beneath her pink hood. Her mother ran after her and caught her by the hand when she was less than ten feet from me. The woman must have read something in my face, because she said, "Come, Rachel, let's not disturb the nice boy," and tried to pull her child away. The little girl grabbed hold of a fence slat and held tight.

"You're not disturbing me," I said. "She's cute."

"Thanks." The mom nodded warily. Then, hesitantly, "Shouldn't you be in school?"

"I don't feel well."

I could see her wondering whether she should start a conversation or just move away with her kid. She was a very pretty woman, with crystalline blue eyes and high cheekbones. If she smiled I could imagine how it would light up her beautiful face, but she looked cautious and even a bit nervous. "If you're sick, you probably shouldn't be outside on such a cold day," she ventured.

"I'm not sick," I told her. "I just don't feel well." I could tell that I had confused her, and that once again she was considering moving off. I felt like talking, so I said quickly, "I see you're from New York."

"How do you know that?" she asked, wary but curious.

"Your Lexus. The license plates."

She relaxed a tiny bit. "Oh. Yes. Of course. You're very observant. Yes, we're visiting some friends here. Do you live here?"

"Yes."

There was a pause. I could see her searching for some positive thing to say about Pineville. "It must be a nice, safe place to grow up," she finally said.

"That's why my parents picked it," I muttered, and she heard something in my tone, because her gaze sharpened.

"Rachel," she said, "it's getting cold. Come on, sweetheart. One more swing and we should go."

"So do you live in Manhattan?" I asked.

She began gently prying the girl's fingers off the fence. "Yes." She nodded.

"That must be great, to live with so many people and so much excitement all around."

"It is fun. But it's also nice to know all your neighbors. There's nothing like a small town. Nice talking with you . . ."

"Jeff," I said.

"Jeff," she repeated. She finally had the girl free of the fence and was ready to lead her away. Only then did she smile at me, and even though it was a small smile and meant as a goodbye present, it warmed up her pretty face and was much appreciated on that cold morning. "Nice talking to you. I hope you feel better." Then she added softly, "Whatever it is, I'm sure it will pass."

"Thanks," I said.

I watched her lead the little girl over to the swing, and soon they were laughing and playing their little game again. I didn't know exactly what was waiting for me in school, but I had been through this once before, years ago, and those memories were still deep and sharp.

As I watched the woman and child, I found myself taking refuge from the present by fantasizing about my future. That may sound a little strange—I get the feeling that most people retreat into happy memories from their past. But the past has never been a refuge or source of comfort for me, and it certainly wasn't on that cold morning. So I threw my imagination the other way, escaping to the years yet to come.

One day soon I would be the age of the blond woman. One day I might have my own kid, a bright-eyed innocent child with a laugh as soft and sweet as powdered sugar. I might be far away from this town with its supermarket gossips and its eager-beaver local police and its pathetic newspaper printing petty hearsay stories on the front page. Perhaps I would move to a city like New York where I could chisel any life I wanted out of my own talents and ambitions, and live in a nondescript skyscraper where even my neighbors wouldn't know my name or my personal business. I would marry a woman like this blond woman, and if Troy ever called or came to see me . . .

The fantasy faded away and I got slowly to my feet. Even in my daydreams, I couldn't pretend that there would ever be such a thing as a completely fresh start. Not with a family secret like mine. No way. Never.

I headed off to school, and as I trudged across the parking lot I heard the blond woman shout "Boo" behind me, and the girl give one last delighted peal of laughter.

 **15**

This is a place I have been before.

No, not as a teenager, and not in a south Jersey high school surrounded by dozens of friends and hundreds of acquaintances and a reputation as a good guy. I had dug that foundation beneath me here in Pineville over the last five years, put up that ring of insulation against guilt by association. It was sheltering me precariously as I walked down the corridor that day, or sat in class and tried to pretend I was listening to the teacher. The stares I felt raking my back lingered, but the ones to my face were quick and carefully concealed; the bursts of whispered speculation and gossip were guardedly muted.

But the feeling was the same. Yes, I had been here before. Soon the stares would sharpen, the whispers grow louder. And then would come accusations and punches.

The last time I was in this place I was twelve years old. In my mind's eye I could picture a scared sixth grader, small for his age, clutching a Buffalo Bills lunchbox to his side like a life preserver as he swam through the crowded hallways of his elementary school. He wore the same green sweatshirt day after day, with a drawstring hood that he began tightening over his forehead in a futile attempt to hide his face and drown out the whispers.

There he is! Did you read about it in the paper? Uh-huh, I heard that, too. His older brother! My mom says his parents are strange. Yeah, a folding knife with a seven-inch blade. He must know more than he says. It was his own brother, so of course he knows!

Survival instincts that I thought I had tossed away half a decade ago unexpectedly boomeranged back to me. The instinct to hurry through school hallways. To duck into bathrooms and stay there till the halls were empty. No, walk normally. Try not to look panicked. You haven't done anything wrong. The instinct to avoid looking people in the eye. If you don't look at them, they won't gawk at you. Pick a spot on a far wall and stare at it as you pass. In class, bury your face in your books. The instinct to avoid friends even more than enemies. Don't test friendships at such a time. Don't put them in that spot, or you'll regret it.

"Hey, Jeffsky, what's the rush?" As I hurried down the crowded first-floor hallway on my way to the locker room to change for gym class, Smitty materialized out of a doorway. He reached out an enormous hand and snagged my elbow. I instinctively tried to jerk away, but he held me in his firm grip as securely as a turtle entwined in a long line.

"Hi, big guy," I said back.

"So, what's new?" he asked brightly.

I figured he must know what was new, so I shrugged and said, "I'm not feeling so well."

"Could be flu," Smitty suggested helpfully. "I think that's going around." He was pissed off, I could tell that much. I wasn't sure how angry, and I wasn't sure why.

We reached the stairwell and headed down. The stairs were less crowded than the first-floor hallway, but I could feel a dozen eyes watching my reaction as Smitty said in a loud voice, "So I read about your bro."

There was no easy way out. No door to dash through, no hood to pull over my head. "I'm sorry you had to read about him," I replied softly. "Sorry I didn't tell you."

"Tell me what?" he asked, and it seemed to me that he was walking more and more slowly. I wanted to speed up and take those stairs two at a time, but Smitty was still holding my arm, so I had to force myself to match his plodding pace. "What are you sorry you didn't tell me?" he demanded. "That my dad hired a convicted murderer? That my mom and sister have been working after hours next to a guy who was sentenced to life in prison for gutting some kid with a knife? The good news is that none of my family members have been stabbed yet. Hey, don't lose any sleep over it. It probably just slipped your mind."

The staring eyes of those kids in the stairwell seemed to swirl around, and I felt dizzy. I gripped the banister and searched the face of my best friend, always so jovial, always so concerned about everyone's well-being, from turtles to swordfish to his teammates. His fury almost melted the big fake plastic smile he had stuck on his face.

"I'm sorry, but it wasn't my secret to tell," I explained in a low voice. "Your dad knew all about it. He could have told you. Can we talk later, Smitty?"

We reached the basement landing and walked out into the dingy windowless corridor. Rows of old green lockers stood on either side like soldiers at attention. His hand, as big as a bear's paw, released my arm and clamped tightly onto my shoulder.

"No, let's talk now," Smitty shot back. "True, my dad knew about your brother. But he also knew that you and I were best friends." I noticed he used the past tense in describing our friendship. "So of course he hired your bro. The thing is, Jeff, I introduced you to my dad. Your family got to know my family at our soccer games. I was the connection. Our friendship created this freaky situation. But I guess you and I weren't good enough friends for you to tell me the truth so I could have headed it off. You had to protect somebody, so you chose to protect your brother. Who could blame you for that?"

"I'm really sorry," I told him. "I did try to tell you a little about Troy the other night at the mall—"

"No." Smitty cut me off, and his fingers dug into my shoulder. "*You told me absolutely nothing.* I had to pry it out of you."

I pulled away with an effort and headed for the locker room. He trailed me by a step. We were late—lots of the guys were already pulling on shorts and T-shirts. I found my locker and began dialing the combination, trying to concentrate on the little numbers.

Smitty's locker was near mine. "I guess all sorts of things are going to come out now," he muttered. "You know they're here in school right now?"

I couldn't resist asking, "Who's here?"

"The cops. They've set up an interrogation room, and they're hauling in members of the soccer team."

"Yeah," Kerry Vaughn chimed in from nearby. "I know they talked to Coach Wallace this morning."

"And they're talking to girls, too," another guy added. "Beth and Pam and lots of Lisa's friends."

"They'll find what they're looking for," Smitty said with quiet certainty.

I finally got my locker open and stared into its dark interior, shutting out the outside world.

I made it through gym class, and dodged and ducked and skulked my way through the rest of the day to sixth-period biology. I figured I would linger outside the classroom till the last possible minute and then dart inside, but when I made my move toward the door I found Beth waiting there. "Hi, Jeff. I thought maybe you weren't coming today."

The bell rang, signaling the start of sixth period. "We're gonna be late," I pointed out.

"We need to talk. You don't look so good," she said.

"I don't feel so good," I replied truthfully. "Okay, Beth, what's up? You haven't exactly wanted to talk to me much lately."

She shrugged and was quiet for a long minute. She turned her head away, and it was only when I saw something gleam on her cheek that I realized she was crying. I stepped forward to hold her, and she gently but firmly pushed me away. "I was just wondering . . ." she began. She took a breath. "Why you gave my name to the police?"

140

"They wanted to know why I fought with Fraser at the soccer game," I answered softly. "Beth, I had to tell them the truth."

"Okay. What is the truth?" she asked, and her beautiful hazel eyes were sharp as razors. "Why did you start a fight with a friend and teammate?"

"Because I was jealous."

"Of Tommy? Why?"

"Because I thought you liked him."

"Of course I like him," she said. "We've been friends since we were in kindergarten."

I glanced at the door. "We should go in."

"The police came to my house," Beth said. "They talked to me for an hour. They grilled my father. My neighbors saw their cars outside. My dad's grounded me for the next thirty years and is thinking of locking me away in some kind of nunnery. I think I'm entitled to an explanation. Why were you jealous of Tommy?"

"I thought you liked him . . . more than as a friend," I admitted. "Things between us weren't so good, Beth. And he came to your concert. And Smitty said some guy we know saw you and Fraser walking together. So I thought . . ."

"That I was going to end everything between us without even talking to you, and start going out with Tommy Fraser? Is that really what you think of me?" The question was whispered, but I could almost feel the anger behind it.

"No," I said. "That's what I think of me. You're so beautiful. And Tommy's so handsome. I guess I was insecure. I just . . .

got jealous. And then I had to tell the police the truth. I'm really sorry I brought your family into it."

"Me too," Beth said. "Thanks for the explanation." And then she said, "I wish I had never gone out with you." She turned and walked through the door into bio class.

I stood in that hallway for two or three minutes, pulling myself together. I was completely alone there in the very center of our school, with kids and teachers in classrooms on all sides of me, going about their normal school day. I thought of just running out the side door and going home, but there seemed no point—things couldn't possibly get any worse. So after five minutes I walked to the classroom door, opened it, and stepped inside.

Mr. Tsuyuki was at the blackboard, writing paper topics in a long list. As if cued by my entrance he said, half-jokingly, "So by now you should have all decided whether or not you believe there is such a thing as evil." Bam, the door slammed closed behind me, and everyone turned to look. I stood there for a second, taking in their curious and angry faces. Beth. Smitty. Pam, who had apparently been interrogated by the police. Mr. Tsuyuki, who must have read the paper and looked like he had some idea of what I was going through. "Take a seat, Jeff," he said quickly. "We've already started." And then he plunged back into his lecture.

I sat down and pretended to read the list of paper topics on the blackboard. The truth was I didn't understand a word of what Mr. Tsuyuki was saying that day. He must have sensed how out of it I was, because even though he was firing off questions and calling on students at random, he left me alone with my thoughts.

My conversations with Smitty and Beth kept replaying in my mind—really the same conversation, just variations on a theme. The theme was trust, and how much truth you owe people who love you. I couldn't blink away the image of Beth standing there with a tear gleaming on her cheek. And then what she had said to me. The kindest person I had ever known saying the cruelest thing to me . . .

"Jeff? *Jeffrey?*" Mr. Tsuyuki was looking at me. All the kids in bio class were staring at me.

"I'm sorry," I managed. "I didn't hear the question . . ."

"I didn't ask you a question," he said gently. "Someone at the door for you. I think you need to go."

It was Claire Sills, the office monitor, a young woman who had just graduated from our high school last year. She was standing right behind my desk. I didn't have a clue how long she had been there or what she had said. I stood up and followed her out into the hall.

"What's the matter?" I asked.

"I don't know," she said. "Mrs. McKinley said to get you right away."

I followed her in silence to the front office, where she turned me over to her boss. Mrs. McKinley had been the face of discipline in the front office for half a century. She always sat in the same black vinyl swivel chair near the window, with the big clock that ticked off the minutes of our school day directly behind her. She reminded me of a gnarled old tree that has taken deep root in a forest clearing and grows there through the years as the seasons change and generations of animals come and go around it.

She peered back at me through her black-rimmed eyeglasses, and I noticed the morning paper on her desk. It was open to the local news section. Tommy Fraser smiling in his soccer uniform, lining up the penalty kick.

She saw me glance down at it, and then I looked quickly back up and our eyes met and she wet her lips with the tip of her tongue. "Dr. Baker wants to see you," she said.

"Now?" I asked.

"Immediately," she responded, and nodded very slightly with her head toward the back.

I walked to a wooden door marked PRINCIPAL'S OFFICE and knocked. "Come in," a voice directed me.

I entered the office and stood there awkwardly, blinking at afternoon sunlight that streamed in through a row of windows. A dozen or so old fountain pens and a clutter of papers sat on a big wooden desk.

Dr. Baker had his back to me. He was squeezing a lemon slice into a cup of tea. "Shut the door," he said.

I pulled the door closed.

He turned and we studied each other. He was a well-dressed old gentleman with a grandfatherly face who always wore a suit and kept his tie on, even in the hottest days. "Sit, Jeff," he said, gesturing me to a chair.

I sat and he sat down facing me, and took a sip from his teacup. "So?" he said.

I looked back into his eyes and kept silent.

"I read the paper this morning," he went on. "Some of what appeared was unfortunate, wouldn't you agree?"

I shrugged. "That's what newspapers do. They print news."

"To me it was old news," he said, fishing out his tea bag and carefully depositing it into his garbage can. "The police kept me informed of their investigation over the weekend. I knew they had talked to your brother. They asked me all about you, too. Chief Mayweather is a very thorough man. Did you know that he was a student of mine?"

"No, sir. I didn't know that."

"One of my best." The kindly face suddenly wasn't so grandfatherly anymore. "I wouldn't cross him. I wouldn't withhold information from him."

"I'm not."

"I didn't say you were," Dr. Baker corrected me. "I said I wouldn't. Would you like to know what I told him?"

"Okay," I said. "Sure."

"I said you were a good student with no history of discipline problems. You have not distinguished yourself at our school, but you have also done nothing wrong. Slightly above-average grades. Regular participation in extracurricular activities. You have friends. Your teachers have nothing bad to say about you. Your performance at Pineville has been positive but unremarkable. Fair?"

"Fair," I agreed.

Dr. Baker seemed to hear something in my voice or read something in my face that he didn't like. His eyes gleamed as he leaned forward. "Mediocrity is nothing to be proud of, Jeff. Is it? But then we can't all be world beaters. They also serve who only stand and wait. Yes?"

I had no idea what he was talking about, but I nodded.

"Is there anything you'd like to say to me?" he asked.

"No, sir."

"Is there anything about your family you'd like to discuss with me? I can be trusted to keep a confidence."

"There's really nothing. You sent for me."

He folded his hands together on top of his desk. "That's right, I did, Jeff," he said pleasantly. His hands unfolded and drummed the tabletop. "So what do you think happened to him?" he asked, studying my face. And then suddenly his fingers folded together into two old fists that pounded the polished wood hard enough to make the fountain pens jump. *"What happened to Tommy Fraser?"*

"I have no idea," I said, looking back into his steady gaze. "I hope he turns up."

"Curious turn of phrase," Dr. Baker observed, unfolding his fists and slowly flexing his fingers, as if to restore circulation. "One might imagine an old sock suddenly turning up, but not a lost boy. Do you think he'll turn up, Jeff? I'm not compromising the investigation by telling you the police have found neither hide nor hair of him so far. Do you have any reason to think Tommy Fraser will turn up?"

"No, sir. I just hope he will."

"Me too," he said. "Listen, there's a problem at your home. A small but shameful act of vandalism."

I found myself standing up.

He waved a hand for me to be calm. "Nothing serious. No one was hurt. But this is why I said the newspaper article was unfortunate. Pineville is a tight-knit community. People are worried about Tommy. I'm sending you home. Right now. Your mother needs you. Go."

 **16**

The street outside our house had been turned into a police parking lot. Half a dozen policemen trudged methodically back and forth over our front lawn and the neighboring yards, scouring the grass for clues. I spotted several more cops going door-to-door, asking our neighbors if they had seen anything.

Mrs. Baines stood on her front porch, coaxing details out of one young policeman. He was holding a pad and pen, but it looked like she had turned things around and was now interrogating him. She was a well-known gossip, and she waved at me as I walked by and flashed me a smile, as if to thank me for bringing so much excitement to the neighborhood. I gave her a quick wave back and hurried up our walk.

I identified myself as a family member to the policewoman at our front door. She let me in but told me not to disturb anything because the investigation was still going on. "Maybe you can give us a little help with your mom," she suggested. "She's had a scare."

The rock was about the size of a grapefruit, so I figured whoever had chucked it through our picture window must have had a pretty good arm. When I walked into our living room it was lying next to our green sofa, where it had landed an hour earlier in an explosion of broken glass.

Two policemen were trying to keep my mom from sweeping up the key evidence. She waved a dustpan and brandished a broom, and kept repeating, "Please, I need to sweep up the glass before somebody gets hurt."

"Lady, nobody's gonna get hurt," a police sergeant told her. "You can't clean anything up till we're done."

"But this is my house . . ." Mom protested.

"Hi, Mom," I said. "Are you okay?"

She turned at the sound of my voice, and attempted a smile. "Hi, Jeff, I'm fine," she said. "It just missed me, thank God. I was walking near the window and . . ." The faint smile quivered and died on her lips, and was replaced by a pleading look of nervous confusion. "They won't let me clean it up," she said, looking around at the police as if she didn't understand what they were doing in her living room but was too polite to ask them to leave. The brittleness I saw in her face scared me—it looked like another rock or even a loud sound might shatter her, too, at any second.

Chief Mayweather emerged from our kitchen and nodded at me. "Your dad's on his way home. You and your mom might want to wait upstairs while we finish doing our job here."

"Sure," I said. "Come on, Mom," and I gently led her away. It occurred to me as we climbed the stairs that the heavy police presence might not be just to investigate the rock throwing. And Chief Mayweather might not have asked me to escort Mom upstairs out of concern for her well-being. Troy was still the main

149

suspect in Fraser's disappearance. The chief might want us out of the way so that he could have a look around our house without a search warrant.

Well, fine, I thought. If he finds something to link this to Troy, at least that will be progress on the case. At least this nightmare will be a few minutes closer to resolution.

Mom let me lead her into her bedroom, and then she pulled free and sat on the side of the king-sized bed. She put her head in her hands and bent forward, like someone who's feeling sick on an airplane. I didn't know what to do, so I touched her shoulder and asked softly, "Mom, are you going to throw up? Do you want me to call a doctor?"

"No, I'm fine," she said. "Would you get me a washcloth with some cold water."

I hurried into the bathroom and let the water run till it was ice-cold. I wet a cloth and wrung it out so it wouldn't drip, and then I carried it back into the bedroom. Mom took it from me and held it over her face, pressing it over her eyes with both palms.

The bedroom was warm and still. A buzz of police conversation drifted up from downstairs.

"Dad's on his way home," I told her.

"Yes," she said. "That's good. We should all be together." She took the washcloth away from her face, folded it neatly in thirds, and placed it on the rug by her feet. "Come and sit with me, Jeff."

I sat down next to her on the bed.

Mom put her arm around me and pulled me close. We're

not the kind of family that hugs and kisses all the time, and it had been years since I cuddled next to her this way. "I think a lot about when we were all together," Mom said softly. "The other day I was going through some of the old albums. There are ones you've never seen, I bet. I found pictures from the summer we traveled across country, when you were just three. You were such a cute little fellow."

"All mothers think that about their kids," I said. I could feel her body trembling between breaths.

"You were both cute and oh so sweet and polite," she said. "Every word out of your brother's mouth was 'Thank you' or 'Please.' That summer we drove all the way to California and back, and at every campground some lady would remark what gentlemen you two were, and how lucky I was. My little angels. That's what I called you. Little angel number one and little angel number two."

"I was number two?" I asked.

She nodded absently, and her hand stroked my hair. "I taught you every song I knew, the corny folk ballads and the religious hymns and the patriotic anthems. Your favorites were religious tunes. 'Swing Low, Sweet Chariot.' 'Amazing Grace.' Those songs have been running through my head the last few days. I can picture the two of you giggling and kicking the front seat and singing 'Oh, When the Saints Go Marching In' louder and louder till your father screamed from the front to hush it up back there."

"So that's where I learned the words to all those songs?" I asked her. "Hey, Mom, would you like a glass of cold water?"

"We drove west in the big old Chevy station wagon," she went on, very far away from me. "Do you remember that car, Jeffrey? It was never any good from the day your father bought it, just a junkmobile, but it sure did have room in the back. We filled it up with suitcases and pots and pans and the tent. Your father got so good at setting up that tent he could have it standing in twenty minutes from the time we pulled in to a campsite. He gave you boys jobs to help him. Your job was to find the rocks to drive in the tent pegs. You were just three, but you used to find flat rocks and your brother would knock those plastic pegs in, and we tented all the way out to California and back, rain or shine. Seemed like more rain than shine."

"I remember it a little bit," I told her. "I remember the lightning storm at the Grand Canyon."

"Do you remember the bear?" she asked.

"No. A real bear? What happened?"

"One night, in the Grand Tetons, we heard people screaming nearby. Somebody had seen a bear. We thought about leaving, but it was pitch-dark and we couldn't decide if it was safer to go or just to stay put.

"Then we heard a loud growl, right nearby. Such a deep and angry sound, it made my heart jump. Your father, bless his heart, picked up the ax he used to chop wood, and he stood outside the tent holding it ready for God knows what. I could see his silhouette through the tent in the moonlight. I called him to come back in, but he stayed out there, standing slightly crouched like a batter in a baseball game, holding the ax ready for a swing. And then I saw your brother. He was just seven, but

152

he had picked up a steak knife and was holding it in his little hand like a sword, and he said, 'Don't worry, Mom, if the bear tries to hurt you, I'll kill it.' He had such a serious look on his face when he said that." My mom broke off for a second. "And that was the first time I think Troy ever held a knife as a weapon."

She was quiet for a minute. I stroked her shoulder. "Mom," I asked softly, "you think he did it, don't you? You think Troy did something to that kid at school?"

"I don't want to think so," she whispered, and her body trembled again. "Jeff, I remember a time in Youngman's Market in Buffalo, when I was shopping for groceries and all of a sudden I saw Mrs. Shea, just standing there staring at me. I had been avoiding her for months, and suddenly there she was in the dairy section. I was buying eggs, and I nearly dropped them on the floor. Oh, Jeff, the misery in her face! Before I could think what to do she shouted, *'Why did he do it? You tell me why?'*

"I left my cart loaded up with groceries and I ran down the aisle to get away. She came after me, not running but somehow keeping up, and shouting over and over, *'My sweet little Billy. Tell me why?'*

"I remember running past the lines at the cash registers and everyone turning to look at me. I almost knocked over a little girl who was standing with her mother. I ran out into the parking lot, and a car jammed on its brakes and almost hit me . . . And—"

My mom stopped talking very suddenly and lay back on the bed, turning her face away from me as if afraid what I might see there. I pulled the curtain closed to block the afternoon sunlight, and then I said, "Ma, I'm gonna get you a glass of cold water. I'll be right back."

When I got down to the kitchen, my father had just arrived. He was talking to Chief Mayweather, but he stopped when he saw my face. "Where is she?" he asked.

"In the bedroom," I told him.

Without another word Dad headed up the stairs, taking them two at a time.

An hour later he came back down and said Mom had taken a pill to relax, and was sleeping. The police had left, so we swept up the broken glass and taped up cardboard to cover the hole in the window. We worked without speaking. It was a chilly night, and a cold wind seemed to blow through that hole and whistle around our living room, as if to remind us how vulnerable and open we now were to the outside world.

Troy got home from work about nine. He said he had heard about the rock-throwing incident, and had already made some plans that he wanted to fill us in on. "Let me just wash up and then we should all talk," he suggested.

Ten minutes later the three of us gathered around the kitchen table for a late dinner of leftovers. There was half a roast chicken and some string beans from the night before, and assorted cheeses and coleslaw. We sat there having a strange little picnic while the wind howled around our house. Troy didn't waste much time in announcing his intentions. "First of all, it's important for me that you both know that I didn't do anything wrong," he began. "Dad, I know you believe me, and Jeff, I know you don't, but I never touched that Fraser kid." He looked right at me as he said Tommy's name, and I returned his gaze without blinking. "But I'm leaving in the morning," he finished.

"If you didn't do anything wrong, then you shouldn't leave," my father started to object.

"*Dad*," I cut in, "he knows what he has to do."

We hushed up as the first stanza of "Swing Low, Sweet Chariot," floated down from the second floor. Footsteps descended the stairs and plodded toward us across the creaky floorboards. My mom walked into the kitchen in her yellow bathrobe, feet in slippers, hands tucked in pockets. "Sorry if we woke you," my father said gently. "We were having a late snack. You should go back to sleep." He attempted to steer her away, but she shook his hands off.

"If one of my sons is leaving my house, shouldn't I know why?" she asked, and she sat down at the table.

"I'm going because Jeff's absolutely right," Troy told her, and then he looked at my dad. "And he has been from the beginning, Pop. I shouldn't have let you bring me back here under your roof. It was too dangerous, too selfish of me. I wanted to believe in a fresh start, but the truth is I have too much history behind me. It follows me around like a bad smell I can never wash off, and now you guys are stinking of it, too. I'm so sorry."

"You have nothing to apologize for," my father said. "Look, when you first came home none of us knew quite what to expect. But you got a job, and you haven't made any trouble for us. You say you haven't done anything wrong outside our home, and I believe you. So you belong here, with your family. Whoever threw that rock through our window is a coward and a bully, and we shouldn't even think about giving in to him."

Troy put a hand on my father's shoulder. They looked so much alike it was uncanny. How could two such different people share the same features, the same eyes? "I really appreciate your faith and loyalty," Troy told him. "But it's my decision and I've already made it. When they start throwing rocks through the window, it's time to stop standing on principle and get out of Dodge, or in this case Pineville. I've found a place over in Waretown—a friend of a guy who works at the grocery has a basement apartment he rents out. He described it to me over the phone, and it sounds nice enough."

"Are you going to keep your job?" Mom asked.

Troy nodded. "Your friend Walter is a loyal guy, too. He said I could keep working at his grocery, but not at a cash register anymore, at least until this blows over. He's gonna put me down in the stockrooms, out of the public view. We'll see how that goes. I was going to move out tonight, but I think it will be better if I go in daylight, so whoever threw the rock sees me load up my things and take off. I told the police about my plans so they won't think I'm trying to escape. They have my new address. So things are all set . . . "

He turned to me. "Most of all, I know I've caused you trouble, Jeff. I'm truly sorry. It was never my intention to wreck your life here. Maybe by moving out I can undo a little of the harm I've done. I hope you still have some brotherly love for me somewhere in your heart."

I looked back at him and I could hear the cardboard patch slapping against the window in the night wind. "You're doing the right thing to move out," I told Troy. "But Waretown's only five miles down the road. Something like this Fraser mess can follow you a lot more than five miles. And continuing to work at the grocery doesn't sound like such a great idea either. You should make a whole new start, Troy."

My father tensed up at this, but he didn't say anything.

Mom looked at me with sad red eyes, and then turned those eyes on her firstborn to hear his response.

Troy's own eyes flashed, but I couldn't tell whether he admired my courage or was pissed off that I hadn't been taken in by his apology. "Maybe I should," he acknowledged. "I appreciate the advice. But one step at a time is the way I like to travel, brother. Now maybe I'd better go pack."

 **17**

The coaches' office was in fact not really an office; it was a converted supply room in the basement, near the phys ed department. The coaches of five different fall sports shared the space, so it was brimming with an odd combination of old and half-broken sports equipment. Torn soccer goal netting spread across the floor like a fungus near deflated footballs that crawled out of cartons as if seeking daylight, while chipped field hockey sticks waved sadly out the one dusty window at the teachers' parking lot.

Coach Wallace stood by that small window, chewing on his mustache. "I don't see why you have to quit, Hastings."

"I don't have to. Nobody's making me. I want to."

"You've been on our team for three years."

"And I've enjoyed it, and now I think it's time for me to do something else after school."

"Like what?" Coach asked.

"I don't know exactly," I confessed. "But I do know that the team will be better off without me. And I'll be better off, too. So it's a no-brainer."

"You're doing this for the team?" he asked suspiciously. He

glanced at the shut door, and then dropped his voice to a whisper. "Jeff, does this have anything to do with an ugly incident that happened yesterday after practice?"

I kept my face blank and my voice empty. "Nothing happened yesterday."

"I heard some of the guys got on your case. I meant to talk to you about it, but you beat me to it."

If you wanted to talk to me about it, you had all day to find me, I thought to myself. But what I said was: "Nothing happened yesterday. It's just time for me to go. Please don't make this hard for me."

"Is that a red mark on your forehead? Jeff, did somebody take a swing at you?" He squinted at me in the bad light. "Jesus, you got a scratch on your arm, too." He was getting angry now. "Somebody grabbed you and held you—"

"I banged my head walking into a door," I told him. "Coach, I've enjoyed playing and I've still got friends on the team. I can't blame some of the guys if they're worried about Tommy and don't completely trust me anymore." I felt my eyes tearing up, so I turned away and said in a burst, "You always taught us the importance of the team, and how we shouldn't just think about ourselves. So let me do something for the team. The guys have five more games left. I'm just a distraction. Let me go. Please."

Coach Wallace's stubby fingers sifted through torn soccer netting while his eyes studied me. I had never thought of him as a particularly perceptive man, but coaching for thirty years probably teaches you a few things. "You don't have the foggiest idea where Tommy Fraser is," he said. It wasn't a question. He knew.

"Of course not."

"You must be going through sheer hell," he said. "I read about that brother of yours. Sounds like a piece of work. I've got a few relatives I wouldn't mind sending back to the store myself. But if you quit the team now, Jeff, do you know how it makes you look?"

"Guilty," I answered.

"As sin." He nodded. "Don't go down that road, Jeff. If you act like you're hiding something, people are going to keep trying to find it. Stand proud and look them right in the eye and tell the truth. I'll make sure nobody on the team bothers you again."

By way of reply I rummaged in my bag and held out my two shirts for him. "Here are my jerseys, home and away. I washed them last night." He didn't make a move to take them. "You won't be doing me any favors by trying to keep me on the team. I don't need my character built that way. The truth is, I've come to realize that I don't like soccer."

"You just realized that, after playing all these years?"

"I've probably known it all along, but I just admitted it to myself in the last two weeks," I told him. "I think I'd rather run cross-country." Coach Wallace had a long-standing rivalry with the cross-country coach, and I hoped telling him this might do the trick. I held my shirts out again, and sure enough, this time he took them.

"Go run. But if you change your mind . . ." he began.

"I won't. Good luck with the rest of the season."

I left the coaches' office and made my way through the halls, survival instincts on full throttle. These are the dangerous places that have to be skirted. Rooms where you can be dragged into and beaten on. Doorways far from other doorways. Supply closets with steel doors that slide shut, sealing you in. Dark throat-like basement stairwells that can swallow your screams for help.

The pressure at our school kept building day by day and hour by hour. I could feel the anxiety going up, like a barometer before a hurricane. If something had happened to Fraser, strong and capable as he was, it could happen to anyone. If Tommy could disappear, anyone else might vanish, too, into the misty bay or the endless stunted pines.

Feeding this fear was the complete mystery of what had happened to Tommy. If he had dropped dead on a soccer field of a heart attack, our school would have mourned but everyone would have understood. Now no one understood, and that was scary. The principal's phrase rang in my mind: "So far the police have found neither hide nor hair of Tommy."

But there had to be an answer. Tommy wasn't the type to have been beamed up onto a UFO by aliens. He was Franchise Fraser, Golden Boy of Pineville High. He had been born and raised in this town, as had his father and grandfather before him. His roots were planted deep in Pineville's sandy soil.

Whether he was wrestling or playing soccer or just walking down the hallways of our school, there had always been a lively cockiness to Tommy. "I am here, I am at the center of all the action, stirring things up and loving it," his glittering black eyes had seemed to say. And now he was gone. Poof. Vanished into the autumn like the smoke from burning leaves.

There had to be an answer, and the police were determined to find it. Two patrol cars took up residence in the guest spaces at the edges of our parking lot, as if riding herd on all the students' and teachers' cars. A policewoman with a cheerful face began standing guard at our school's front door, welcoming us in the morning and learning many students' names. More town cops trolled for clues inside the school. Chief Mayweather chose his younger officers for this duty, and they could be seen in the halls and the cafeteria, chatting with students and teachers in a relaxed and friendly fashion.

The gleaming black Ford sedan with the blue flasher that I had noticed weeks before returned and parked in front of our school. I figured it had to be some sort of unmarked FBI car. Its driver, the short man whose uniform seemed to be khaki pants and a blue blazer, I imagined to be an ace special agent. I spotted him with Chief Mayweather three or four times, always talking seriously.

The chief was coming under fire for not making progress on the case. Our local newspaper questioned whether a small-town police force could handle this disappearance, or whether it was time to bring in state or federal law enforcement.

There had to be an answer. That was the reason why, twenty minutes after a perfectly normal soccer practice had ended, five kids had suddenly pushed me back into the shower room, pulling my towel away so I was naked and defenseless.

Three football players and two of my soccer teammates. Faces I knew. Two of them went around turning on all the showers to create a cascade that would drown out our voices. The other three blocked the only exit. "We don't want to hurt you, Hastings. But we need to know what happened to Tommy. And you're gonna tell us right now."

My answers and excuses sounded even lamer now than when I was twelve. "Guys, Tommy was a friend of mine. I wish I could help, but I don't know anything. I swear I don't."

I saw an opening in the wall of bodies and tried to dart out. Hands grabbed at me. Nails raked my arm. I pulled free and screamed, but the showers drowned my voice. BAM, a punch thudded into the side of my face. The yellow shower room tiles swirled. I spun down to the wet floor and covered up, my body curled above a drain.

"*Where the hell's Tommy?*" a voice demanded loudly.

"*Tell us or we'll beat your face in.*"

"*Let's cut his nuts off if he won't talk.*"

"*Where's your brother? Did he take off?*"

Then a lookout's voice shouted a warning: "*Teacher's coming!*" They all ran out of there. I got slowly to my feet and decided it was time to quit the soccer team.

There had to be an answer. That was why I was singled out, picked on, and watched so closely by people who barely knew me. They thought I had that answer, or even that I was that answer.

Surely that was the reason a tall man in a work shirt who I had never seen before stepped in front of me on a deserted stretch of Edgewood Drive. There weren't any houses here—that was why I had chosen it as my route home from school. Just woods and bramble, and the muddy foundation and first-floor skeleton of a house going up.

"Hey, you. Hold it, buddy," the tall guy said.

I registered that he didn't even know my name. "What?"

"Boss wants to talk to you."

He turned toward the muddy construction lot and pointed to a blue bulldozer that had already chewed out part of a hillside. It was sitting at an angle, so that it looked like it might tumble down the slope at any second.

I had a pretty good idea who might be sitting atop the bulldozer. I considered walking away, but I knew he was up there watching and I didn't want him to think I was a coward.

I picked my way across the rocks and the mud to the foot of the big blue bulldozer. Mr. Doyle waved down to me from the driver's platform. "Climb on up, Jeff."

I hesitated, partly because he wasn't exactly my favorite person and also because I had no idea how to climb on a bulldozer.

"Step on the tread," he shouted down.

I stepped on the tread, pulled myself up, and swung onto the platform. Mr. Doyle was sitting on the only seat, in front of a bristling array of levers. He looked at ease up there, high above the muddy ground that fell away steeply, like the chute of a ski slope. I was struck by what a big man he was—his shoulders and arms seemed to fill up the driver's cage. "Thanks for coming up," he said. "I heard about that rock somebody tossed through your window, and it really ticked me off. Your parents didn't get hit?"

"No, sir," I said. "They're fine. Thanks for asking."

"That's disrespecting a house," he said. "Did you know I renovated that house? I put in that window."

"I didn't know that."

"About ten years before you folks moved in. One of the first I ever worked on. Still standing up okay, huh?"

"It leaks now and then, but it's doing okay," I told him.

"It leaks, huh?" he said and then he threw a punch at me. I ducked back quickly, raising my own fists, and realized too late that his blow was meant as a playful feint. He grinned and said, "Hey, hey, look who's willing to take me on. Let's not fight up here, Jeff. I always liked you, son."

"You had a strange way of showing it," I muttered, unclenching my fists and feeling a little foolish.

He shrugged his broad shoulders. "I'd do anything to protect my little girl, but that was nothing against you or your folks. Your brother, on the other hand, sounds like a whole different breed of dog. But that's not your fault."

"I'm glad you realized that," I said. "How's Beth?"

Mr. Doyle seemed surprised by this question. "Don't you see her in school?"

"She won't talk to me. You made her promise not to."

"Good girl." He nodded approvingly. "She's fine, Jeff. Miserable but fine." His small, hard brown eyes glinted strangely. "She still keeps your picture by her bed. Guess she really must have liked you." I couldn't tell if he was taunting me or

165

paying me some kind of compliment. "She's resisting my efforts to send her away to school," he went on, "but I'll find a place she likes."

"You're gonna take her away from all her friends?"

"Beth never had any trouble making friends," Mr. Doyle pointed out. "And the kind of school I'm thinking of weeds out bad influences. Take that Fraser boy, for instance. He was nothing but trouble. He once worked for me, and I caught him stealing. I should have kicked his lazy butt right there. But I just fired him."

"I don't believe Tommy was a thief," I said. "He worked at the diner and he always had plenty of spending money."

"That doesn't mean somebody's not a thief," Mr. Doyle said as if he knew a lot more about the world than I did. "I saw that chump for what he was, and he could never stand that. He wanted to take me on. I could see it in his eyes. The day I fired him he almost got up the nerve to come after me. God, would I have loved that excuse. But he was smart that way. He knew what would have happened."

A breeze blew through the construction site, whipping canvas tarps against concrete blocks. "What would have happened?" I asked him.

Mr. Doyle chuckled, enjoying the suggestion buried in my question. "Not what did happen, Jeff. Making people disappear is not my style."

"It sounds like you're gonna make your daughter disappear from our high school," I said back quickly.

His grin vanished and his voice became a lash. *"You watch*

that wise mouth." He took a few breaths, and I could see him willing himself to calm down. "You're tougher than you look," he finally said. "I kind of like that. I never understood what Beth saw in you, but now maybe I do." He studied me, the way I bet he studied a house for structural flaws. "Speaking of taking on Fraser," he went on, "I hear you tangled with him just before he disappeared. I gather he whupped you pretty bad."

"He just knocked me down," I said.

"And then he disappeared. Jeff, we're just sitting up here shooting the breeze, but I figure you and your brother would be a good team for making someone disappear," Mr. Doyle mused. "You'd be the brains. Him the muscle."

"Making people disappear is not my style either," I told him. "I think Tommy's gonna turn up."

"I don't," Mr. Doyle said with such certainty that it was like he was slamming a door. "Just a hunch," he added quickly. "Look over there." He pointed out at the blue water visible to the east. "One thing about living near the ocean. Lots of real estate to hide a body. Tie on a few weights and let the fish have a new friend." He grinned at me as if we were sharing a secret. "Just out of curiosity, does your family keep a boat, Jeff?"

"No," I told him, and moved to the edge of the driving platform, ready to swing down. "But you have lots of digging equipment. I got into a fight with Tommy because I thought he was hitting on Beth. You wouldn't have liked that either, would you?"

"He wouldn't have dared," Mr. Doyle growled.

"I think he would have," I told him, looking right back into those small and hard brown eyes. "And I think you would have done anything to protect your daughter from a guy you hated."

"Anything," Mr. Doyle agreed in a low rumble. His small eyes gleamed. "Let me show you how this digging equipment works."

He switched on the ignition and his hands moved expertly on the levers. Before I could climb down, the bulldozer growled to life. Its treads began to turn, and it lurched forward. I clung to a side of the cage as the metal behemoth rolled down the steep slope to the rocky flat of the construction site.

Mr. Doyle pulled more levers. The bulldozer's great scoop blade descended and bit into the rocky earth, and lifted two hundred pounds of rocks and mud. The roar from the exhaust stack behind my head sounded like the growl of an angry dinosaur. Mr. Doyle seemed to be enjoying himself as he steered the bulldozer in a wild and jerky circle, and I was amazed at how fast this monster could spin around. Then the great scoop blade came down, dumping out its load in an ear-shattering explosion of mud and gravel.

I climbed down, jumped onto the tread, and ran for the street.

18

The first whisper I heard of Troy's vindication came from an unlikely source. I was sitting by myself at a back table in the cafeteria, nibbling on one of the worst meatball grinders ever assembled by human hands, when I glimpsed Mr. Tsuyuki hurry in. I had my algebra book standing open in front of me to give the impression that I was cramming hard for an exam, so he didn't see me right away. He checked out the soccer team table and ran his eyes over several other tables before finally spotting me. I don't think the open algebra book fooled him for a minute, but he was too nice and too polite to ask why I was sitting all alone. Instead he said, "Hi, Jeff. Can we talk?"

I snapped the book shut and pushed the grinder away. "Sure. What's up?"

"Let's take a walk," he said, and suddenly I knew something big had happened. An empty corner table in a noisy cafeteria is private enough for most conversations.

I gratefully winged the meatball grinder into the nearest garbage can and followed him into the corridor. He headed for the science department and led me quickly through an empty classroom to the supply room in back.

It was a small space, crammed with enough apparatus to explain everything from the Theory of Evolution to the Laws of Motion. A chart of the order Coleoptera was draped awkwardly over a prone plastic human skeleton so that beetles with long antennae and bright metallic bodies seemed to crawl over ribs and femurs. A stuffed owl with an impressive wingspan perched on a table, its yellow eyes glinting in the fluorescent light as if searching for prey among the jars of chemicals and glass beakers that were stacked floor to ceiling on metal shelves. The supply room door swung shut, and we were alone.

"What's up?" I asked him again.

"I wanted to give you some good news," Mr. Tsuyuki told me. "At least, it's news that I think will be a great relief for you. I get the feeling that things have been a little tough lately, so I wanted to tell you even though there's been no official announcement." His eyeglasses almost slid off his nose, and he leveled them with a finger. "I'm probably breaking rules by telling you this, so I'm not going into much detail, and I don't want you to tell anyone else till it becomes public knowledge—"

"Did they find Fraser?" I cut him off.

"No," he said.

"But they found out what happened to him?"

"Not exactly. But they did find out some things that point in a direction. And it's a very different direction from your brother."

The air in the small supply room suddenly seemed so thin and stale that I reached out and grabbed a shelf to steady myself. "What kind of different direction? What are you talking about?"

Mr. Tsuyuki was relaxed and funny in class, but one-on-one he was a formal, shy man, and I got the feeling he didn't often break rules. "I can't say more. There's been a serious problem at this school for a while. It's been under investigation. Tommy's disappearance seems to be linked to that problem. Which means that it's not linked to your brother or to you." He added quickly, "Not that I ever thought that you had anything to do with it."

I figured it out in about five seconds. Something about his voice and choice of words tipped me off. There could only be one type of problem in our school under long-term investigation. For months I had heard rumors of Ecstasy and methamphetamines taken by some of the wilder kids, and even passed around at parties. I recalled Tommy on the roof of the school during intermission of the fall concert, lighting up a joint. "Drugs?" I guessed.

Mr. Tsuyuki glanced at me, as if wondering how I knew. He didn't confirm it—he just stood with his thin arms dangling awkwardly down and a sad look on his face. "Let's just say this school's not in great shape," he whispered. Behind him the old owl seemed to spread its wings a little wider as if preparing to burst through the supply room window and fly screeching around the hallways. "You'll know the full story soon enough," he promised. "What's important is that you and your family are off the hook."

I let out a long breath. That was indeed what was important. No more rocks aimed at our window. No more beatings in the shower room. But on some level I had trouble believing the good news. The mystery of Fraser's disappearance seemed to require a deeper explanation than just a school drug problem. "You're sure about this?"

"I wouldn't have told you if I wasn't. The police are following up lots of new leads."

"Okay. Thanks for telling me," I said. "You're right—I needed some good news. I appreciate it, and I won't break the confidence." Mr. Tsuyuki didn't move toward the door, so I didn't either. Instead we stood for a few seconds in silence. "Is there something else?" I asked.

He nodded. "Yes. I want to give you some advice."

"What kind of advice?"

"Personal advice," he said. "You know I'm Japanese. My parents were both teachers in Japan. There it's expected that teachers will take a close interest in the lives of their students. And if they see a student having trouble, it's their job, almost like surrogate parents, to try to help. You were a good student in my class."

"You just used the past tense," I noted.

"You've zoned out and stopped taking notes," he said. "You've missed a bunch of homework assignments, and you're the only student who hasn't chosen a paper topic."

I nodded. "Sorry. It's been a hard time . . ."

"I understand. Jeff, I hear you quit the soccer team. I heard why, too, not that we need to go into it."

"Good. Let's not," I said.

He looked embarrassed to be probing into my life, but he had started this conversation and I guess he felt he had to finish it. "And I always used to see you with friends. Or with Beth. And these days I see you alone a lot. Again, I understand why, and it's none of my business."

"So what's your advice?" I asked him.

He hesitated and then he surprised me, veering off away from me and toward himself. "Let me tell you a story. A true story about something that happened to me when I was six or seven years older than you are now. I was a serious physics student in those days. A very eager beaver. I practically lived at the lab." He grinned and shook his head at the memory of his earlier self.

"For my degree, I had to write a thesis. Instead of choosing a safe topic, I got wrapped up in one of my own ideas. I thought it was brilliant and even revolutionary. I kept it secret and wrote it up, and when it was ready I turned it in to my adviser, who was a famous scientist, and my role model. Well, he thought my idea was revolutionary, too, but he didn't exactly think it was brilliant."

Mr. Tsuyuki turned his head sideways and looked away from me, as if concentrating on a beetle on the Coleoptera chart. "In fact, he thought it was hilarious. He said it was just about the silliest idea he had ever come across. Even now, twenty years later, I can hear his laughter."

"Did you write another thesis?" I asked.

"No. I dropped out of that program. And I followed another direction."

"You became a teacher?" I guessed. I had always wondered how someone of Mr. Tsuyuki's intellect had ended up at our lousy high school.

"The point is," Mr. Tsuyuki said, "I had a calling to be a scientist. But I let him knock me off my stride."

"I don't have a calling to be a scientist," I told him. "I don't have any kind of calling. The phone must be disconnected."

He didn't smile at my feeble attempt at a joke. "This is not about having a calling. You are a friendly and smart kid with a good future." Mr. Tsuyuki looked right into my eyes and added in a low voice, "And I get the sense that you're fighting to be happy, which is a very brave thing to do." Staring back at him, I suddenly wondered if despite his calmness and perpetual good humor Mr. Tsuyuki was, in fact, a desperately unhappy man. He didn't wear a wedding ring, and he never talked about friends or family. Did he have a wife or a girlfriend or kids to come home to? Was his sailboat the main passion of his life?

"Jeff, I've heard about your brother," he went on in a low voice. "And I've seen how much you've been keeping to yourself lately. Here's my advice, for what it's worth." He paused and then spoke his few words of advice very distinctly and with a noticeable tinge of anger: "A person can ruin your life only if you let him."

I sensed that the wisdom he had just shared with me had cost him a lot of pain. "Thank you," I said. "I'll remember that. But I'm not sure I have as much control as you think. You don't know my brother."

"I don't have to know him," Mr. Tsuyuki snapped almost

174

angrily. "It's not about him. *It's your life, Jeff. Your one and only life.* Don't give anyone the power to take it away from you."

BING, BING, the bell. Mr. Tsuyuki pushed open the supply room door, signifying that our conversation was over. We crossed the empty classroom together. "Thanks for the good news," I said, my hand reaching for the doorknob. "And for the advice." I started to open the door and then looked up at him. "Oh, and I've chosen a paper topic. If it's okay, I'd like to write about evil."

Mr. Tsuyuki's eyebrows took a surprised little hop toward his receding hairline. "That's an interesting subject. But it's much too broad."

"I'll find a way to focus it," I promised him, and headed off into the stampede of teenagers who no longer seemed quite as threatening as they had an hour ago.

That afternoon I asked Mr. Terry if I could run with the cross-country squad. He had been a pretty good runner in his day, but he was now the size of a walrus, with a booming roar of a voice to match. He said the season was half over, so it was too late to run in races, but I was more than welcome to do road-work with the team.

So I ran with them. I didn't know any of them very well, and they clearly weren't that interested in making friends with me. But I followed them over a ten-mile course without too much trouble, and I enjoyed the solitary challenge of long-distance running on a crisp fall day.

The long trek took us up hills and along winding town roads. As we pounded through Waretown, I suddenly realized we were only a block from the apartment my brother had rented. It was a run-down and depressing neighborhood in what was otherwise a nice town. At intersections, liquor stores with security glass and barred windows faced small delis advertising lottery tickets. Dilapidated two-story houses stood side by side on tiny, weed-choked lots.

I pictured Troy walking these narrow streets and buying food in these sad shops. Did he cook for himself after long days at the grocery? I could understand him living at home while my mom cooked for him, but why was he sticking around in such a dull and depressing place and working long hours at a dead-end job? It didn't make sense to me, and anything about Troy that I couldn't figure out was a new reason to worry.

We turned toward the water, and the houses started to get nicer. I tried to block out all thoughts of my brother, and concentrate on my running rhythm.

We were soon on a long stretch of bay beach. The sand and gravel were hard on my legs. This was the beach closest to Troy's new home. Did he come here in the evenings and walk these long stretches of sand? Did he light up his evening cigarette here, beneath the moon and stars? Did he still watch passing ships, and imagine himself sailing away to distant ports? As my feet sloshed through tide pools, I mulled over Mr. Tsuyuki's big news.

On some level I didn't believe it. I felt in my heart Troy must be responsible for Fraser's disappearance. And I couldn't get the image of Mr. Doyle out of my mind, sitting atop the bulldozer, his big hands operating the levers as he dug up a hillside.

If Tommy had been involved with drugs and brought this all on himself, then Troy and Mr. Doyle were completely innocent.

Dinner that night was torture. My mom made lasagna, and the three of us sat at the table with four chairs, trying to make small talk. Mom's eyes were red from lack of sleep, and she barely touched the pasta. I wanted to tell them the news so that the weight I could almost see pressing down on their shoulders might be lifted. But Mr. Tsuyuki had asked me not to tell anyone, and I had to honor his request. If what he told me was true, in a town as small as Pineville the story would leak out on its own.

Sure enough, the next day rumors were all over school. I heard the whispers, but in my isolation I didn't get the full story till after school. Smitty was waiting by my locker, already in his shorts and shirt for soccer practice. I was surprised to see him there, because he hadn't said one word to me since we had quarreled on the way to gym class. It had been a tough time for me, and I had expected more from a former best friend. Still, when he asked if I had heard the news, I was too curious to resist. "What news?"

He told me quickly. I had been right: drugs were the key to the mystery. The police had been piecing it together slowly, but they had gotten the break they needed when Lisa Sullivan had reluctantly come forward. She had been Fraser's girlfriend for years, so she hadn't wanted to name him as a drug dealer. But she had finally realized that finding him was more important than anything else.

Franchise Fraser had been selling Ecstasy and meth for

nearly a year. He had kept his part-time job at the diner for cover, but it was the drug money that had bought him the new van and all the snazzy clothes. Fraser had kept the drug dealing secret from his family and even his girlfriend. Lisa had only found out about it a few weeks ago, when he tried to borrow money from her. He had gone into debt to his suppliers, and he was scared what they might do to him if he couldn't come up with some cash. Lisa had broken up with him, but had not told anyone his secret.

"It's still a mystery without a solution," I pointed out when Smitty finished. "Why did Fraser disappear? Are you saying they killed him because he owed them money?"

The big guy shrugged as if I had brought up a minor detail. "I'm sure the police will solve this now that they have suspects and a motive."

I nodded. "Well, thanks for telling me."

"What are friends for," he said.

"I don't know. What are they for?" I asked him back.

The hall had emptied and we were pretty much alone. "So you quit the team," he said.

"Yeah, I'm running cross-country now. I like it."

"You don't miss soccer?"

"Not one bit. But you're gonna miss practice if you don't hurry. Better go."

He took a step away and then turned. "Jeffsky, I'm sorry we had a fight. I still think you should have told me the truth about your brother working at our store. But it seems like he had nothing to do with this Fraser thing. He's a hard worker, and he doesn't seem like such a bad guy. My dad's been a little ill, and your brother has sure helped us take up the slack."

"I'm sorry your dad's been sick."

"It's nothing serious. But your bro has really pitched in. We've worked together a couple of weekends and he's been trying to make friends, asking me questions about my work at the marine wildlife refuge, and the soccer team, and most of all about you. I've pretty much blown him off, but my dad says he deserves a second chance, so I'm gonna try to give him one."

"He doesn't deserve anything," I said, nervous that Troy had been asking questions about me. "Don't give him anything on my account."

Smitty nodded, and his big hands folded into fists. "I feel bad about what happened the other day after soccer practice. I didn't hear about it till it was over, or I would have tried to stop it. You know that, don't you?"

"It's over," I told him. "Forget about it. Now I have to get changed for cross-country. See ya later, Smitty."

 **19**

Troy's vindication was splashed all over the paper the next morning. MISSING PINEVILLE TEEN WAS DEALING DRUGS, ran a headline in the local news section. The article had some new details. An investigation into drug use at five area high schools had been going on for months. Tommy's disappearance had brought it into the open. Police suspected the drugs had come from down south, and law enforcement agencies were trying to track them to their source. The police hoped the people who supplied the drugs to Tommy would know what had happened to him.

"This is one case when bad news is good news," my dad said at breakfast. "I hate to think of a kid your age selling drugs, but maybe whoever threw the rock through our window would like to take it back." He lowered the paper and gave me a searching look. "Jeff, did you know there was a drug problem in Pineville?"

"No. I mean, I heard rumors, but there are probably drugs at every school in America."

"But this kid was a teammate of yours. I'm just asking the question a father needs to ask. You never . . ."

"No, I never," I told him.

"Good," he said. "I believe you. Let's hope they find Tommy and lock up whoever was supplying the stuff."

The news brought about a radical transformation in my mom. Instead of being tired, worried, and withdrawn, she suddenly buzzed about our house with nervous energy sweetened by a surface cheerfulness. She focused on the upcoming holidays, and how they would be a great chance to bring our family together. "We haven't had a real Thanksgiving, a fun family Thanksgiving, in years," she said.

I thought of our last few Thanksgivings and how they had seemed real and fun to me, but I didn't argue with her.

"I'm going to do it up this year," she promised. "A turkey and all the trimmings. And just wait till Christmas! I'll get out all the ornaments I have boxed away and we'll have a great big tree with presents for all of you, just like we had years ago in Buffalo."

Kids at school seemed to digest the news on two very different levels. On one hand, everyone figured out pretty quickly that if Tommy had been selling drugs, someone must have been buying them. The police had spent days roaming our school's hallways asking questions about Fraser. Word spread that the short man in the khaki pants who had driven the black Ford had been from a state narcotics task force. Surely now that this was all out in the open, arrest would soon follow arrest like a toppling chain of dominos.

On the other hand, everyone was glad that the mystery of Fraser's disappearance had been at least partially solved. We no longer had to worry that our school's Golden Boy had been swallowed up by some mysterious Bermuda Triangle–like force deep in the Pine Barrens. Drugs were a familiar evil, at least through movies and TV shows. If Tommy had gotten into trouble with drug dealers, it meant that the rest of us who had no contact with that world were safe.

I felt the change almost immediately. People who had been mean to me or given me the cold shoulder started to thaw. Smitty struck up several conversations with me, and mentioned a couple of new action movies I might want to see. I didn't make any plans with him, but it was hard to stay mad at a guy so good-natured.

I had a very strange conversation with Beth. She bumped into me one morning near my locker—I'm not sure whether she was lurking there or it happened by chance. She surprised me with a slight smile and a friendly "Hi."

"Hi, back," I said. "It's nice to hear one syllable of your voice, even if you're sorry you ever met me."

She looked surprised. "You must know I didn't mean that," she said. "Jeff, you can't give girls' names to the police and expect them not to be angry." And then she shocked me by saying, "I met your brother."

"Where?"

"At the grocery. He doesn't seem beyond redemption. In fact he was really polite."

"You don't have to talk to me if you want, but don't talk to him," I told her. *"Ever. For any reason."*

She looked at me curiously. "I wasn't planning on making a

habit of it. But for what it's worth, he knows how you feel about him, and he's sad about it. I got the feeling he's working hard to rebuild his life, and his greatest wish is that he could repair things with you." People turned into the hall and Beth walked off quickly, leaving me to wonder what she had been doing talking to Troy at the grocery and why he had told such lies to her.

Finally Chris Parker, one of the football players who had pushed me into the shower room and demanded answers about Fraser, surprised me by stammering out an apology. "It was nothing personal against you. Everybody knows you're not a bad guy. We just thought you might know something about Tommy. Sorry it got rough."

I figured if Smitty could thaw, if Beth could smile at me, and if Chris Parker could find it in his heart to apologize, there was something I needed to do also. It's not that I thought Troy was innocent—he had blood on his hands that he would never be able to wash off. But I had to admit it looked like he had had nothing to do with the disappearance of Franchise Fraser. And Beth's words stuck in my mind, so that I found myself brooding about him more and more and understanding his behavior less and less. Why had he told her he cared about patching things up with me? And why was he asking questions about me of Smitty? Why was he sticking around? What did he want here?

That Saturday morning I copied down the address my parents had written on the pad near the phone, and biked the five miles to Waretown. As I entered his seedy neighborhood, I once again wondered what Troy was doing here. If he really hadn't been responsible for Fraser's disappearance, why had he left our home for this? Sure, moving out had been the decent thing to do, but since when had Troy ever acted decently? And if he had done something to Fraser, why was he sticking around? The sudden focus on drugs at our school would have given him a perfect chance to slip away. Either way, his behavior made no sense to me.

It was ten in the morning and most stores were still closed, but I found a corner deli that was open and I bought a quart of orange juice and some doughnuts. Holding the breakfast bag in my right hand, I pedaled to Troy's house.

I don't always lock up my bike, but on that narrow street with the ill-kept yards and decrepit houses, I threaded the chain through both wheels and the frame before locking it around a rusty sign pole. The house was so shabby that I checked the address twice before descending three stone steps to the basement door and knocking.

At first there was no answer. I knew from Troy's routine when he had lived with us that Saturday was his day off and he didn't go out in the morning, so I knocked again, louder. I had the sense that I was being studied through the peephole. A few more seconds ticked by. Then, just as I was getting ready to give up, the door was yanked open.

Troy was wearing Jockey shorts and a T-shirt, and I could tell he had just woken up. "Brother Jeff. What an unexpected surprise," he said, his quick eyes taking in the orange juice and doughnuts in my hand, and then flicking out to the street, where they spotted my bike. "But you're a little early."

"It's ten. I thought maybe we could have breakfast."

For a minute I didn't think he would let me in. Then he stepped back and to one side. "File this away," he grunted. "Saturdays I sleep late."

His apartment was small and sparsely furnished. The floor was covered with a shabby gray carpet, and there were bars over the windows. He had a rickety card table and some folding chairs, a hot plate to cook on, a portable TV, and a mattress on the floor. I couldn't help wondering how much smaller his jail cell had been, and how closely he had re-created his prison decor. It kind of felt like a cage.

By the mattress I saw a jump rope, two twenty-five-pound iron barbells, and a few empty beer cans. That was all, except for the books and the drawings. There seemed to be books everywhere, on shelves and in piles on the floor. Troy had always read a lot, and I guessed that the prison library had offered him an escape during his five long years. Now it looked like his small but steady paycheck had allowed him to raid the nearby paperback book shops. There were old novels and art books and stacks of boating magazines, and several books for learning Spanish.

"You have enough books here?" I asked him, nearly tripping over a small tower of novels.

"I never have enough books," he said. "Try not to step on all of them, Jeff."

And then there was the art. His art. Troy had always been talented, but the years had clearly sharpened his disturbing gift. I say disturbing, because I don't think Troy ever drew anything that didn't have some capacity to shock. There were no pretty landscapes to be found in this dark little apartment. His only subjects were people and animals, and he drew them in such a way that it was often impossible to tell which was which. His humans frequently had fierce animal features. And his beasts always looked eerily human in intelligence and cunning. They were all over his apartment, a menagerie of unsettling images, stampeding across the floor or taped to the walls in savage flocks of five or six.

I noticed one particularly horrifying image that he had drawn over and over, as if trying to get it right. It was always sketched darkly, in pen and ink, emerging from shade or retreating into shadow. The creature had a human face, the body of a dragon, the wings of a bat, the feet of a pig, and a long forked tail. But it was the eyes in that human face that made me shiver. They weren't just human eyes—they were unmistakably Troy's eyes. "What is that?" I asked him. "Some dragon from one of your nightmares?"

He laughed. "Study your local history. That's the Jersey Devil. Come, let's have breakfast."

I didn't budge from the wall of horrors. It occurred to me that Troy had inherited my father's eyes, so that the devil he was sketching over and over had the eyes of the most gentle and saintly man I know. "I've heard of the Jersey Devil," I told him. "I thought it had a horse's head."

"The legends vary," he said. "Come on, let's try one of those doughnuts."

I sensed that Troy was trying to lead me away from his artwork. On instinct I looked around and saw an easel that had been dragged into a far corner, facing two walls. I remembered standing outside his door and feeling that he was watching me through the peephole. And then the long seconds that had ticked off before he'd opened the door. Had he used the time to conceal something? Weeks ago Troy had barged into my bedroom looking at things I didn't want him to see. "Let's see what you're working on now," I said and started over to the easel.

He caught my arm. "Leave it," he said. "It's bad luck to look at a work in progress."

"Since when have you been superstitious?" I asked, and yanked my arm free with an effort. Before he could stop me I stepped to the easel. A cover had been flipped over on top of the drawing there. I flipped it back, and froze.

It was a drawing of Beth. There were no beastlike features on display, and yet his entire drawing made me think of a wild animal. He had drawn Beth lying down on what looked like a cot, not completely naked but wearing very little. An almost feverish sexuality and a kind of caged eagerness oozed from her expression and her pose. Her body was pictured in a way that accentuated her nubile ripeness—her long bare legs, her jutting breasts, her thick and slightly parted lips.

"I told you not to look at that," Troy said. "Now, don't get pissed off. It's not like she modeled for me. I drew it from memory . . ."

But his words barely registered. I had noticed one small detail. To the side of Beth's navel, Troy had drawn a tiny rose tattoo. It was not just some figment of his imagination: Beth had one there in real life. He might have seen it in the summer if he saw her in a bikini, but he could never have glimpsed it in the fall, when she wore shirts and sweaters. The sight of the intimate detail made me completely lose it.

I grabbed a pen from the easel and attacked him, jabbing at his eyes with its sharp point. There's no doubt in my mind I would have stabbed him to death with it if I could have, but of course that didn't happen. My attack caught Troy by surprise, so he was a little late ducking out of the way and the steel point of the pen nicked the side of his cheek. Then he caught my wrist with one hand and pivoted, and suddenly I found myself flying through the air.

I landed hard on my back on his floor. The thin gray carpet provided no cushioning at all, and the impact stunned me. Troy was on top of me in an instant, one hand still holding my right wrist and the other reaching for my throat. I tried to slash up at him, but he slammed my right arm to the floor three times and finally knocked the pen loose. Meanwhile, his fingers closed on my throat, shutting off my air supply. I bucked wildly and tugged on his arm with my free left hand, but I couldn't break his grip.

Black and silver spots spun before my eyes. Troy didn't let go. In fact, his grip got tighter. You are going to die now, I told myself. Without conscious thought, I found myself arching my back and rocking wildly as if my body itself was making one last spasmodic effort to throw him off. He stayed on top of me, pinning me down. I started to black out.

Troy's hand, clamped to my windpipe, eased off, and a

tiny bit of air found its way to my lungs. I revived ever so slightly—just enough to hear myself choking and gagging. Blood from a cut under Troy's ear dripped down into my eyes, blinding me. Troy was saying something to me in a very calm voice. "I could kill you now, brother. Do you know that? I could kill you right now. Are you aware of that, and do you accept it?"

"Yes," I said, but it came out like a choking sound. "Yes," I gasped again, more loudly.

"Do you want to live?" he asked, as if it was the most natural question in the world. His face was so close to mine that I could feel his hot breath on my nose and cheeks.

"Yes," I repeated desperately. "Please. Yes."

His fingers were still around my throat, and blood dripped from his cut onto the bridge of my nose and slid down the side of my cheek. Looking up into his eyes, I saw a battle going on between an angry impulse to squeeze just a little harder and finish me off, and his own growing certainty that he should let me go. "Okay, then," he finally whispered. "Do you know why I'll spare your life?" He leaned even closer. "Because I love you, brother." He kissed me once on the tip of the nose, and then let me go and stood up all in one motion.

I got to all fours, gagged, and retched.

"You're okay," he said. "Just try to breathe normally. I, on the other hand, need a little patching up. I never thought you'd go for me like that, little brother." He walked to the sink, ran some water, and washed his cut. "You actually drew blood. There's hope for you yet."

I got to my feet a little dizzily.

He turned from the sink, holding a wet paper towel to his cut. We faced each other.

"What do we do now?" I asked him.

He smiled and suggested pleasantly, "Why don't we sit down and have breakfast."

20

S o, should I tell you about your girlfriend?" Troy asked as he munched on a chocolate doughnut.

I could breathe normally now, but I still felt a little dizzy. Troy was acting as if nothing unusual had happened, but it's not every Saturday morning that someone nearly chokes me to death. "If you want."

"Actually I don't want to," he said, "but I think we need to clear the air about that before we can progress to more important matters. It's simple and perfectly innocent. She came to see me at the grocery. Asked if she could talk to me. I could tell she was very nervous, but I figured that was understandable given what you'd probably told her about me."

"Yeah, I did talk to her about you." I nodded.

"I'll bet you weren't too complimentary, brother," Troy said, and took a big swig of orange juice. He had put a Band-Aid over his cut, and when he moved his head I could see that it had soaked up a lot of blood. "So I took her to a stockroom and asked her what was on her mind. She was concerned about your soccer teammate."

"She asked you about Tommy Fraser?"

"Yup," Troy said. "She was worried about him. I guess they were friends. She figured I must know something. She's very bright and up-front. She asked me to my face how I could expect her to believe it was just a coincidence that a murderer comes to a small town and right away somebody disappears. I told her that's the strange thing about coincidences—they're coincidental. She didn't buy it for a minute. She practically accused me of killing her buddy and dumping him in the ocean."

"I imagine you didn't like that," I said.

"How little you know me, brother. I find confrontation very . . . stimulating." I got the sense Troy almost used an even more suggestive word, but changed his mind at the last second. "We made a deal. I told her I wanted to draw her, and asked her if I could make some quick sketches. I promised that if she agreed, I would tell her what she wanted to know." Troy's gray eyes sparkled. I could tell he was playing with me as he narrated this story, enjoying my discomfort at the thought of the two of them alone in a stockroom.

"What did you tell her?" I asked.

"That's between me and the young lady. But obviously she didn't run to the police, so you can conclude what you want. After we were done talking I drew a few quick pencil studies of her, and she went her way. And that's all."

"That's not all. How did you know about her tattoo?"

"Ah," he said. "Suspicious, are you? Don't you trust her? She has a very pert beauty, but at the same time it's a fairly common look for a pretty teenage girl. I simply asked her if she had any unique features—little things like a mole or a birthmark or a

192

missing tooth, that I could use to unlock her personality and make her unique. So she showed me her tattoo. She seemed eager to do it—even proud of it."

That made some sense, even though I hated to admit it. Beth was proud of that tiny rose. She called it her freedom flower, I think because it showed that she could stand up to her dad. When she got it, he had been so angry he had grounded her for a week.

Troy finished off his doughnut, washed it down with a big swallow of orange juice, and wiped his face with a napkin. "Thank you, brother Jeff. That wasn't exactly the most nutritious breakfast I've ever eaten, but it tasted okay."

"I'll bet it wasn't the least nutritious breakfast you've had, either," I muttered, still pissed off at the thought of Beth unbuttoning her shirt to show him her tattoo in a basement stockroom.

"You're referring to my incarceration?" Troy asked with a smile. "Don't underestimate prison food. The state mandates a certain calorie requirement. It may taste like cardboard, but it won't kill you. You done?"

I nodded. He washed my glass and his own, and turned back to me, wiping his hands on a dish towel. "Now, let's get down to business and move from my prison days to my attempt at rehabilitation. I don't mean to be judgmental, Jeffrey, but let me say that it didn't escape my attention that you weren't exactly pleased as punch to see me come home and try to begin a new life. And while I have done nothing to hurt you, you have done nothing to make me feel welcome. In fact, you've given me the distinct impression that if I had stayed in prison and rotted there, you would be happier. True?"

I looked back at him, and my eyes jumped from the bandaged cut on his cheek to his gray eyes. I didn't want to agree to such an awful thing, but I couldn't deny it.

"Come on," he said, "let's try to be honest with each other. True or not true, you would have preferred it if I had stayed in prison?"

"It's not that I wanted you in prison," I said. "I just didn't want you here, screwing everything up for me."

"So it was self-interest that made you treat me like a leper when I came home needing love and compassion?" he asked. "You barely talked to me, Jeff. You didn't introduce me to any of your friends. You didn't include me in your life in any way. You suspected me of murder. When I moved away to protect our family, you didn't seek me out. And then ring-a-ding on a Saturday morning, all of a sudden here you are with orange juice and doughnuts. Well, I enjoyed our little breakfast, although I could have done without the physical assault with a deadly weapon. But I am just a bit curious. What are you doing here?"

He had moved our conversation to such a level of brute honesty that the only way I could answer him was to speak the cold truth. "I guess that's why I'm here," I told him. "Because I'm curious, too. Yeah, I didn't include you in my life because I don't want you in my life. But I need to know what you're doing here."

"Where?"

"Here. Living in this dump. Talking to kids I know from school. Drawing pictures of my girlfriend. Working a dead-end job at a store in my town. What the hell, Troy?"

"I'm rebuilding my life," he said.

"Crap," I snorted. "Don't give me that."

"Not necessarily crap," he shot back. "Do you have any idea how difficult it is to function in our society once you've been convicted of a felony? Something tells me you don't, little brother."

"I may be your little brother, but I still know crap when I smell crap," I told him. "For most people who get out of jail, that might be true. But you, with all your brains and talents, could make a fresh start anywhere. Maybe that's why you came home at first, but why have you stayed?"

"Family love," Troy said, but it was said almost as a question—a trial balloon he sent up to see if it would fly.

"More crap," I said. "Aren't you the one who said we should be honest? Okay, tough guy, be honest." I caught his arm and held it tightly and looked right into those mocking eyes. In a strong, loud voice I asked the question I had been brooding about for so long. *What are you doing here?*

For a minute I thought he might push me away or even hit me. Instead, his thin lips turned up and he chuckled, and then the chuckle became a full belly laugh—a rarity with Troy. "I am so happy you came here this morning, brother," he said. "I have been so alone in the world, and you are in your way a kindred spirit."

"I am not. Don't say that. We are nothing alike."

"We are everything alike," he said, and suddenly he was holding on to me as tightly as I was holding on to him. "And you know I'm right, and that's why you're so afraid of me."

"If I was afraid of you, would I be here?" I demanded.

"It sure took you long enough to come," he said. "But I understand. I'm glad you finally got up the balls to show up. And I have a suggestion. You have questions for me, and I have a few for you, too. But most of all I think you want to get to know me and vice versa. So let's spend a little time together. Let's take a drive."

"On bikes?" I asked.

"I have a car," he informed me.

I looked back at him. "Since when?"

"Since two days ago."

"How did you get the money to buy a car?"

"Well, my suspicious brother, I didn't rob a bank or strangle some old woman and take her life's savings. I bought it through the sweat of my brow. It's not exactly a Rolls-Royce, but it will serve."

"Do you have a driver's license?"

"A learner's permit," he said. "Issued by the state of New Jersey. It's all perfectly legal. I'm remaking my life, credential by credential. Jeff, we haven't had much chance to get to know each other in the past few years. And we may not in the future, so maybe we should grab this opportunity. It looks like a nice enough day. Shall we take a drive?"

"Where?" I asked.

"Let's find some action," Troy said. "Since you came here to get to know me, are you ready to take a walk on the wild side?"

"Which wild side did you have in mind?"

"How about Atlantic City?" he suggested. "It sounds like the nearest fun place."

"No way. Mom and Pop won't like it if I go . . ."

He reached out and tapped my cheek with his index finger. "You are nearly eighteen years old, little sparrow. Why don't you start making some decisions for yourself?"

I knocked his hand away.

He picked up the phone, and before I could stop him, he'd dialed my home number. "Hi, Dad. It's Troy. Jeff's here, visiting. That's right, at my place. We just had a nice breakfast. Listen, I wanted to take my new car for a test drive to Atlantic City. I promise I'll be careful and get him home safe. Would that be okay? We haven't spent much time together, and it would be kind of fun for us to take a trip as brothers. Sure, I promise. Here, I'll put him on."

"Jeff? Do you want to go?" My father sounded worried but intrigued and even happy that Troy and I were finally doing something together.

I looked back at Troy. I was scared and at the same time tempted. He smiled back at me, and his mocking gray eyes dared me. I understood suddenly and on a deep level that if I got on my bike and rode back home to my parents I would

197

never know why Troy had come home, never learn what he was doing staying here, and never understand what made him tick. I exhaled a long breath of air. "Yes. Sure."

"Let me just check with your mom," Dad said. He was gone for a long minute, and I heard muted conversation in the background. I think he was holding his hand over the receiver. "Okay," Dad finally said. "But be careful and don't get back too late. Oh, and have fun."

21

Troy was not being modest when he said his car wasn't exactly a Rolls-Royce. It was an old black Ford with a powerful V-8 engine and about a million miles on the speedometer. It looked like a police car except that no police department would put a cruiser with so many dings and scrapes and rust marks on the road. But Troy seemed to like it, and he drove it skillfully enough as we wove our way south on Route 9, past a string of small bay towns.

We rode in strained silence for a while. Our fight was still very much between us. My throat felt tender, and I noticed Troy touch the Band-Aid on his cheek several times as if checking to see whether blood was leaking out. He turned on the radio to a hip-hop station, and the thumping music gave a rhythm to the endless parade of streetlights and gas stations and chain stores as Manahawkin gave way to Mayetta, which led on into Staffordville.

It felt very strange to be sitting there in the front seat of that old Ford next to Troy, when we hadn't been alone together for any length of time in years. I wanted to talk to him, and I wondered what he was thinking about me. I glanced at him, and as if reading my mind he leaned forward and switched off the radio. "So, brother," he said, "here we are together, like Cain and Abel on a road trip. I know you've got all kinds of questions and dark suspicions, so why don't you just fire away."

"Okay," I said, unsure where or how to start. "First of all, I owe you an apology. I thought you were somehow involved with Fraser's disappearance, but it turns out he was mixed up with drug dealers and owed them money and . . ."

"And what?" Troy prodded me.

"I guess you weren't involved after all. I'm sorry I thought that about you."

Troy lit a cigarette and rolled his window down. "Do you mind?" he asked.

"No. It's your car."

"It is, and I don't need to be lied to in it by my dear brother," Troy said, exhaling smoke out the cracked-open window. "Don't apologize unless you really think I'm innocent, and I'm not getting that vibe. You're no fool. We both know that just because Fraser was selling drugs doesn't mean I couldn't have been involved with his disappearance."

"So . . . were you?" I asked.

"Was I what?" I could tell Troy was enjoying my fear of confronting him directly.

I took a breath and then dove in. "Did you kill Tommy Fraser and dump his body in the ocean?"

Troy grinned at me for exactly repeating Beth's question. "To tell you the truth," he said, "oceans aren't the best place to dispose of dead bodies. Corpses swell and become buoyant and wash up onshore."

"Not if you weight them down," I pointed out. "That's what they do on TV and in the movies."

"Don't believe it," Troy told me. "Even if you weight them down, they have a way of surfacing. There's an old saying 'The ocean will yield up its dead.' That actually happens surprisingly often."

We drove in silence. He smoked, and I closed my eyes and imagined Tommy Fraser's bloated body rising through the waters of Barnegat Bay, and then floating belly-up toward the Pineville pier. In my mind's eye, Tommy's handsome face had been half eaten away by crabs and other crustaceans, and his long shock of black hair trailed behind him like seaweed. The big Ford churned southward. The towns we passed were separated by bristling barriers of pine forest. Road signs provided frequent updates on the decreasing mileage to Atlantic City.

"So how would you dispose of a body?" I finally asked.

"Bury it," Troy responded, stubbing out his cigarette. He didn't seem to mind the question at all.

"Isn't that risky? Someone might see you do it, or some animal might smell the body and dig it up."

"True," Troy agreed. "And bodies can float up through soil just as they float up in water. Did you know that?"

"No," I said.

Troy nodded. "You do learn some useful things in jail, brother," he said, and then waved his hand out the window. "But look at that."

I looked and saw nothing. "What?"

"That!" He gestured again.

"You're not pointing to anything."

"Bingo," Troy said. "Nothing at all. One million acres of national reserve. Pine trees and sandy soil. You could bury a body fairly deep in under an hour."

"No," I responded softly. "But maybe *you* could."

Troy nodded. He was playing with me and enjoying the game. "Would you like to know how I'd do it?" he asked. "I mean just hypothetically."

"Sure, if you want," I said.

"I'd find a remote spot off a little-used road," Troy began, looking around at the Pine Barrens as if to emphasize that such spots now surrounded us. "I'd dig the hole with the body concealed in case someone happened to come along. Once the hole was ready, I'd pop the body in, cover it up as fast as I could, and roll a big rock on top. The lucky part is it's November. We've got a couple of cold months coming when the earth is gonna freeze and man and dog stay home in their warm houses. The odds of anyone finding him till the spring would be pretty low."

"Sounds like you've thought a lot about this," I whispered, watching his eyes in the rearview mirror.

"You should see your own face, brother," Troy said with a laugh. "Anyway, you asked the question, so I answered. Burial beats dumping in the ocean. Now I have a suggestion. Since we're starting to get reacquainted, maybe we could begin with something warm and fuzzy and work our way to my preferred method of hiding corpses."

I tried to think of something warm and fuzzy to ask him, but I couldn't get his description of burying a body out of my mind. It hadn't sounded like he was making it up—it sounded like he was describing something that he had actually done, right down to rolling the big stone on top. "Why Spanish?" I finally managed. "I saw all the grammar books at your place."

"I picked a bit of it up in prison," Troy said. "Had a cellmate who spoke it. I figured rather than let it go, why not really learn it. Never know when it will come in handy. And you know what they say—to learn a second language is to gain a second soul."

"I didn't know you even had one soul," I responded. I meant it as a joke, but it came out sounding pretty nasty.

Troy sped up slightly. We were in the final stretch run to the expressway that would take us right to the casinos. "Which brings up one of my questions to you," he said. "I watched you praying in church. Do you really believe that gunk?"

"What gunk?"

"Immortal souls. Heaven. Hell. God Almighty."

I felt myself hesitate for a second, and rushed to fill the silence. "Sure. Absolutely. Maybe I don't believe in all of it anymore, but . . ."

"You've let go of Santa Claus?" Troy mocked me.

"Yeah, I finally let go of Santa. But when it comes to God I definitely still believe. What about you, Troy?"

"Prison pushes people in two directions," Troy told me. "It either makes you super-religious or it makes you know once and for all that the whole thing's a crock. Not that I didn't think that already. But now I know it."

"How can you possibly know it for sure?" I asked him.

Troy didn't answer right away. He turned onto the expressway. Billboards advertised casinos. There were pictures of dice, and sexy women. I was nervous but also excited. Mom and Dad don't like gambling, so even though we had taken a few family trips to Atlantic City over the years, we had spent most of our time on the boardwalk and the beaches, and just ducked into the casinos for lunch.

Troy finally answered me, and his eyes, scanning the expressway, sharpened into knife points. "If you had seen some of the things I've seen and heard some of the things I've heard, you'd know it was a crock, too, brother." He pressed the gas pedal, and the big engine roared. The black car rocketed toward the casinos that were now visible in the distance. "Men being tortured in ways you don't want to know about. Crying out all night for mercy till their throats crack and the last whimpers fade, and everything from manhood to life itself has been taken from them. There's no mercy. No divine intervention. No miracles. The will of the stronger prevails. This world's a brutish place, Jeff. An ugly place. What God could put us here? How dare he? Is he a sadist?"

"Maybe his reasons are unknowable," I ventured, conscious of the gold crucifix on the chain around my neck. "Maybe it's a test . . ."

"Yeah, a test of sheer stupidity," Troy snorted.

Did I dare? I had come on this trip with him. He was making fun of my beliefs. So I whispered, "And heaven and hell? Don't you feel in your bones that the good are rewarded and the bad are punished?"

"No, throughout history the good have been taken advantage of and the bad have had more fun," he shot back. I could feel his sudden anger. "But you're not talking about the general case. You're bringing up specifics?"

"I was just asking . . ."

"Yeah, brother, I've been to hell and back," Troy growled. "You're saying that I did wrong, so I was punished. I got what I deserved? And then I caught a lucky break to get out? Well, for your information, I just spent five years in hell for one reason— I was stupid and I got caught."

"Maybe," I said softly. "Or maybe you spent those years in prison because you did wrong, Troy. Maybe your life would be better if you admitted that to yourself. You killed a kid." The big Ford suddenly seemed so quiet that I could hear its wheels going round and round on the expressway. "If you hadn't, Billy Shea would be alive."

"It's a hard thing to kill someone with a knife," Troy said back in a low, hard voice. "You feel them die. But Billy had it coming to him." Troy flapped his pinky on the steering wheel. It had a broken joint, and waved at an angle. "You know they caught me with a gang. Held me down. Stomped on me. Busted my hand."

"You said that at your trial," I reminded him. "But you could never prove Billy Shea did anything to you. And anyway, a life for a finger?" I had thought about this for years, and I couldn't restrain my anger.

"It seemed like a pretty fair bargain at the time," he said in a low voice. "I think that's enough questions, little brother. Here we are."

Troy guided the Ford off the expressway onto local streets. I kept silent. What he had just told me about a kid I had known made me feel cold all over. But Troy seemed to have already forgotten about it.

Gaudy casinos rose up on all sides. "Look at this place," he said. "Like a glass and chrome Oz. But just two or three blocks in from the casinos it's all pawnshops and tattoo parlors. Let's get a little bit away from the strip, and we can find parking on the street." Troy made a couple of quick turns, and we were soon on a back street where there were indeed pawnshops. He seemed to know exactly where he was going.

"I thought this was your first time here," I said softly.

Troy glanced at me. "I read up on it," he told me. "Seemed like the nearest interesting place to Pineville."

"You sure seem to know your way around."

"We'll see whether I do or not." He steered the Ford into a parking spot near an abandoned lot and shut off the engine. "Now, we've discussed corpse disposal and whether I deserve to burn in hell. What do you say we have some fun together?"

"Okay," I said, unbuckling my seat belt. "What did you have in mind?"

22

I was grateful for the cheeseburger, because it gave me an excuse to look down. Troy kept talking to me, and I couldn't avoid glancing up at his face occasionally. When I looked at him I saw the blond lady five feet behind him, nearly completely naked, staring right back at me as she gyrated around a brass pole.

I didn't know what to do or how to act. Should I meet her eyes? Should I just ogle her body the way Troy did as he devoured his own cheeseburger, the grease slicking his lips? I had never been in such a place before and I had never seen a naked woman up close this way. I felt aroused and slightly sick to my stomach at the same time.

"They'll never let me in," I had said to Troy as he led me toward the door. "The sign says you have to be eighteen."

"You're tall for your age, little sparrow. Just walk in right behind me and look like you belong."

"But I don't belong. Troy, let's go to a McDonald's. Or we can eat in one of the casinos. I'll pay."

"No, this whole trip is on me," Troy said. "If they don't let you in, we'll find someplace else. When we go in, try to talk to me about something innocuous."

"I don't know what that word means," I admitted as we approached the door.

"What do they teach you in that school?" Troy asked.

Before I could answer we reached the heavy door and Troy yanked it open. I heard music thumping. Troy entered nonchalantly and I followed him inside. "I don't know how you can say the Jets still have a shot at the playoffs," Troy said loudly, as if we were in the middle of an argument about football.

" 'Cause they still do," I mumbled back, giving it my best shot. "They just have to turn things around."

An enormous bouncer perched on a stool inside the door glanced up from a newspaper and looked us over. I figured he would demand to see some I.D., but instead he grunted, "The Jets suck," and waved us in.

It was a cavernous place, with dim lighting and several long stages that sat in darkness because the place was mostly empty during the afternoon. One stage was lit, and a thin blond woman wearing a red thong and nothing else danced around on it, grinding her hips and shaking her breasts for the benefit of a dozen or so sad-looking men who sat on stools sipping drinks. Troy found us two seats near the action, and a waitress took our order.

The music pounded.

The blond woman removed her red thong.

One of the sad-looking men let out a whistle.

Our burgers arrived, with a root beer for me and a real

beer for Troy. I played a hockey game on my plate, pushing around pieces of beef and bun, hoping Troy wouldn't notice my discomfort. But of course he did, and he enjoyed it.

"Don't worry, Jeff," he said, his eyes on the dancer. "She's probably not going to show up in this place."

"Who?" I asked.

"Your third-grade teacher," he answered with a laugh. "Or your librarian. Or Mom. Or your sweet little girlfriend who ditched you. Or whoever it is you're so afraid might see you here."

"It's not that," I said. "This place is . . . cheesy. Let's get out of here."

"Soon as I finish my burger," he promised. "Meanwhile, a little sleaze will probably do you good. Don't you think she's pretty?"

"I don't know," I said.

"Well, look at her. She won't mind. That's what she's up there dancing for."

I glanced at her. She was so thin her ribs showed. Her round breasts looked like balloons that had been overinflated and might burst at any minute. "No," I told him in a whisper. "Not to me."

"Well, she is to me," Troy said. "But then I spent a lot of time in . . . shall we say, deprivation . . . while you were with that cute honey of yours." Troy glanced from the dancer to me. "I could tell even from the photo on your desk what she was like. And when I saw her in person at the grocery, I knew I had to draw her. She has a feral, inhibited, but almost primeval sexuality that's hard to catch."

I didn't know what a lot of the words Troy was using meant, but I understood his tone. *"Don't talk about Beth in here."*

"This is just a place like any other," Troy responded with a laugh. "And I'm not saying anything bad about her. I sketched her too realistically, that's all. She needed a Gauguin."

"A what?"

"No," Troy corrected me. "A *who*. Paul Gauguin? Doesn't ring a bell?"

I shook my head.

"Jesus," he said. "Postimpressionist painter. He was a stockbroker in France. Gave it up to become a painter. Went off to Tahiti and had a wild time there. He tried to capture the essence of it in primitive art—flat forms, violent color, untamed nature. That's the way your Beth needs to be drawn. Hey, bro, did you just hold her hand, or did you two ever get it on?"

I looked back at him.

"What a shame," Troy said, wiping the grease off his lips with a napkin. "You sweet, cowardly fool. It's so obvious that she's tired of playing the nice girl. And I think you're probably ready to explode, too, so—"

I stood up off the stool. "I'm out of here."

"Sit," he said. "I'll be finished in one minute and we'll find some less objectionable place. Please sit. I'm sorry if I offended you. That wasn't my intention."

A waitress came by to see if we wanted more drinks, and Troy asked her for the check. He left twenty dollars for the burgers, and as we headed out he handed a five-dollar bill to the blond dancer, who smiled and blew him a kiss.

Then we were outside on the run-down street, passing pawnshops and discount stores and jewelry exchanges with signs proclaiming WE BUY GOLD. "I really didn't mean to embarrass you or insult your ex-girlfriend," Troy said. "I thought that's what brothers talk about. Sex. Dating."

"Maybe some brothers. Not us."

We walked in silence for a few minutes, and the strangeness of our being together there was so heavy I almost felt like running away. The glittering casinos were visible a few blocks away, rising up over the shabby two-story brick buildings like a shimmering mountain range.

"So why didn't you go to Tahiti?" I asked Troy.

He stopped walking, intrigued. "What?"

"I heard it in your voice when you were talking about that French painter. That's what you really want. To get away from everyone and everything you despise. Us. The stockroom. You used to watch boats at night, and I could tell you wanted to be on one, sailing away. That's what I don't get about you staying near Pineville. Why don't you just go off to some beautiful place where you could have fun, live cheaply, and make your own rules?"

Troy smiled at me and his eyes gleamed. "It's so strange," he said in a low voice that had odd traces of warmth. "Sometimes I'm convinced you're a total fool, and then you have true insight into me. You're the only person who does. I'm touched. I truly am. Come, brother."

As if on impulse, he grabbed my arm and led me through a narrow doorway into a tattoo parlor. It was just a one-room shop, with jasmine incense burning and pictures of different tattoo designs on the walls. There were common ones, like skulls and flowers, and far more complicated ones like dragons in flight. I saw Troy running his expert eyes over the display. "Not bad," he said.

"What are we doing here?" I asked him.

A bald Asian man came out of the back and looked us over. He was wearing black jeans and a black T-shirt, and wiping his hands on a white towel. "Hi. Need help?"

"This is my dear brother," Troy said. "I want you to tattoo his initials onto my arm."

"Troy, that's crazy," I objected.

"Your honey got a tattoo. You didn't think it was crazy when she did it."

"She got a flower."

"She got what she wanted," Troy said, "and I'm gonna get what I want." He looked at me shrewdly. "Or do you hate me so much that the thought of me carrying your initials on my skin for all eternity is disturbing to you?"

If I had some insight into Troy's mind, he sure as hell had some into mine. Sometimes he seemed to know exactly what I was thinking, and he wasn't afraid to call me on it either. "I just wish you wouldn't do it," I said.

"J.H.," Troy told the tattoo artist, sitting down in what looked like an old barber's chair. "Right here on my upper arm."

"If you put it up there, it will get a lot of sun," the bald man warned. "The colors may fade."

"No colors," Troy said. "Just black. How long will it take?"

"Less than an hour," the man said. "It will hurt a bit."

"All things worth having do," Troy replied, looking at me as if he was teaching me some kind of lesson.

It actually took less than half an hour. I stood next to Troy, watching. I hadn't been with Beth when she got her rose, so I had never seen this done before.

First the artist sketched the letters on Troy's upper arm. When Troy approved the size and design, the man pressed a copy on carbon paper. He swabbed Troy's arm with alcohol and then used the carbon to transfer the design back to Troy's skin. "You've got muscles," he said. "You must lift weights all the time."

"Now and then," Troy told him. "Let's do this."

The tattoo artist fired up what looked like a little paint gun except that it made a buzzing sound. "The outlining hurts more than the shading," he said. "You want some gum to chew on?"

"No, just get on with it," Troy told him.

Troy tensed when the man approached him with the whirring gun, and when it first touched his skin he sucked in a breath, and his fingers dug into the leather pads on the chair's arms. Then he forced himself to relax, and he said in a conversational voice, "You should feel honored. I'm a virgin canvas. I did lots of tattoos for people in prison. But I never got one of my own."

I didn't know whether he was talking to me or to the artist. "I don't feel honored," I said. "This is nutty. You're never going to be able to take it off."

"You can get it off," the tattoo artist said as he continued to move the gun around. "But it's not easy."

"I don't want to take it off," Troy said, and now he was clearly talking to me. The tattoo artist was sitting right next to him, concentrating on the work, but Troy was ignoring him and focusing on me as if we were the only two people in the room. He began saying personal things—things that it was embarrassing to have someone else hear. Maybe talking to me this way helped him deal with the pain. "I want you to always be with me, brother," he said. "I really am very fond of you, however much you hate me. There haven't been too many people in my life who understand me on any level. Hey, why don't you come to Tahiti with me? We could have some wild times in paradise together."

"Tahiti is just a big Club Med," the tattoo artist grunted. "I know people who've been there."

Troy registered the information but ignored the artist and continued speaking to me. "It wouldn't have to be Tahiti. There are lots of places you can still go to get away. Mexico, Cuba, Thailand, the Philippines."

"I'm happy in Pineville," I told him.

He laughed. "Are you really happy, brother? With the

telescope at your window and the maps on the wall and the golf clubs peeking out of the closet?"

"What's wrong with a telescope and maps?" I asked.

"They're like props from a bad movie," Troy said, and winced as the tattoo gun hit a tender spot. "That's not you for one second. Why hide? Why not live your life?"

"I don't need you to tell me what's my real life," I said, and walked away to inspect the tattoos on the walls.

Twenty minutes later Troy stood up from the chair. "Check it out," he said, showing me the black letters. There were my initials, boldly engraved on his upper arm. "That's you, brother Jeff. You're my right-hand man now." He paid the tattoo artist fifty dollars, and tipped him ten. "Where are you getting all this money?" I asked him.

"Jeff, I've been working my brains out. Ten-hour days in that damned stockroom for weeks. Let me have a little fun." He took me by the arm and we headed out of the tattoo shop. "Come on. It's time to see the Emerald City of Oz."

 **23**

Three short blocks brought us into a completely different universe. The shabby streets with their tattoo parlors and seedy bars and pawn shops seemed light years away from these glittering glass-and-chrome palaces that rose up side by side along the wide wooden boardwalk.

We tramped through them one after the other, with Troy leading the way and me following a few steps behind. The electric energy of the casinos seemed to charge him with ten thousand volts—I had never seen him quite like this before. He pointed out details to me, from the fancy cars outside to the crowded gaming tables, as if he was giving a guided tour.

"See that limo with New York plates! Thirty feet long—like a cruise ship on land! Those fat cats rented it in Manhattan and partied all the way down here." A group of eight people got out of the limo—overweight balding men in dark suits and attractive younger women in slinky outfits. "Must've cost five hundred bucks, but what do those old goats care? They're gonna get what they want." Troy craned his neck to peer in as we walked past. "They've got a bar inside, and a color TV. That's the way some people live, Jeff, while others sit rotting in jail cells."

"A car is a car," I said. "And you're a free man."

"Yeah, well, life is short and death is forever," Troy muttered back. "And a stockroom is a lot like a jail cell."

We reached a casino's entrance and Troy circled in through the revolving door. I followed him and was blinded by a whirl of neon and mirrors and polished chrome. I stumbled along behind Troy, and bumped into a cocktail waitress who was wearing a uniform that looked like a bikini with wings. "You almost tackled her," Troy laughed, taking me by the arm and steering me quickly forward.

"See that chick with the long legs at the bar, looking so friendly at us?" he grunted with a nod. "Casino hooker. Two hundred bucks an hour, plus what you pay for the room. A girl like that will do some really unusual things for you, little brother."

"Probably give you some really unusual sexual diseases, too," I whispered back, wondering how he knew so much about her, right down to her hourly price tag.

"Aren't you the life of the party," Troy said.

We wandered through a maze of slot machines, their red lights flashing and bells ringing as they paid out small and large jackpots so that it sounded like everyone must be winning all the time. But the people seated in front of the machines clearly weren't winning. They were old—some looked to be seventy and even eighty. They sat on stools, fishing quarters out of paper cups and pumping them into slots one after the other. "One-armed bandits," Troy said with contempt. "Casinos rig up a few to win, and all the rest to lose. You might as well pour lighter fluid on your money and set it on fire."

217

"When did you become such an expert on casinos?"

"I told you, I read up on this place," Troy said.

I didn't let it go. "You read books about slot machines and the going price of casino whores? It feels like you've been here before, Troy."

Troy looked at me. "If you weren't so meek, you'd be dangerous, little brother. But I'm starting to get a kick out of your suspicious nature. Let's go find some action."

We hurried through an exit, and the bells and whistles faded, replaced by the soothing wash of nearby Atlantic surf. The boardwalk was deserted. Shuttered malls. Empty benches. Christmas wreaths hanging from lampposts. A few hungry gulls circling overhead. I sucked in a welcome breath of cold air and tried to clear my head. But Troy was on the move again, heading for an even bigger casino whose sign flashed out a fancy Italian name in bursts of neon that seemed brighter than the afternoon sunlight. "This is the one," Troy proclaimed. "Lady luck, smile on your two humble supplicants."

"What are we going to do in there?" I asked him as we approached the impressive main entrance.

"Win a fortune and corrupt you," he said. "You play cards, brother?"

"A little poker with my friends," I said. "But, Troy, we don't have nearly enough money to gamble at this—"

He cut me off. "Forget poker. Blackjack is the game. The only one where you actually can have an advantage over the casino, if you play correctly. And I've studied the odds."

"Nobody has an advantage over a casino . . ." I objected.

Troy stopped just outside the doors and took me by either arm. "For one day, for one hour, I want you to do two things," he said. "Stop being so afraid. And try to believe in me."

I obediently followed him in through massive doors, past great marble pillars that looked like they belonged in a cathedral. We wandered around between craps tables and roulette tables and blackjack tables, and Troy seemed to be sniffing them out, trying to catch a scent that he liked.

"Bingo," he finally said, and sat down at the one empty seat of a ten-dollar-minimum blackjack table. The dealer was a very nice-looking young woman with red hair and green eyes whose name tag identified her as Bridget.

Troy pulled a hundred-dollar bill out of his wallet and threw it down on the green felt.

"Hey, we've got a big spender," Bridget said with a smile.

Troy smiled back at her. "Irish?"

"And proud of it," she said, raking in his hundred and giving him a stack of chips.

"It's a lovely name," he told her. "It means High Goddess of wisdom and poetry."

I bet pretty dealers in Atlantic City hear all kinds of lines twenty-four hours a day, but she blinked her green eyes at that one. "Does it really? How do you know such a thing?"

Troy looked right back at her and didn't answer. They locked eyes. Her long red hair fell around the shoulders of her black dealer's outfit, which was cut low in the front so that her cleavage gleamed in the bright lights.

"He knows things like that," I told her.

"Enough chitchat," a tall man in a leather jacket said impatiently, tapping his bony fingers on the leather table rim. "How about dealing some cards, honey?"

"Victoria," the pretty dealer called, summoning a waitress. "Get a drink for our new high roller. And his friend."

"Dear brother," Troy said.

"And for his dear brother," Bridget corrected herself, and then dealt, her small hands deftly pulling cards from the shoe and flicking them around the table.

Troy drank, and he bet ten dollars a hand, and he won. He didn't win every time, but he won steadily, and soon he had more than five hundred dollars in chips sitting in front of him in tall stacks. He was draining one scotch and soda after another, tipping the waitress five dollars a drink, and flirting with Bridget whenever possible.

She returned all of his one-liners with little jokes of her own, and when he tipped her twenty dollars after a big win, Bridget threw him a smile as bright as the entry lobby with all its mirrors and neon. "Thanks, high roller."

"Troy," he said. "Like the city in Homer's *Iliad*."

She threw him a quizzical look. "You're really something, huh?" I couldn't tell if she liked him or was just humoring him.

There was a break in the game as Bridget shuffled, laying the cards out on the table in small piles. Players at our table used the break to get up and go to the bathroom.

"I'd like to draw you," Troy told her.

"I bet you say that to all the girls," she teased.

"I already sketched you. Take a look." He had done a few quick pencil studies of her face on a bar napkin.

She glanced down at the napkin and sucked in her breath. "Wow."

"You want to run away with us, Bridget?" he followed up. "My brother and I are going to Tahiti."

"Sure," she said with a laugh. "Count me in. When are we leaving?"

"Soon," Troy told her, and I heard something serious in his voice for a second. "I picture you running half-naked down a gleaming beach."

"Keep it clean," she told him. And then to me, "You're lucky to have such an interesting brother."

"You said it," I told her softly.

"Are you always the quiet one?" she asked.

"No, he's the scared one," Troy said, counting his stacks of chips. "He's in hiding. Has been for years."

Bridget glanced up from her shuffling. Her green eyes studied me with interest. "Who are you hiding from?"

"I don't know what he's talking about," I told her. "And neither do you. Troy, let's get out of here. Quit while you're ahead."

"The afternoon is still young," Troy said. "Deal 'em up, Bridget."

Bridget went on break, and was replaced by a serious man who didn't talk to the players as he dealt. Suddenly the whole table went cold. Troy kept pulling fives and sixes on his first cards, and busting on his third ones. The towers of chips in front of him soon became small piles, and then one small stack.

Bridget came back from her break and gave Troy a warm smile. "You're still here, high roller?"

"Waiting for you to bring me luck," he told her. "Deal me in, and get me another drink."

"Victoria," she shouted, "another scotch and soda."

When the last little stack was almost gone I said, "C'mon, Troy, let's go."

"You know your problem? You never believed in me. Never," Troy said, taking the last hundred-dollar bill out of his wallet. "He never believed in me," he told Bridget, slurring his words just a tiny bit. "None of them did. They tried to lock me up and throw away the goddamned key. My own flesh and blood. Can you believe that?"

Bridget kept silent and concentrated on her dealing.

Troy lost that second hundred in about five minutes. He suddenly looked kind of pathetic sitting there with his winter coat over the back of his chair, wearing a black T-shirt, his oversized arms up on the lip of the table as his hands went back and forth from his drink to his dwindling pile of chips.

When he lost the second hundred, I touched his shoulder. I was thinking that in the stockroom he made minimum wage. Each bet he lost was nearly two hours of work. "You can't afford to lose this much. C'mon, let's go home."

Troy knocked my hand away hard, and pulled two fifties out of his sock. He changed them for chips and bet them one by one, sitting up straighter and following the cards as if his life hung in the balance with every deal. When he picked up his last ten-dollar chip and put it on the table, he said to Bridget, "Be good to me, sweetheart. It's a long road back, but I know about long roads back."

She dealt him a six and a nine, and she flipped over a ten for herself. Troy pulled a queen and busted, and as she raked in his last chip she said, "Sorry, high roller. Wasn't your night."

Troy climbed off his stool a little unsteadily. "After you get off, why don't you have a drink with us? We can talk about Tahiti?"

"I don't socialize with customers," Bridget said. "But I'll give you some good advice. Don't drink when you play cards for money, and don't bet more than you can lose. Are you gonna be okay driving home? I'll get you free coffee."

"Go to hell, bitch," Troy growled at her, and headed away from the table. I followed him out of the casino, past the rows of slot machines that were still jingling by the front entrance, onto the boardwalk. Troy walked to the rail and stood there, motionless. I didn't know what to say, so I just kept quiet.

"Let's go home," he finally said.

"A cup of coffee might not be a bad idea," I whispered.

"I'm fine to drive," he assured me.

 **24**

Troy drove in silence through the gathering shadows of the late afternoon. We had come on a local highway, but he opted for the Garden State Parkway for our homeward journey. He veered into the left lane, and was soon passing cars. I checked to make sure that my seat belt was buckled, and I sat with my right arm gripping the armrest. "Why are we taking the parkway?" I asked.

"Quicker," he said.

I couldn't tell whether Troy was drunk or sober, truly angry or merely pissed off and a little embarrassed that his road trip had taken such a bad turn at the end. I felt the need to say something, to reach out to him. "Troy, listen to me. It wasn't so much money."

"No, it wasn't," he agreed. "You happy now, brother?"

"Happy for what?"

"That I lost," he said bitterly. "That that flame-haired bitch blew me off. Now you're going home to your safe warm bed with Mommy and Daddy in the next room."

This is what he's really like, I thought to myself. This is the bitter path he walked back and forth on in his mind during his years in the jail cell. He's kept it hidden till now, but here it is. You wanted to see what makes him tick, and now he's showing you. "No, Troy, I'm not happy that you lost," I told him. "I never—"

"Do us both a favor and shut your mouth," he growled.

So I shut my mouth. We were speeding through the Pine Barrens now, miles of twenty-foot-tall scraggly trees that the gathering dusk turned into an endless tide of dull green. Occasionally a leafless black oak would rise above the vast sea of pitch pines like the lone mast of a lost ship. Then the pines would take over again, so still and uniform they could have been painted onto the darkening horizon.

Troy drove very fast and in complete silence for what seemed like an eternity but was probably just fifteen minutes. I could feel his seething anger—at himself, at me, at everyone. His shoulders were hunched over the steering wheel, and his eyes were locked onto the highway that unrolled ahead of him. His hand movements on the wheel seemed a bit jerky, but he had the car under control.

"Barrens is a good name for this," he finally said. "It's the only thing about this mind-numbing hell hole you guys chose that I find at all interesting. I walk in them sometimes, right about now. It's easy to believe there's a monster lurking around."

I nodded, glad that we were speaking. "Yeah. Sometimes it gives me the creeps."

"Not me," Troy said. "But then I've always liked monsters."

I remembered the hideous pictures on the walls of Troy's

apartment. The human face, the body of a dragon, the wings of a bat, the feet of a pig, and the forked tail. "That's why you draw so many pictures of the Jersey Devil?" I asked.

"Self-portraits in a way," Troy grunted, and swerved to pass a station wagon with what looked like six little kids squeezed into the back. "We're kindred spirits."

I remembered now that the monster Troy had drawn had human eyes—Troy's eyes. "How so?" I asked to keep him talking.

"Born to be wild," he said, his voice thick with anger and self-pity. "Fated to be hated. But you know the story, brother. You're a big part of the story."

I tried to keep him focused on the Jersey Devil. I figured the more we talked about the monster and the less he brooded about himself and me, the better. "I don't know the story of the Jersey Devil," I told him. "How was it created?"

"Not created," Troy corrected me. "*Born.* You should know the legends of your own piss pot of a state." He told me the story in a quick, flat voice, and he seemed to speed up slightly with every line, so that we were soon flying down the twisting highway. "Three hundred years ago there was a very poor woman named Mrs. Leeds, who lived at the edge of the pine forest. She was trying to raise twelve starving children. When she found out that she was pregnant again, she cried out, 'I don't want any more children. Let it be the devil!' Sure enough, when it was born, it had wings and the body of a serpent and a long forked tail. It crawled out from her womb, slithered up the chimney, and flew out into the Pine Barrens, where it's lived ever since, feeding on livestock and small children."

Troy spoke of the birth of the creature with a kind of savage glee, as if savoring every horrific detail. When he ended with the beast flying off into the Pine Barrens, he accelerated so that the Ford jumped forward down the parkway.

"Troy, slow down," I begged softly. And then, "You were the first baby. Our parents wanted you very badly."

"And they wanted me desperately to be like them," Troy shot back. "When I wasn't, they turned on me. If I couldn't be like them, then I had to be a monster."

I couldn't take my eyes off the speedometer needle as it touched ninety. "They never turned on you, Troy. They went to your trial. Dad visited you in prison. They took you back. *You're going too fast. Please slow down.*"

When he screamed I could tell how close he was to crashing the car. *"Five years!"* he shouted, and pounded the dash with his right hand. "*Five years* with only one letter on my birthday, and one letter at Christmas. Dad only visited me in jail when he knew I was getting out. Till then they were perfectly happy to throw away the key. And do you know why? Do you know how a parent can do that to his own flesh and blood? Because they had the perfect son at home."

"I'm hardly the perfect son," I whispered.

"Tall," he spat out, and steered us around a curve without slackening speed, so that the tires shrieked in protest. "Good-looking. Good grades. Friends. Polite. Churchgoing. Nice girl-friend. *Normal, normal, normal...*"

"I'm not perfect and I'm not happy and I'm not normal," I shouted back, pleading for my life by telling the truth about myself. *"I'm miserable.* And you could do anything I've done and more. You could go back to school. You've got the talent to do anything. Troy, you're gonna have to slow down or we're gonna go off the road. Troy . . ."

"It's a hard thing to slow down," he said. "It's a lot easier to speed up. But you wouldn't know about that." His voice came bubbling up from a deep, dark place, a geyser of pure bile. "Some of the things I've seen and some of the things I've done and some of the things that have been done to me. You don't know what any of it's like. You're still sleeping in the bed you slept in when you got out of your crib. Everything that I should have had has been handed to you . . ."

"So what are you going to do?" I asked. "Kill us both right now? Would that make you feel any better?"

The car was in the high nineties now. The shadows of trees whipped past us. "I might just," Troy said. "Not much holding me onto this highway. I'd like to see their faces if I crashed us. Do you think they'd bury us side by side, brother? Do you think our sanctimonious father would deliver a prayer for both our souls? Do you think the crash would hurt or would it be the best feeling . . ."

We skidded wildly and almost went off the road. I threw my hands in front of my face, but somehow Troy managed to keep us on the highway.

My voice came out hoarse and low. "The day somebody threw the rock through our window, I took Mom up to her bedroom. She sat on the bed, and I sat next to her and held her hand. And she talked about you, Troy. About what you were like when you were young. She talked about the summer we drove across country. She called you her angel."

His biceps flexed as he gripped the steering wheel. He seemed furious at himself for feeling what he was feeling. "She's a fool," he said. "A pathetic creature, scared, stupid, on pills half the time . . ."

"You did that to her," I told him. "She's like that because of how much she loves you. Loves you, loves you. On your birthdays I used to hear her crying long into the night. I've never heard anyone cry like that. Hour after hour. Like she'd lost a part of herself. She loves you, Troy. Always has, always will."

The skin stretched tight over Troy's cheekbones as he pursed his lips outward and clenched his teeth. Bit by bit, the big Ford began to slow down. I held my breath, my body tense, and didn't say another word. The needle crept down past eighty, past seventy-five. When it reached sixty-five, he turned off the parkway onto the ramp of an all-night rest stop.

As we drew near the rest stop building with its parking lot lights, I saw that Troy was drenched in sweat. "I always knew you were every bit as smart as me, but you hide so much of the time I almost never see it," he whispered. "But that was smart of you to bring up Mom. That was damn clever."

As soon as the car rolled to a stop, I jumped out the door and ran ten feet away. "What're you doing that for?" Troy asked. "I'm okay now. I'll drink some coffee and I'll be just fine."

I shook my head. "No more."

"What do you mean, no more?"

"I mean, I'll get home by myself. Goodbye, Troy."

"You're crazy," he said. "You think anyone'll give a stranger a ride now that it's getting dark? C'mon, fool."

I turned away from him and walked to the rest stop. A family was coming down the steps—a father and mother with two small kids in tow. "Excuse me," I said. "I need a big favor. I know it's risky to pick up a complete stranger, but I really need a lift home."

"What happened to your ride?" the man asked.

"My friends were drunk," I said. "My parents always told me if I was with kids who were drunk I should just get out of the car. So I did."

The husband and wife looked me over for a second—the way I was dressed, the way I was groomed, the way I stood there talking to them politely and respectfully. Normal, normal, normal, as Troy would have said. "You did the right thing," the man told me. "Sure, we'll give you a ride. Where you going?"

"Pineville," I said, and started walking across the parking lot with them.

I saw Troy in his big black Ford watching me in disbelief as I reached their car, and got into the backseat with their children. When the door closed, Troy peeled off into the gathering darkness.

25

Winter hit suddenly, with a hard one-two punch.

First the weather turned bitter, and we registered a new state record for low temperatures. Kids put on four layers—long underwear, flannel shirts, sweaters, and coats zippered from belt to chin. I wore wool gloves under thermal mittens, and my hands were still so cold that I had to bang them together every few blocks on the way to school.

The Siberian temperatures turned Pineville High into a ghost school. Dozens of kids stayed home with colds or the flu. For those of us who came in, it seemed like it took most of the day just to get warm. When classes changed, the halls were half-empty and oddly silent, except for echoing coughs and endless miserable sniffles. I noticed that Beth was absent, and asked Pam if she had the flu. "I don't know where she is," Pam told me with a trace of anger. "I left her a bunch of messages. She's not returning my calls."

In our mostly deserted school library I found a book of Gauguin's paintings and carried it to a chair between two rows of shelves. Feeling embarrassed, but also intrigued, I flipped through it. Island colors flashed—yellows, reds, and browns.

Native women with flowers in their hair smiled back at me. The nudes were drawn as if they had not been posed but rather captured for a second during an everyday life without clothes. They looked happy and comfortable in their strong and sensuous bodies.

Had Troy understood something about Beth that I had never glimpsed? Was she ready to explode, and had I really been a gentle, cowardly fool? I remembered the evening when I had told her about Troy coming home. The way she had kissed me under the pier and pressed her body tightly up against me. Thinking back now, there had been a few other moments like that during the summer—when she had looked a little wild and might have been ready to roar ahead, but I had found a reason to put the brakes on.

And what had Troy meant that I was living my life in hiding? He had repeated it several times, and it was the kind of comment about yourself that you can't shake out of your head. Tahiti. Ripe fruit. Endless sunshine. Bare, jutting breasts. I heard our school librarian's footsteps, and closed the book quickly as if hiding something shameful.

The cold snap was so numbing and life-draining that two events that would otherwise have gotten lots of attention slipped by almost unnoticed. First, Charley Hu returned from his suspension. He had always been friendly and talkative, a model student who helped other kids with their homework. His suspension for fighting, and the practical joke that had caused him to flip out, seemed to have completely changed him. He barely talked to anyone—old friends, former teammates, or even teachers. Charley paced through the halls with his jaw set and his body rigid. He had been betrayed by everyone he trusted, so he wasn't going to give anyone a chance to victimize him again.

I felt like he and I had been through something similar, and I tried to reach out to him. On his second day back, I went over to the table in the cafeteria where he was studying alone. "Hey," I said. He didn't look up. "Hey, Charley."

He glanced up. "Go away. I'm studying."

I sat down. "I'm sorry about what happened," I whispered. "I knew about it and I should have told you. Peer pressure can make people act cruel. But it was never anything personal about you. It was just a joke that went way too far. You must have gone through a lot of hell. I'm sure you'll still get into some great colleges."

Charley looked back at me, not saying a word, not moving or blinking. I almost gave up and walked away. But instead I found myself reaching out to him a different way, talking about myself instead of him. "I know this school can be a very tough place. You might have read or heard about what's happened to me and my family. Somebody threw a rock through our window. A couple of guys on the team tried to beat me up. I guess the thing I really wanted to say is that . . . I'm sorry if I treated you the way those guys treated me. I've been through it myself, and I'm really sorry." I ran out of words, so I just watched him and waited.

Charley opened his mouth, and for a second I thought he might accept my apology or at least say something about what we had both gone through. Instead he snapped, "Go away, I'm studying," and looked back down at his book.

The second event at Pineville High that slipped by without too much fuss was that two seniors were arrested for meth use. One was a football player, well known for popping pills and picking fights at parties. The other was a geeky loner who got stoned in school bathrooms and spent all his time playing violent video games. With those two arrests, word spread that the drug investigation had concluded. A lot of kids who had tried meth or Ecstasy once or twice had been questioned, but the police decided not to press any more charges. There was a feeling of relief at our school: the guiltiest had been punished and closure had been achieved just in time for Thanksgiving.

Then the second punch hit. The sky turned white, and there was a dry heaviness in the air that you could smell and taste on your tongue. It started to snow and it didn't stop. We get sprinklings a few times every winter, and two or three inches are not uncommon, but we rarely get blizzards. We soon had more than a foot on the ground, with drifts that you could sink into up to your waist.

As I shoveled the snow from our walk on Thanksgiving morning, I remembered what Troy had told me during our road trip—hypothetically, as he put it—about burying a body in the Pine Barrens. Crunch, my shovel bit through a high drift. Was Tommy Fraser really at the bottom of a hole in the snow-shrouded forest, with frozen earth sealing him up in an icy tomb, and a big rock rolled on top of him like a gravestone without dates or endearments?

Troy had explained that the earth wouldn't thaw till the spring. Was that a hint about his plans? Thinking back on our nightmarish trip to Atlantic City, it was pretty clear to me that he hated all of us, and that he planned to escape fairly soon. Would it really happen in the next couple of months? If so, what exactly was Troy waiting for?

"Jeff?" my father called, apparently for the second or third time, because he tapped me on the shoulder and asked, "Have you got snow in your ears?"

"Probably," I said, turning.

Dad was wearing a ridiculous fur hat, and holding two cups of steaming hot chocolate. "Your mom thought this might thaw you out."

"Too late," I muttered, taking the hot chocolate and sipping it with chapped lips. "My frostbite has frostbite."

"I'm gonna grab a shovel and help you in a minute," Dad promised. "But let's drink this while it's hot."

"Why don't we go inside and get warm?" I suggested.

"Nah, let's stay out here and freeze," Dad said. And then, "Jeff, your mom has put a lot of work into today."

"Meaning?"

"Let's have a nice Thanksgiving."

I looked back at him. "Meaning?"

Dad lowered his voice even though we were the only two people nutty enough to be out shoveling snow in this blizzard. "I know in some ways Mom has seemed better the last couple of weeks," he said. "But in some ways she's been worse. She's very much on edge. The doctor has increased her medication. She's built up in her mind this fantasy of a perfect family Thanksgiving and Christmas. She's kind of fragile, Jeff."

"I know," I said softly. And I also knew how tenderly my father was taking care of her. "I'm sorry."

Dad sipped his hot drink, and blinked flakes of snow away from his eyes. "Look, I don't know what happened between you and Troy in Atlantic City. Since neither of you has told me, maybe it's not my business. If you reached out to him and something bad happened, that's unfortunate."

I didn't answer. I just sipped hot chocolate and looked back into those kind gray eyes. *If you only knew how much he hates you,* I thought. *All of us, but you most of all, dear sweet father. But I can't tell you that. I don't dare. It would hurt you too much, and you'd never believe me anyway.*

"I know Troy has left messages for you and tried to come by and talk to you several times," Dad continued softly. "My impression is that he's been trying to give you an apology. Jeffrey, it's good for the soul to forgive. Especially during this season."

"Yeah, deck the halls," I muttered.

"Don't be that way."

"Okay, sorry. Dad, I'm freezing. Can we just get back to work? I think my spine's about to freeze."

"We wouldn't want that," Dad said with a slight smile. "Can't shovel snow with a frozen spine. Listen, all I'm asking is that you be polite today. Cordial. Let's have a happy holiday. Let's give your mom that."

"Fine," I said. "Now let's shovel snow." I dumped the rest

of the hot chocolate on the snow, but my dad reached out and grabbed the pole of my shovel and held it fast.

He looked at me, and I could see the pain and worry I had caused him as he said very softly, "Jeff, we are none of us innocent. We are all sinners."

"Not you," I said back to him with a sincerity that seemed to catch him by surprise. "You're a good man. The best I've ever known. That's what makes this all so tough."

He shook his head. "No. I have done things in my life that I'm terribly ashamed of. It's part of being human." His humility and simple goodness seemed to shine through his eyes and for a minute I forgot the freezing wind and heard only his pleading question: "Jeff, why do you hate your brother so?"

"Believe me, you don't want to know."

"I do."

"No you don't. If I said it, you wouldn't hear it."

"Try me." Dad let go of my shovel and brought his hands together. I don't know whether it was a gesture of pleading or if he was just trying to restore circulation. "Please."

I didn't mean to speak, but the words exploded out of my mouth. "I hate him because he hates you," I said quickly, looking back into those kind gray eyes. I could almost feel his whole body wince, but I kept on. "Because he's the exact opposite of you. He despises everything that you stand for, everything that you've taught me. And he's going to rip it all down."

"No," Dad whispered, but what he really meant was stop. Enough.

I didn't stop. I kept going. "Yes. He's gonna repay your trust

237

with pain. He's going to hurt you as deeply as he can. Mom, too. He's going to destroy her because he loves her and he hates that in himself. Dad, he's planning something awful. Something terrible."

"What?" my father managed to ask.

"I don't know."

"When?"

"I don't know."

"He told you this?"

"Not in so many words."

Dad grabbed me by the arms. Our faces were inches apart. "If he didn't tell you, then how can you know?"

"Because I know. Don't give him the chance to do this."

For a moment I saw a tiny crack in the perfect glaze of trust and decency that gave such a lovely shine to my father's world. I saw doubt and even fear—strangers to that perfect world, odd and unwanted interlopers. And then, as I watched, Dad seemed to draw himself up in height, and I could see his faith rolling back in like a wave and sweeping away the unwanted doubts. "Be careful," he warned me softly. "With what measure ye mete, it shall be measured to you again."

I knew he was quoting the Bible. I tried to interrupt: "I don't know what that means, but I know—"

He went on as if I hadn't spoken. "And why beholdest thou the mote that is in thy brother's eye, but considerest not the beam that is in thine own eye?"

"Stop it," I said to him. "There's no beam in my eye. I didn't kill anyone."

"You stop it," he said. "Anyone can be made to sound suspicious. It's beneath you to say such vile things, that you can't prove. I brought Troy home under hard terms, and he has met those terms. He's worked his butt off. He's never told me a single lie. He's stayed out of trouble."

"Have you forgotten the rock through our window? Next time they'll probably burn down our house."

"I won't hear any more of this, Jeff," my father said. "Not a word. Not a syllable."

"You asked," I reminded him.

"I won't ask again," he said. "Trust your fellow man and he will reward your trust. That's all that I know about life, and it has stood me in good stead for forty-six years. Now let's shovel some snow."

So we shoveled, moving off in opposite directions, and the snow fell around us. Soon the path was clear and we were far apart.

Troy showed up at about two o'clock in the afternoon, nicely dressed in corduroy pants and a pressed white shirt. He came through the door singing, "On the first day of Christmas," with a bottle of French wine in one hand and a box of Swiss chocolates in the other. He kissed my mom and handed her the chocolates. "Sweets for the sweet," he said. Then he saw the dining room table, set with silver and china. He grinned and inhaled. "Someone's been cooking a turkey."

"I hope it's big enough," Mom said. Underneath her apron she was wearing a lovely blue dress. She had put on pearl earrings that I had never seen before, and she had done up her hair in a way that made her look ten years younger.

"Something tells me it will be," Troy assured her. And then, gently, "You look lovely, Ma."

"I don't."

"Thanks for doing all this," Troy said, and the words caught in his throat. "It means a lot to me."

"You don't have to thank me," she told him, and reached out to stroke his face very gently. "My baby," she whispered. "My angel."

Troy let her fingers linger on his cheek for a second, and then he spotted me watching from a corner of the dining room and pulled back as if embarrassed. "Hi, Jeff," he said. "Happy Thanksgiving, brother."

"And to you," I replied with noticeably less enthusiasm.

"Well, I'm going to run and check the turkey," my mom announced nervously, and hurried off into the kitchen.

I was alone with Troy for the first time since our trip to Atlantic City. "How've you been keeping, Jeff?" he asked, stepping toward me.

"Well. Thanks for asking."

"I've called a few times," he said, and I felt his searching gaze.

"Yeah, so I heard. I've been busy."

"No doubt," Troy said. And then in a lower voice, "Look, I'm sorry for what happened. I had a bad night."

"Let's have a happy Thanksgiving," I said.

"That's not exactly accepting my apology," he pointed out. "Surely I'm allowed one rough night."

"Let's have a happy Thanksgiving," I repeated, and tried to walk by him.

He grabbed me by the arm, hard. "I drank too much and behaved like a damn fool. I never would have crashed the car. You believe that, don't you? You're my brother and I love you. What more can I say?"

"You can say whatever you want." I tried to pull away from him, and for a moment we struggled.

Then we heard footsteps, and he let go of my arm just as our dad walked in, carving knife in hand. I think Dad heard us arguing, but you couldn't tell it from his face. "Happy Thanksgiving, Troy," he said. "And a cold one it is. You were lucky enough to come late and miss all the snow shoveling."

"Smart, not lucky," Troy corrected him. "Hey, watch where you're going with that sword." Troy feigned dodging out of the way of the carving knife, and handed Dad the bottle of wine. "Happy Thanksgiving, Pop."

"Looks like a fancy bottle," Dad said. "You shouldn't have. I better go carve up the bird." Dad took a half step and then turned back. "Hey, did you hear the good news?"

"What good news?" Troy asked.

Dad answered him, but he was now looking at me. "About your friend Fraser? I just heard it on the radio."

Troy stiffened, and for a moment I glimpsed something pass across my brother's face that I had never seen there before. Dad was still holding the carving knife, and over the glittering blade edge I watched unmistakable fear flicker in a single pulse beat through Troy's eyes. Then it was gone. "They found him?" Troy asked in a level voice. And before Dad could answer, he posed another question with what sounded like real concern, "Is he okay?"

"No, they haven't found him yet," Dad responded, "but they found his van in Washington State, up near the Canadian border. They think he probably sold it for cash before crossing the border 'cause he knew there were people looking for him. The radio says there are a lot of police up there now, trying to pick up his trail. I'm sure his parents will be relieved. I can't think of anything more terrible than a child you love just vanishing. Well, I'd better go carve that bird."

"Thanks for the good news," I said, watching Troy's face.

He looked back at me as he said to Dad, "Yes, I'm sure they'll find him very soon. By the way, in case you've forgotten, Pop, I like dark meat."

26

"Let us give thanks," my father said. The four of us joined hands around the table and bowed our heads. I was glad that I was seated opposite Troy, so I didn't have to touch him. My mom's hand felt small and warm in my own. Dad clasped me firmly, almost as if in a handshake, and when he began to pray, his voice was rich with emotion. "Dear Lord," he intoned, "we thank you for this Thanksgiving dinner, for the food on our table, and for the gladness in our hearts. Most of all we thank you for bringing our family back together. We remember the poor children all over the world who don't have enough to eat, and we ask that in the coming year you not only bless us with health and happiness but give us the chance to serve our fellow man. Amen."

"Amen," I heard Troy echo quickly from across the table.

I mumbled my own "Amen," but before I could let go of my parents' hands, Troy asked, "Dad, can I say a few words?"

"Of course," my father told him.

Troy lowered his head solemnly, and my parents did the same. As Troy began to speak he peered upward through half-opened eyes, looking right at me. "Dear Lord," he said, his words and his tone an almost perfect copy, or should I say mockery, of my father's. "When I walked through the valley of the shadow of death, you stood by me. Your rod and your staff, they comforted me."

I looked back at him and remembered his comments on the ride to Atlantic City about how religion was gunk and anyone who believed in it was a fool. He sure was spreading it on pretty thick.

"I want to thank you, Lord, for bringing me home to those who love me despite all my sins," Troy said softly, and for a second as he looked at me his lips seemed to twitch in an almost imperceptible smirk. "I ask you to make me worthy of the wonderful parents I have, and of a brother who is the living embodiment of all the good things I aspire to. Amen."

"Amen," my father repeated. "That was well said, Troy."

I felt my mom let go of my hand a little too quickly, and I glanced over at her. She picked up her dinner napkin and dabbed away a tear. "Amen," she whispered.

Troy unfolded his own napkin and draped it over his knees. "Now let's eat," he said. "I don't know about the rest of you, but I could eat a horse."

"Then we're in trouble," Mom said, "because I didn't do the horse recipe this year."

My dad laughed first, and then Troy, and I joined in. It wasn't a great joke, it wasn't even a good joke, but it was the first one Mom had told in a very long time.

That laughter, forced and faked though it might have been, ushered us into a Thanksgiving dinner that seemed as perfect as even my mother could have wished for. Snow fell outside the window, coating the tree branches. A fire crackled in our fireplace. In the background, a Bach cantata played softly. There were more bad family jokes, and lots of good food to make up for them.

My mom had made pumpkin soup, sweet with the rich flavor of autumn. As spoons clinked against china, the dinner conversation drifted easily from the heavy snowfall to a movie my parents had seen the previous weekend to a chronic leak in the basement. "I could probably fix it for you," Troy ventured. "I borrow tools from the store sometimes, and do odd jobs for people. I'll take a look after we finish."

"How are things going at the store?" Dad asked. "It must be getting on to the busy season."

"You said it," Troy told him. "With the holidays coming, I get all the overtime I want."

"So I heard." Dad nodded. "Walter says you're there at all hours. Hardest worker he's ever had. You really helped him out when he was ill."

Troy looked down into his soup bowl for a moment, as if embarrassed by the praise. "I'm trying to put away a little savings," he finally said, almost as if making a confession. And then he looked up and added softly, "I've been thinking about maybe trying to take some college classes."

"Oh, Troy. That would be wonderful," Mom gushed.

"Maybe we could help out some," Dad offered.

"Absolutely not," Troy told him. "If I do it, I'm going to pay for it myself. I figure I'll work harder that way."

He was telling them exactly what they wanted to hear, and I wondered if any of it was true. How well he knew them, and how skillfully he manipulated them. I wanted to press him: What college, Troy? Have you picked up any applications? What are you planning to study? Don't you have other plans that involve disappearing to some faraway paradise? But I had promised Dad a cordial Thanksgiving, and I spooned the last tiny puddle of soup out of my bowl and held my silence.

Out went the empty soup bowls and in came the turkey, with chestnut stuffing and cranberries and braised Brussels sprouts to keep it company. There were candied yams and homemade coleslaw. Soon we all had heaping plates, and Troy raised his wineglass and smiled at my mom. "To the mother of the feast," he said.

We repeated the toast and clinked glasses, all looking at my mom, whose face seemed to glow with contented beauty. She raised her own glass. "Come again next year," she whispered back to us. "Same time, same place."

Dad and Mom rarely drink. Maybe it was the French wine or perhaps it was the family holiday that they had both wanted for so long, but as the dinner went on, they grew more and more nostalgic. They recalled a Thanksgiving in Buffalo when the turkey had been larger than Troy, and he ran around and around the table in a Pilgrim hat, banging on a toy drum with a turkey drumstick. "I had to take it away from you because you were getting grease all over everything," Dad recalled. "How loud you screamed!"

"If you try to take away my drumstick I'll still scream,"

Troy threatened, sliding his plate a few inches away from Dad. "Confess, you just wanted to eat it yourself."

"He might be right about that," my mom kidded.

Laughter over my dad's denials. More sips of wine. Mom's pearl earrings glinted in the candlelight. I watched them having fun. They were willing to talk about dinners before I had been born, but they stayed far away from mentioning any Thanksgiving when Troy had been in prison.

"Did I ever tell you about your mom's and my first Thanksgiving together?" Dad asked. "I had just met her a few days before. I was a junior; she was just a freshman."

"Freshwoman," my mom corrected him.

"Whose story is this?" he demanded with mock anger.

"I just want to make sure you get it right."

"My memory's pretty good in this area," he assured her. And then, to us, "I met your mom on the second floor of the college library at two-thirty in the afternoon."

"How can you possibly remember the time?" Mom asked.

"I remember everything about that day," he said. "I had been reading a statistics textbook for three hours straight. I looked up just as you walked out of the elevator and crossed the hallway into the stacks. You were wearing dark slacks and a green sweater, and you were the prettiest thing I'd ever seen in my life."

Mom smiled at him and said softly, "Anyone would look good after three hours of statistics."

"You were holding a Russian novel in one hand," Dad recalled, "and a cup of tea in the other."

"*Anna Karenina*," Mom supplied.

"A shaft of winter sunlight slanted in from a high window and lit your hair," Dad continued in a faraway voice. "And I said to myself, 'I'm gonna marry that girl.' "

"Frank," my mom whispered, blushing but smiling.

Dad grinned back at her. "So I waited for you to sit down, and before you could start studying I went over and found some clever reason to strike up a conversation."

"You asked me if I knew the time," Mom said. "But you were wearing a watch. And there was a big clock on the wall."

Troy and I laughed. "Suave, Dad," Troy said.

"Obvious though I may have been, you didn't exactly tell me to get lost," Dad fired back at her. "Anyway, that's how I remember that it was exactly two-thirty. I ended up sitting down and we talked for a long time . . ."

"Hours." My mom nodded. "They went by like seconds."

"And when she found out that my folks were in Cleveland and I wasn't going home, she invited me to come to Syracuse and have Thanksgiving with her family." Dad looked at Troy and me, as if something about the memory still puzzled him. "It made no sense at all," he said. "I didn't even know her. What were her parents going to think? But I could never say no to those pretty eyes . . ."

RING, RING, RING, the front doorbell interrupted the sweet story.

"Now, who could that be bothering us on Thanksgiving?" Mom asked.

"I'll get it," Dad offered, but I was the closest to the front door. I popped up and hurried through the vestibule.

RING, RING. Whoever it was, they were impatient. KNOCK, KNOCK, KNOCK. And rude.

I opened the door and saw Chief Mayweather standing there in street clothes, with a balding older man next to him.

"Hi. I need to come in," the chief said. "Are your folks home? Your brother . . ."

He started to walk in, and somewhere I found the courage to step in front of him. "Listen," I whispered, "my mom's put a lot of work into this day, so couldn't you just—"

"No, I couldn't just," Chief Mayweather cut me off. "I don't know how you're involved in all this, but that sweet and innocent act never fooled me. Now get out of the way."

Suddenly my father was standing next to me. "Why are you speaking that way to my son, and what's this all about? It's Thanksgiving and our turkey's on the table—"

"And my turkey's in the oven warming and probably getting dried out," Chief Mayweather said back to him. "And my family's sitting around hungry, so let's get right to it. Is your son here? Your other son?"

I had never seen Dad challenge authority before. He did it with firmness and dignity. "I'm going to have to ask you to please leave my house," he said. "Now."

My mom's voice drifted in from the living room. "Who is it? The turkey's getting cold . . ."

Chief Mayweather took a document out of his pocket. "You're free to examine this."

Dad didn't even glance at the paper. He was looking back into the chief's eyes, asking a favor man to man. "Don't do this now. My wife's not well."

"It's a search warrant, authorized by the court," the chief told him. As if following up on this, he stepped by my father and began walking through the vestibule.

Dad and I followed him into the dining room.

My eyes were first drawn to Troy, who had bolted up at the sight of the chief, his knife and fork still in his hands.

"Let go of the knife," Chief Mayweather said to him.

Troy opened his hand, and the knife clattered to the floor.

"I don't understand what you're doing here," my mom said in a polite voice that quivered just a bit. "We're in the middle of our meal. Surely this can wait . . ."

"Sorry, but it can't," Chief Mayweather told her. "I have here a search warrant to be executed today . . ."

Dad walked behind my mom's chair and put his hands on her shoulders. "Then go ahead and search," he said. "We have no secrets. My son doesn't even live here anymore. *Go, search, turn the place upside down.* And then get out so we can finish our dinner."

"We're not here to search your house," Chief Mayweather told him. "It's not that kind of search. The court order is for a DNA sample." He turned to Troy, who hadn't moved. "My technician here is going to take a scraping from inside your cheek."

The small bald man took a swab out of what looked like a small kit. "Please sit down, tilt your head up, and open your mouth," he said.

Troy did not sit down. He hesitated for a second and then squared his shoulders and said to Chief Mayweather, "Let me see that court order."

The chief handed it to him, and spoke quickly as Troy's eyes moved across the official form. "You probably heard they found Tom Fraser's van up north. What you didn't hear is that there were blood splotches in the back of the van. We want to see if your blood matches. Now, are you going to sit down and let my technician do his work, or are we going to have to restrain you?"

For a second Troy looked like a trapped animal, and I thought he might make a run for it. He glanced quickly at my father, and then at my mom. "He can't do this. Don't let them do this to me . . ."

As if in answer to this plea, Mom suddenly let out a low moan. We all looked at her. She had taken her fork and jabbed it into the back of her arm. As we watched in horror, she dug it up toward her elbow, so that three lines of blood appeared on her pale skin.

"Linda?" My dad reached for her.

But my mom jumped up before he could touch her, knocking over her chair, and ran out of the room.

"Damn you to hell," my father said to Chief Mayweather, and then ran after her.

Chief Mayweather stepped toward Troy, who looked back at him as if sizing him up for a fight. Then, without a word, Troy very calmly sat down in his chair, tilted his head up, and opened his mouth.

 **27**

I heard the knocking a few minutes before midnight. It was stormy outside, with gusts of wind that blew spatters of rain and rat-tat-tats of hail against the windows. I was working late into the night on my report for Mr. Tsuyuki on evil and human behavior. Articles cluttered my desk, while file cards on which I had jotted notes lay all over the floor.

The last few days had been painful, so I was glad to have this paper to distract me. Mom had gone to bed early, disappearing into her room without even a good night. After our disastrous Thanksgiving dinner she had spent a few days in the psychiatric ward of a hospital. While it was great to have her home again, it didn't feel like she was completely here. She said very little, and I knew her quietness and the amount she slept had to do with her new medications.

Concentrate on your paper, I commanded myself. I had plowed through a dozen articles explaining the latest theories on human behavior. Some claimed people act the way they do because their genes point them in that direction. Others made convincing arguments that a person is really just a big machine carrying out commands from nerve cells that chemically have no choice but to react a certain way to stimulation. Still others talked about how people's actions as adults are predetermined by their psychological makeup and history, so that a childhood tragedy or severe trauma to the head may explain a person's actions much later in life.

Tap, tap. I dismissed the knocking as hail, or perhaps a branch that was being raked against the pane by the wind. It was a good night to be inside a safe, warm house.

Yet even as I thought this, I knew that all was not well in our home. I pictured Dad in the bedroom down the hall, stroking Mom's hair while she drifted into a drugged sleep, and then watching TV with the sound off till he finally fell asleep himself, with his clothes on. Something deep in the foundation of our family had been pried loose in the last few days, and the whole structure now felt shaky.

I forced myself to stop worrying and focus on the note cards for my paper. The more I read these hyper-modern arguments for how people's behavior could be explained by genes or chemicals or psychological trauma, the more they reminded me of a much earlier argument—one that had raged two thousand years ago.

I had done a search online for evil and human behavior, and scanned through dozens of sites having to do with religion and philosophy. The most interesting sites were historical and referred me back to the early Church arguments over free will and predestination. Those arguments boiled down to this: if God is really all-powerful and all-knowing, then how can people who do evil things be blamed? God created them a certain way and knew everything that would happen, but he chose not to stop it. So how could people be sent to hell for punishment or rewarded by heaven if they were really just acting out what God had predestined them to do?

I remembered Troy driving back from Atlantic City, and claiming in fury that our parents had turned on him. "They wanted me desperately to be like them," he had said bitterly in the speeding car. "And when I wasn't, they turned on me. If I couldn't be like them, then I had to be a monster."

His words had made me feel sorry for him, and also a bit guilty. I always knew deep in my heart that Troy was different from the rest of us. Apparently he felt the same thing. And that difference had made his life miserable, and landed him in jail, and while I blamed him for it, he blamed us and . . .

Tap, tap. I glanced quickly at the window. No stars, no moon. Nothing but blackness. A hellish night.

So did Troy deserve prison, or even eternal hell? I glanced at one of the most interesting articles I had downloaded. Augustine of Hippo, a Church philosopher who lived nearly two thousand years ago, was asked why God gave humans free will, since it enables us to sin. He replied that it was a necessary condition for virtuous action. There could be no sins and no good deeds without free will, and so there could be no punishments and no rewards.

It seemed to me that after two thousand years, all these scientific articles attempting to explain human behavior raised the exact same question. It doesn't matter whether it's God dictating our actions, or neurons and synapses. Once you believe that people are not responsible for how they behave, you remove good and evil from the equation. And you also remove rewards and punishments, blame and prison.

I wasn't smart enough to sort through all the scientific theories or to argue my way through all the logical twists and turns. But I knew what felt right: acts of cruelty that hurt or kill people require blame and punishment. Sure, I was tremendously sorry for Troy because he had been born with a different nature, a dark side. It was a part of him, engrained in him, just as deeply as his artistic talent and his cleverness. I couldn't blame him for it any more than I could blame a shark for having sharp teeth.

But I also believed that Troy had no right to take the life of Billy Shea. He deserved life in prison for that. And if he had killed Franchise Fraser, he deserved the hottest hell there could ever be . . .

Tap, tap, tap. *Knock. Knock.* It wasn't just rain or hail. It was a persistent knock. A demanding knock. Open the damn window and let me in, the knock was saying. Someone was out there!

I jumped out of my chair, already fairly sure who it must be. When Troy had first entered my room, I saw his eyes drawn to the tree outside my window. Who else would come knocking on a night like this? Was he being chased by the police? He had kept a low profile since Thanksgiving, only coming by a few times. I peered out the window. It was hard to see anything through the ice that frosted the panes of glass, but I could just make out a form waving to me. An arm reached out. *Tap tap.* Let me in before I freeze.

I got the inner window open easily, but the outer one wouldn't budge. I pried with all my might, and it gave. Swoosh, the cold air came streaming in. I saw a figure two feet away, bundled from head to foot in coats and scarves and a hat. He leaned toward me and I grabbed an arm.

For a minute he dangled, and I thought he would plummet. He kicked and I pulled, and all of a sudden he came sprawling into my room like a great fish over the side of a boat.

Off came the hat, releasing waves of long brown hair. Round and round the scarf undraped itself, revealing red cheeks and bright hazel eyes. Not a he but a she. "What took you so long to open the window?" Beth demanded, with a shiver for a question mark.

For a few seconds I was too surprised to answer her. "Sorry," I finally managed to get out. "I didn't expect you to be in my tree. During a hailstorm most people enter through the door. Are you okay?"

She nodded and shivered again. A few tiny hailstones catapulted from her eyelashes. Off came a parka and ski pants. Beth had still more layers on underneath—a thick sweater and what looked like nylon leggings. She had dressed for an Arctic expedition. "Most people ring the doorbell, and I didn't want to do that," she explained. "I figured your parents were sleeping."

It wasn't a question, but it seemed somehow to require an answer. "Definitely." I nodded. "Mom's been out for hours. And Dad conks out watching *The Late Show.*"

"Good," she said, pulling off her sweater. Watching her tug it off over her head made me excited, embarrassed, and curious all at once. Why had she come, and what did she want? She had worn a lot of layers, but she was definitely getting down to the bottom ones. I looked away politely, and then I slowly looked back and met her gaze.

"Even with all those wet clothes off, I'm still cold," she said. She stepped forward and kissed me on the lips. Her cheeks were freezing, but her lips were warm. She pulled away and I felt a little dizzy. "Do me a favor?" she asked.

"Sure," I whispered, steadying myself with one hand on the corner of my desk. A few file cards explaining human behavior fluttered to the floor. "What?"

"Go make me some hot tea."

"Milk, sugar?"

"Both," Beth said. "Thanks, Jeff."

I pulled my bedroom door closed just in case Mom or Dad happened to wake up and go for a stroll down the hall. I hurried downstairs and put a kettle on. As I waited for the water to boil, I tried to deal with my own rising temperature. I didn't know why Beth had come or what she wanted, but it's not every winter's night that a beautiful ex-girlfriend climbs through my window and begins peeling off her clothes.

I filled a large mug with hot tea and tiptoed carefully back upstairs. At the second-floor landing I glanced down the hall. My parents' bedroom was dark and still. I took a deep breath and turned back toward my room.

 **28**

I knocked softly on my own bedroom door and entered. Beth's coat, sweater, ski pants, and other winter gear had been piled near my bed. I didn't see her for a minute, and then I spotted her standing by the mirror. She was wearing my blue bathrobe, and was brushing out her long hair. "I hope you don't mind," she said. "I needed something warm and dry."

"It looks better on you than me," I told her, which was an understatement. I could see the curves of her body beneath the terry cloth. I flashed to Troy's drawing of her—the long, bare legs, the jutting breasts. "Beth, here's your tea." My voice played tricks on me. Some words came out loud and slow while others turned whispery somersaults.

She took the mug and sipped. "Mmm. Perfect. Thanks."

I stood there a little stiffly, my arms at my sides, watching her drink. The bedroom door was open a crack, so I reached out and pushed it shut.

A tiny smile flitted across Beth's lips. "So is all quiet on the Western Front?"

"Excuse me?"

"Your parents asleep?"

"Yeah," I said, and hesitated. "Beth, I can lock the door from the inside." She looked a little surprised. "I just meant . . . if you're worried about my parents walking in . . ."

"Sure," Beth agreed. "Lock the door."

So I did, and turned back to her. Our eyes met. Now we were locked in together.

"You really must like privacy," Beth observed.

"I got the lock when Troy moved in. His room was right under mine and . . ." My voice trailed off.

Beth sat down on the rug Indian style and sipped her tea. "When I met your brother at the grocery," she said, "I finally understood why you were so scared and angry that evening under the pier at Seaside Heights. There's something dangerous about Troy. He follows no rules. It's frightening, but it's also kind of thrilling."

"There's a lot dangerous about him," I corrected her. "And the closer you get to him, the more you see it."

"Have you gotten close?" she asked. And then, softly, "What did you see, Jeff?"

I sat down opposite her and described the trip Troy and I had taken to Atlantic City. I told her how he had teased me about burying Fraser in the Pine Barrens, and how it felt like he'd been to Atlantic City before. I ended by describing Chief Mayweather bursting into our Thanksgiving dinner.

"I'm sorry about your mom," Beth said.

"Thanks."

"She's better now?"

"More at peace," I said softly. "That doesn't always mean better."

Beth reached out and stroked my cheek very gently. "You think your brother killed Tommy?" she asked in a whisper so low it seemed to flicker like a candle flame.

I could hear the wind outside gusting around the roof and whistling through the bare tree branches. I nodded, slowly and sadly.

"But the blood they found in the van didn't match Troy's," Beth pointed out. "Otherwise they would have arrested him."

"I knew it wouldn't match," I told her. "If there had been any doubt in Troy's mind that even a drop of the blood in the van was his, he would have run for it after the chief left our house. He must've known the blood was all Tommy's."

"So what happened to Tommy?" Beth asked.

"I don't know exactly," I admitted. "I have some suspicions. I can't prove any of it. My dad says I shouldn't talk about things that I can't prove."

"You can talk about them to me," Beth said. She took my hand in her own. "We used to trust each other a lot."

"That was a long time ago," I told her. "You haven't been here for me, Beth."

"I'm here now," she said. "Real close."

I folded my fingers over the back of her hand. Suddenly the suspicions I had been storing up for weeks came spilling out. "Troy likes to walk through the Pine Barrens," I told her. "My bet is that Fraser had some place in the forest where he parked and hung out and sold drugs. And Troy ran into him there after they fought at the soccer game."

Beth opened her mouth as if she was tempted to add something. Then she closed it and nodded. "So you think they met again that day just by coincidence?"

"Maybe it wasn't a coincidence," I told her. "Maybe Troy had seen Fraser parked at that spot before. Or maybe Fraser was driving through the forest and he spotted Troy, out for a walk. I don't know. But that afternoon, one way or another, they ended up alone in the Pine Barrens. They had just fought, and Fraser's pride was hurt. He would have confronted Troy. Maybe he had a weapon in his van, since he was dealing drugs. A knife. A gun. I don't know."

"He had a knife," Beth said quietly.

"How do you know?"

"I saw it. He kept it in the glove compartment. It was the kind you can throw. Sometimes he would take it out and make it spin through the air till it stuck in a tree."

"So you were with him in his van and you were with him in the pines?" I waited for her answer. Long and awkward seconds crawled between us.

"Okay, so Fraser had a knife," I finally said, giving up the wait. "After five years of prison, I figure Troy knew how to take a knife away from a bigger guy. They struggled, and Fraser got stabbed. I'd like to think it was an accident. Troy had nothing to gain and everything to lose by killing someone. But he could have meant to do it. He could even have enjoyed it."

Beth nodded. She had met Troy. She understood him.

"Then Troy had a problem. There he was in the woods with a corpse. He was a convicted murderer, who had just moved to town. He had threatened Fraser that very morning. Who would believe he hadn't meant to kill him? If he went to the police and told the truth, they would lock him up and throw away the key."

Beth nodded. "So he buried the body?" she asked in a whisper. "Just the way he told you?"

I shut my eyes for a minute and I could almost see Troy standing alone in the Pine Barrens, with a bloody knife in his hands. "No one knew they were there. No one witnessed the fight. So, sure, Troy followed his instincts and buried Fraser. Then he drove to Atlantic City in the van. He sold it for cash to one of those places that don't ask questions."

"A chop shop?" Beth asked. "That's what they call them on TV. They can even get rid of license plates and serial numbers."

"Now Troy had a choice," I said. "He could run with the cash, or he could come home. He spent part of the night in Atlantic City figuring it out, and he chose to come home."

"Why?" Beth asked. "Why come back to Pineville?"

"I don't know," I admitted. "Maybe he didn't get much money for the van. Maybe he has something else planned here in Pineville. It would have been very suspicious if he had gone on the run the same day Fraser disappeared. So he came home, and he's been living with this ever since."

"Wow," Beth said, and we were quiet for a few minutes and just sat there holding hands. "I could tell that your brother has a lot of levels and secrets," she admitted. "It's what makes him interesting."

" 'Thrilling' was the word you used," I reminded her.

"He recommended some art for me to look at and some books for me to read that kind of blew me away."

"I can imagine," I told her, thinking about the Gauguin nudes. As she sat there close to me, I recalled moments from the summer when we had been alone together and she had flirted or kissed me or caressed me. It seemed like a long time ago, and yet here we were, locked in together on a stormy night.

"And he said really nice things about you," Beth added.

That surprised me. "Like what?"

Beth glanced down for a heartbeat, and then back up. "He said he loves you in his own way . . . and that he thinks a lot about times you had as brothers long ago. Sometimes he wishes he could be like you, but he knows he can't. He thinks you're more like him than you let on, but you're afraid of that part of yourself, so you live your life in hiding."

"He told me some of that, too. I didn't know what he meant. Do you, Beth?"

She nodded and squeezed my hand. "I think so." Then she asked, "How was his picture of me? I just saw some sketches. How did it come out?"

"It's like you and it's not like you. Do you really want to hear this?"

"Absolutely," she said. "Don't be embarrassed."

"He thinks you're sensuous, like a caged animal, ready to explode. He told me I was a coward because I couldn't see it and we never . . ." I searched for the words, and she nodded and saved me the trouble. "The picture he drew of you captures that and more. It's sexy and provocative and disturbing. When I saw it I attacked him."

"You punched him?"

"I tried to stab him. I would've killed him."

She looked astonished. "Why?"

"That he saw you like that, even in his mind. And that you showed him your tattoo. Maybe I was jealous."

She moved closer to me across the rug. "Jeff, I came tonight for three reasons. First, I wanted to say goodbye."

"Where are you going?"

"Mount Hopewell Academy. It's a private school in Essex County. We've been away for a few days visiting there and interviewing. It's a really beautiful place. And they're going to take me right away."

"Congratulations," I said. "I assume you want to go?"

"My dad wants me to," she said. "And I kind of owe him. Which leads me to the second reason I came. You deserve an explanation."

"For what?"

"For my dad. And for what I've done. I'm not super-proud of what I'm about to tell you. But I think you have a right to know."

"Then tell me," I said. "As you put it, we used to trust each other."

She nodded. I could tell this was hard for her. She looked back at me and took a few short breaths. "You were right," she finally said. "Tommy Fraser didn't like to sell drugs in town. He said even inside a house or in his van you could never be sure of total privacy. So he liked to drive out into the forest."

"You were a customer?"

Beth nodded. "It's not like I was a hardcore druggie or anything. But I was curious. Pam wanted to experiment, and I went along with it. We just did it a few times. We smoked joints. The first time it made me sick. And then we bought some Ecstasy. I kept it at my house and my dad found it."

I imagined the irascible and overprotective Mr. Doyle stumbling on a stash of his daughter's drugs. "He knew what they were?"

"Oh yeah," she said.

"He knew they were yours?"

"He caught me smoking a joint. The rest of the stuff was right there."

"Must have been a bad scene," I said. "Did he know who you bought it from?"

"He thought you gave it to me," she said. "He thought your brother was corrupting you, and you were corrupting me. I swore to him it wasn't you. And then I think he asked around and began to hear rumors about Tommy. Tommy had worked for him and they had never liked each other."

"No wonder he looked like he was ready to kill Fraser at your concert."

"Dad went a little nuts, and maybe I can't blame him," Beth said. "At first he wanted to go to the police. I convinced him that wasn't a great idea. Then he made me go talk to a therapist. And he made me swear to stop talking to you and Tommy and just about everybody else. And then Tommy disappeared and the police came to our house. That was when my dad decided to give me a fresh start, to use his words. And I had put him through so much hell that I kind of had to agree." Beth fell quiet for a few seconds. "Whatever you might think of him, he's a good dad," she whispered. "He loves me and wants to protect me."

"I can see it from his side," I told her. "Beth, where is the place Tommy used to go in the Pine Barrens?"

She thought about it for a few seconds. "I don't know," she answered with a slight shrug. "He drove. It was just a mile or two out of town along a dirt road."

I pressed her. "It must've been near something? Some landmark? Come on, you grew up here."

"It was out beyond Eagle Rock," she said. "Not near anything. I couldn't find it again if I tried." There was a silent beat. "So that's my explanation, Jeff, for whatever it's worth. I'm sorry I screwed things up so badly, and I haven't been able to even talk to you while you were going through a hard time. I was also going through a hard time at home."

"Okay," I said. "I'm glad you told me. You said there was a third reason you came tonight?"

"I wanted to give you something," she whispered. She looked back at me and her hazel eyes sparkled, and then she stood up. Her hands loosened the belt, and then in one movement she took off the blue terry-cloth bathrobe. She wasn't wearing anything under it.

I don't recall standing up, but suddenly we were facing each other a few inches apart. My eyes ran down her body and then back up to her face, and she blushed bright red but met my gaze. "Your brother might have been a little bit right about me," she whispered. "Is that okay?"

"You're very beautiful," I whispered back.

"Beautiful but cold," she said. "Can I get into bed?"

I nodded, and she got in under the covers and lay there, looking up at me. "Jeff, will you come keep me warm?"

I started to get into bed and she said, "Aren't you going to take off your clothes?"

So I did, and I turned out the light, and then we were side by side under the covers.

"I want you to know something," she said. "Remember when you told me at school, in the hall, that you loved me?"

"Yes. I felt foolish afterward."

"I've thought back to that moment so many times. There was such a serious look in your eyes when you said it. I'll never forget that look. You meant it, didn't you?"

"I did."

"Good," she said. She reached down and took my hands and pulled them toward her, till they touched her breasts. "Don't be afraid," she said. "I've never done this before either. But I love you, too, Jeff. And I think that's the most important thing."

29

"Listen, Smitty, I'll only go if it's one of your truly bad movies," I told my big buddy as we headed to bio class. "A real stinker. The kind you specialize in."

"I don't know what you mean by that," he said, puffing out his cheeks. "I have superb taste in movies."

"Superbly awful," I told him. "So don't hold back. Choose one where the plot makes no sense, everything that moves blows up, and the sound effects shake the walls."

Smitty pretended to be offended, but I could tell he was pleased. "You asked for it and you're gonna get it, pal," he promised. He'd been dropping hints about us seeing a movie for weeks and I hadn't given him much hope. The truth was I'd had a hard time forgiving Smitty for turning on me when I needed his friendship. But I'd decided to forgive and forget, for three pretty solid reasons.

First, I'd watched Charley Hu turn his back on all his former friends. He now marched through the school days as an army of one, without smiling or acknowledging anyone. I understood why he was still so angry, but I also saw what holding on to the grudge would cost him. For four years he had made good friends who cared about him and now felt very guilty about the practical joke. By deciding he couldn't forgive us, he was cutting away a whole part of his life. I got the feeling Charley would forget all the good school memories and look back on Pineville High as an evil place where he had been betrayed. I didn't want to make that mistake.

Second, the story Beth told me that stormy night had made me realize that I was not the only person with secrets. I never would have guessed that she and Pam had bought drugs from Franchise Fraser, or that her dad had found them. Beth's revelations showed me that other people may be acting in strange ways for their own very good reasons. For example, I now had a lot of respect for Beth's dad. All along, when I thought Mr. Doyle had been unfair and even menacing, he'd really just been trying to protect his daughter.

Who knew what was going on in Smitty's life? His dad's heart had an irregular beat, and he had gone into the hospital a few weeks ago for a minor operation. Now that my mom was ill, I understood how vulnerable an ailing parent can suddenly make you feel. Smitty's dad was a wonderful and successful man who had always been the bedrock of their large family. Now he was home recuperating, and a lot of the duties at the store were falling on Smitty's shoulders. Maybe when my friend got so angry at me for not telling him about Troy, he was reacting in his new role as protector of his family.

I had a third, more pressing, reason for wanting to patch things up with Smitty. The pressure on Troy seemed to mount day by day. I knew nothing concrete, but I heard lots of rumors.

The police were reinterviewing kids at school who had bought drugs from Fraser, and focusing on exactly where in the Pine Barrens the sales took place. I even heard a rumor that a section of the forest had been sealed off, and that dogs had been led around to sniff for bodies.

I never talked to Troy about any of this, but if I heard these rumors at school, he probably picked them up at the grocery where he worked. Perhaps that was why when he came by to visit my mom, he looked so uncharacteristically tense. You could see the wariness in his eyes as he sat with her, holding her hand. He flinched every time a phone rang or the doorbell buzzed. They're gonna find Fraser and they're gonna come for you, I thought, watching his fearful vigilance. I know it and you know it. It's only a matter of time.

So why was he sticking around in Pineville? I still didn't know, but I was starting to have a suspicion. It was the kind of thing I couldn't prove, and I might be completely wrong. Still, I wanted to run it by my big friend, and if I was right, to warn him.

"So, Friday night at the mall?" I asked as we neared the bio classroom.

"Can't do it," he said. "How about the early show on Saturday?"

"What's happening Friday night?" I asked. "Hot date?"

Smitty didn't answer for a second, and then he tried to change the subject and I read the truth in his face. I gave him a good solid whack on the shoulder. "Hey, way to go, big guy. Who's the lucky girl?"

He looked around to make sure nobody was listening. "Pam," he confided shyly.

"You finally got up the nerve to ask her?"

"She asked me," he admitted. "She said she was tired of waiting. It takes a lot of courage to ask someone on a first date. I was really blown away that she would take a chance like that."

I remembered what Beth had told me about how Pam and she had bought drugs to experiment. "She may take more chances than you expect," I told Smitty. "Where are you taking her?"

"To a movie," he said. "But not an action movie," he added quickly. "Despite my superb taste in cinema, I decided to let her choose. She picked some soppy love story."

We reached the bio room. Pam was already inside, so we lingered outside the door to finish talking. "Just try to stay awake and say it was romantic," I advised him. "You'll do great. And we'll make up for it with an action movie on Saturday, weather permitting. They're expecting a snowstorm."

"We'll go if we have to travel by dogsled," Smitty promised, and we entered the classroom.

As Mr. Tsuyuki handed back our term papers, I was struck by how much smaller our bio class had gotten. Junior Martinez had been expelled, and Franchise Fraser had disappeared. Now Beth was also missing, headed to Mount Hopewell Academy. Mr. Tsuyuki, always an orderly man, returned the term papers in alphabetical order. He reached Hastings and skipped right over me.

I didn't say anything till he had finished giving back his

whole stack. Then I raised my hand and caught his eye. Before I could ask for my paper, he said, "See me after class, Jeff."

I waited nervously for the period to end. Could my paper have been that bad? I had put a lot of work into it, but also a lot of personal stuff. I had written about Troy, both directly and indirectly, and I didn't know what Mr. Tsuyuki would make of it.

The bell finally rang and everyone got up and headed out. Another class was coming in, so Mr. Tsuyuki led me to the empty Science Department office. His desk was neat, with pens arranged on top and every paper neatly filed away. My eyes were drawn to the picture of his boat, sails flying before the wind. He pointed to a chair and I sat down. He sat on the edge of the desk, looking down at me. "So," he said, "let's talk about evil and human behavior."

"Was my paper so awful that you can't even give it back?" I asked.

"No, it wasn't that bad," he said. He studied me for a few seconds, trying to read something in my face. "Where have you been hiding?" he finally asked in a quiet voice.

"I beg your pardon?"

He took out my paper and passed it back to me. An A was written neatly in the upper right-hand corner. "You must be aware this was rather extraordinary for a secondary school paper. In terms of length."

"Sorry it ran on so long. I got into it."

"Also in terms of depth and quality of thought," he said. "It's far and away the best of its kind I've gotten in years." His eyeglasses had slid far over to one side of his nose, and he slid them back with a finger and peered down at me. "From a student who's never shown me very much before."

"Like I said, I guess I got into the subject."

"I guess you did," he said. "I'm sorry to have to ask this, but no one helped you with this paper, did they, Jeff?"

"No," I said. "Only my brother, in a way, by making me care about the material."

He examined my face and nodded. "I believe you. Congratulations on a fine paper. That's the good news." He jabbed a thin finger at me, and suddenly seemed almost angry. "The bad news is you're out of hiding. Now I know what you can do and I won't let you fool yourself or me anymore. Jeffrey Hastings, it's a terrible thing to hide your light. A shameful thing in a way."

"Then why do you hide yours?" I shot back at him before really thinking about the question.

Mr. Tsuyuki's head shot up. "What?"

I regretted the question, but there was nowhere to go now except forward. "I guess I was just wondering, no disrespect intended, how you can be hard on me for hiding my light, as you put it, when you're spending your life teaching at this school."

Mr. Tsuyuki didn't look pleased. "What's wrong with this school?"

"Nothing," I said. "Forget it."

"No, let's not forget it. I've been honest with you. Be honest with me."

"Look, you're probably the most brilliant person I've ever met in my whole life," I told him. "You understand things that most of us will never understand, like the Theory of Relativity.

You could do anything. Some big-shot professor made fun of something you wrote years ago, so you're wasting your life teaching at our stupid high school. I just think you could do so much more." He looked back at me and said nothing. Seconds dragged by. "I don't mean that in a bad way," I finally added. And then, as the silence became unbearable: "I mean you're a great teacher and we're lucky to have you."

"No," he said softly, and for a horrible second I thought he was going to cry. Thank God he didn't. Instead of sadness or regret, his response took the form of barely contained rage. "No," he repeated, his voice getting louder, "that's all wrong, Jeff. That's all screwed up." He slammed the desk with his fist so hard the picture of the sailboat jumped as if encountering an unexpectedly big wave. "Don't get me wrong, I love America, but what you just said is the one thing about this country I'll never understand."

"What's that?" I asked.

"How can such a great country treat the people who teach in its schools like failures?" he asked and the rage in his voice was mixed with a deep sense of bafflement. "My father and mother were both high school teachers in Japan. Teaching there is no more highly paid than it is here. But people from the best universities go teach in the high schools and the junior high schools for the honor of being teachers. Everyone respects them for the valuable service they provide. They are senseis. They train the next generation. How come in Pineville we're the scum of the earth?"

"I didn't mean to imply that," I whispered. "Sorry."

"You're just repeating what you've heard," he said, trying to calm down but failing. *"But it's so wrong and it makes so little sense.* Jeff, I'm very happy with the way I'm spending my life."

I just nodded and waited for him to let me go. I had the sense that I had said something ugly and stupid that had hurt him even though he believed it wasn't true. When the silence dragged on too long, I decided I either had to run out and leave him there or change the subject. "Mr. Tsuyuki, could I ask you something about boats?"

He blinked. "Boats?"

I pointed to the picture on his desk. "That's yours, isn't it?"

"Yes," he said. "My hobby." He seemed relieved to be focusing on something new. "What do you want to know about boats?"

"I know people sail this time of year," I said. "I mean, I've seen them. And fishermen go out, even in winter."

"Striper fishermen." He nodded. "They're crazy."

"How much does a small boat cost?" I asked.

"It depends on the boat. Are you thinking of buying one?"

"No," I said. "But a friend might be. He'd be interested in a very cheap boat. He'd probably buy one in bad condition and try to fix it up himself. He's good with his hands, and he has access to tools."

"Maybe a few thousand dollars," Mr. Tsuyuki said. "Less if it was in really bad condition."

"And I know this is a strange question, but if he wanted to keep it in a marina nearby, just for a little while, would that be expensive?"

"No," Mr. Tsuyuki said. "Not this time of year."

"And there are other boats around? So he wouldn't stand out too much?"

Mr. Tsuyuki nodded. "A lot of boats sail down from Canada to Florida during the winter. They stop in places like this for a night or two. It's called transient dockage. Like staying in a motel."

"And just like in a cheap motel, you could pay in cash?" I asked. "You wouldn't have to give too much I.D.?"

Mr. Tsuyuki didn't reply right away. He studied me long and carefully. "I don't know about that," he finally said. "But if it was just a few nights, I guess you could probably do it that way. I would advise your friend to have some good I.D. so he wouldn't need to hide."

"Thanks," I said. "And thanks for the paper. It's the first A I ever got." I stood up.

He let me walk two steps away before he asked softly, "Jeff, what's going on?"

"Nothing. Really." I took another step away.

"Is it your brother?" he asked. "Let me help."

"You already have," I said, turning back to face him. "I'm going to try to follow your advice and not let one person ruin my life. But if there's one thing I've learned about evil and human behavior, it's that evil is sometimes a lot more complicated than it seems."

30

Everything that moved had been blown to smithereens, and everyone who ran, walked, or crawled had been shot, punched, or stabbed, so for sheer lack of more ballistics or victims, Smitty's movie mercifully came to an end.

"Wow," he said, "that was freaking awesome."

"They sure didn't hold back." I nodded, blinking away the muzzle flashes and trying to get my ears to work again. "I think I have post-traumatic stress. Should we grab something to eat?"

"Absolutely," he said. "I worked up an appetite watching that one."

A few minutes later we were in the food court, chowing down on pizza. I gave my friend time to tell me about his big date, but Smitty didn't volunteer any details. As he devoured a slice of extra-cheese pizza in four prodigious bites, I decided to subtly interrogate him. "So I see you worked up an appetite last night."

"I'm always this way," Smitty said.

"No, you seem even hungrier than usual," I observed. "Late night, was it?"

"Not especially."

I gave up on subtlety. "Come on, big guy, how did it go with Pam?"

Smitty lowered his soda and looked back at me. A grin as bright as a Christmas ribbon slowly gift-wrapped his face. "It went," he reported. "Except that the movie stank. But I managed to stay awake. I think Pam appreciated that."

"No doubt. So will you see her again?"

He shrugged, and said very casually, "Probably."

That didn't sound too promising. "Like this year or next year?"

Smitty hesitated and glanced down shyly. When he looked back up, the big and goofy grin had returned. "Like tonight," he admitted, embarrassed yet also proud.

"Two dates in two days? You're a love machine."

"We clicked, what can I say." Smitty nodded. "You were right, Jeffsky, I should have asked her out months ago."

I decided to take this as an opportunity to head where I really wanted to go. "Well, I'm not always right about everything. I should have told you about Troy when he started working at your store. You were right about that, and I'm sorry. But I want to talk to you about him now."

Smitty held up his hand to stop me. He had just stuffed what looked like several inches of folded-up pizza crust into his mouth, and he chewed and swallowed and washed it down with a gulp of soda. "No, I'm the one who should apologize about Troy," he said. "I've gotten to know your brother pretty well the last few weeks. Since Dad's slowed down, I've put in a lot of extra hours at the grocery. Your bro practically lives there. He's a

278

model employee—maybe the best we've ever had, including family members. He's learned every job from checkout to stockroom and he does them all perfectly."

"I never said he wasn't smart or capable," I tried to cut in, "but listen—"

"He's also a good guy." Smitty rolled right over me and kept on going. "He talks a lot about your mom and how he feels so bad about what's happened."

"He should feel bad," I spat through tight lips. *"He did this to her."*

Smitty heard the bitterness in my voice and lowered a slice of pizza. "I know this is between brothers, but maybe you shouldn't be so hard on him," he suggested quietly. "He feels torn up about what's happened. Sometimes he can't sleep, so he comes into the store and stacks cans for hours. He says he's gonna go away soon. He likes being near you guys but he thinks that his leaving would be the best thing for your mom. Frankly, I feel kind of bad for him. He doesn't have that much going on in his life."

I looked back at Smitty and said softly, "You sap."

He wiped tomato sauce off his cheeks with the back of an enormous hand. "What's that supposed to mean?"

"I shouldn't be so hard on him? You're gonna tell me about my own brother? He's got you right where he wants you."

"He doesn't have me anywhere," Smitty replied in a low but firm voice. "Maybe you know things about him that I don't. But I'm a reasonably good judge of human nature. And I've spent a lot more time with Troy lately than you have. He's shown me some real character. We spent all day last Saturday together, and he was just great."

"Great at what?" I asked.

"I got a call before noon at the store. Some fishermen I know thought their boat might have hit a sea turtle. They could see it swimming to shore, and they said it didn't look good. I called the Marine Rescue Center, and they said they'd send someone to try to find it. So I figured I'd go see if I could help out. When Troy found out where I was heading, he volunteered to come along and help, even though it was freezing out."

"Where were you heading?" I asked.

"Way out by Edwards Bay, near Oyster Creek. Troy had been asking me about the wildlife refuge for a while. When I told him this turtle was in one of the most isolated inlets, he insisted on giving me a ride out in his car."

"I don't see why Troy would be so eager to help a turtle," I said. "Was anything else going on out there?"

"You are so suspicious of him. I don't think he had any ulterior motive for going out to Edwards Bay with me in the snow and ice. It's the most isolated spot on the whole shoreline. It took us almost an hour to find the turtle. Sure enough, it was a big old loggerhead, bleeding from prop cuts. I put a wet blanket over it to keep sand and parasites from the wound, and I called the refuge guys and told them it was alive and they should hurry up. I think we saved its life. Your brother was great. He seemed really concerned. It was ten degrees and even colder with wind chill. Troy was a real trouper."

"Great, so he helped you save a turtle," I muttered. "That doesn't mean anything."

"It meant something to the turtle," Smitty shot back. "And to me. But I don't want to argue with you." Smitty checked his watch and stood up. "Make love not war is my new motto. Gotta go, Jeffsky. Duty calls."

"What duty?"

"I'm supposed to pick Pam up at three at her house. The love machine's gotta go oil the gears with aftershave."

We hiked back together, crossing the overpass above Route 44 as the light snow thickened. Cars below turned on their headlights even though it was midafternoon. The wind whooshed across the bridge of the overpass like a broom trying to sweep us off, and every step forward was an effort. Neither of us spoke. I was furious that Smitty would try to lecture me about my own brother—especially when I had come out on this snowy day to warn him.

We descended the steps of the overpass and headed home, tromping side by side through sidewalk slush on which freshly fallen powder now gleamed. Smitty glanced at me. He must have sensed my thoughts, because he began to apologize. "Look, Jeffsky, we've had enough arguing, old buddy. You know Troy much better than I do. It's just that I've spent a lot of time with him lately. Maybe I'm wrong. I admit I have a soft spot for people who are kind to animals. Maybe I am a sap. I just don't see what he could want out of me."

"I don't either," I told Smitty. "But I have suspicions. That's why I'm here right now."

"So it wasn't just the bad movie?" Smitty asked.

"Nor the charm of your company," I told him. "I need to warn you about something. Now shut up and listen."

"I'm listening," Smitty promised.

"For weeks I've been asking myself why Troy is hanging around Pineville," I told him. "I know he wants to take off for parts unknown. And now that the police are looking for Fraser's body out near Eagle Rock, the temptation to just cut and run must be tremendous."

Smitty stopped walking. "They're not looking for a body," he said.

"Then what are they looking for, with dog teams?"

"Those are just stupid rumors," he declared, as if trying to hold on to something that was important for him to believe. "Fraser's alive. They found his van. He crossed the border and he's living in some Canadian fishing village, no doubt with some cute French-speaking chick."

"I hope so," I told him. "But don't count on it."

"You really think he's gone?" my friend asked softly. And then he asked the harder question, "You really think your brother killed Tommy?"

I looked back at Smitty and there was a long and tense beat, just as there had been when Beth had asked me this question. The snow fell on my hair and in my eyes, but I didn't blink. "Yes," I said. "I do."

"Have you got any proof?"

"No. And neither do the police. But they're searching out there all the same."

Smitty nodded and exhaled a long breath. It came out like a geyser of steam in the freezing air. "Boy, you must be pretty sure, 'cause that's a hell of a thing to accuse your own brother of. Or else you really don't like Troy."

"It has nothing to do with liking him," I said. "It has to do with knowing him. If I'm right, he has every reason to get the hell away from Pineville as soon as possible. So he must be sticking around for a reason."

Smitty nodded. "Makes sense. What's the reason?"

"What he craves is freedom," I said. "Money is freedom for him now." I looked Smitty in the eye. "Your store is one of the biggest businesses in town."

Smitty was paying serious attention. "You think he's gonna try to rip us off?"

"I keep remembering something my dad mentioned at Thanksgiving. He said the holidays are your busiest season. I was wondering—does your store take in a lot more money just before Christmas?"

"Sure, we have a couple of big weeks," Smitty said with a nod, "but the cash doesn't pile up. My dad takes it to the bank every few days."

"And where is it till he takes it in?"

"In a locked safe. In the basement. There's no way your brother could get in."

"Smitty, he picked the lock of my room."

"Jeffsky, this is a professional-quality safe. Like a small bank vault. It cost three thousand dollars."

I wasn't impressed. "He works there at night. He has

access to tools. Who knows what skills he picked up in prison."

Smitty weighed it in his mind for a long moment. "Okay," he said. "I'd like to think you're wrong about this, but I'll tell my dad. We'll check to see if the safe has been tampered with. And we'll be more careful." He walked a few steps more, turning it over in his mind. "But I have to say, people earn your trust over time, and Troy has earned ours. If he was going to rip us off, he would have done it already. He worked the checkout for weeks and was never a dollar short. And he was all alone in the store some nights when my dad was in the hospital. There was money in the safe. He didn't take it. Tell me why?"

"I don't know why," I admitted. "Maybe he's waiting for the holidays. He knows he's only going to get one shot, so he wants to make it count. Then he plans to disappear."

We neared the outskirts of Pineville. The snow continued to get heavier. Large flakes sifted down from a dull white bowl of sky.

Smitty started to walk a bit faster. I matched him stride for big stride, but he kept increasing his pace and it was soon hard going on the slippery sidewalk. "Slow down, big guy. It's not a race."

"Jeff?" he said.

I knew something was wrong. Smitty never calls me by my name. It's always Jeffsky or J-man. "Yeah, big guy?"

"I don't feel so good all of a sudden."

"You mean you're sick?"

"No, I'm not sick. I'm remembering last Saturday."

"When you saved the turtle?"

"Yeah."

"Why would that make you feel sick?"

"While we were out there, we had a lot of time to talk. And your brother asked me questions about Christmas and the store that seemed innocent at the time. But now that I think about it, they focused on our Christmas bonuses. What I was going to do with mine. And how much he could expect for his."

I took that in, and started to understand why my big friend was suddenly nervous. "Your dad gives holiday bonuses?"

"Yup," Smitty grunted. "To twenty-three employees."

"Big bucks?"

"Everybody gets about a tenth of their annual salary. So, yeah, a lot."

"In cash?"

"That's the way my dad's always done it. He hands out envelopes with handwritten cards."

We reached the outlying streets of Pineville. "Troy knew that?" I asked softly.

"He knew all about it, and what he didn't know he asked. I thought he was just curious and eager about his own bonus. But thinking back on it, it's like he was pinpointing when and where and how much. He was clever. He made me do most of the talking."

"When does your dad take out the money for the bonuses?" I asked.

"In three or four days."

"Then you have a little time," I told him. "Troy's been patient this long. He'll wait till the right moment. Like you said, he's clever."

My words seemed to calm Smitty. He slowed down a bit. "I really hope you're wrong," he said. "Maybe his questions were innocent. Everybody thinks about their bonus this time of year."

"If I were you I'd talk to your dad right away," I told him. "And to the police."

"Believe me, I will," Smitty promised. "I may be a sap, but I'm not a fool. Listen, thanks for telling me all this. It can't be easy to think such things about your own brother, let alone say them out loud."

"I've been thinking them for a long time."

"How's your mom?" he asked. "I heard she's home."

"She's okay," I said. "Thanks for asking."

"She's being treated? Getting better?"

"She's on medication," I told him. "It's not the same as getting better. But we're taking good care of her."

We reached the first stores of the Pineville business district. All was quiet outside the 7-Eleven and the Capitol Cleaners. We hurried past the bakery and the Pineville Pharmacy. And we were just passing Vaughn's Barbershop when Kerry, our soccer teammate, poked his head out the door and said, "Hey, guys, have you heard the news?"

Kerry didn't look so good. His normally happy Irish face was tight and drained of color.

"What news?" we asked in perfect unison.

"It really sucks," he told us. "Right now it's on TV. They found a body out in the woods. They think it's Fraser."

We dashed into the barbershop. There were two men sitting in red chairs getting their hair cut by Mr. Vaughn and his partner. Another man was parked in an old armchair, waiting for his turn. Everyone was watching a small TV on which a local reporter was breaking a story. "Police are releasing few details, but a source confirms that the body found near Eagle Rock is Tommy Fraser, a popular athlete at Pineville High who disappeared..."

She talked on, but I didn't even hear. I turned to Smitty, who looked down from the TV set with fear stamped all over his face. "If he sees this, he has to make his move right now," he whispered to me. "Isn't that right?"

"If he sees it," I said. "Smitty, let's call the cops..."

But Smitty was already running for the door. No, check that, he was already out the door and sprinting for the big family grocery, which occupied half a block of Main Street. And even though Smitty was the slowest guy on the soccer team and I was one of the fastest, he pulled away from me with long and desperate strides.

 **31**

The grocery was crowded with Saturday afternoon shoppers who had braved the snow and winds. I ran in and spotted Smitty, shouting questions at one of the checkout girls. I hurried over in time to hear her tell him, "They went down to the basement about twenty minutes ago, but—"

Before she could say another word, Smitty bolted toward the back stairs. I ran after him and saw him nearly take a spill as he leaped down the steep stone staircase five and six steps at a time.

The basement of the old grocery was dark and cavernous. Narrow halls twisted and turned, opening suddenly into large meat lockers or stockrooms with boxes piled floor to ceiling. Powerful odors of fruits and poultry seemed to cling to the very bricks. I followed on Smitty's heels as he wound his way through this dingy maze and reached his father's basement office.

The office door was closed, and Smitty didn't even knock. He just lowered his shoulder and burst through the door with a crash. It was pitch-dark inside. I heard him flick a light switch, but nothing happened.

A low groan sounded from somewhere nearby. It wasn't a

voice I recognized, but Smitty seemed to know it. "Dad?" Smitty said with alarm. *"Dad?"*

There were no more groans, just ominous silence.

"Stay here, Jeff," he half shouted, and ran out.

I stood in the darkness. "Mr. Smith? Are you okay? Hello? Is anyone here?"

All was quiet and still. Every few seconds I heard a faint rasping sound, as if someone was struggling for breath and losing the battle.

Smitty seemed to be gone for an eternity, but I'm sure it was just a few seconds. I heard his footsteps pounding back toward me, and saw the beam of a flashlight bouncing wildly off the hallway walls. He dashed back in through the door, and swept the flashlight beam in wild circles around the room.

The office was in disarray. It looked like there had been a struggle. Both ceiling bulbs had been broken. The small door to the wall safe was open. I didn't need to look inside to know that it had been emptied.

There was no sign of Mr. Smith.

"Dad?" Smitty pleaded, his voice cracking. "Where are you? *Dad?*"

No response. No sign of him. Nothing.

Smitty ran to the closet and ripped open the door. Nothing. As he turned and his flashlight swung back toward me, I glimpsed two shadowy shapes poking out from under the desk. Shoes. "Smitty, he's under here."

Smitty ran over and crouched down, and I knelt next to him. Mr. Smith looked so fragile lying there that we didn't drag him out—we moved the desk away. His eyes were open, but it was hard to tell if he was alive or dead.

I don't think I've ever seen anyone look as frightened and desperate as Smitty did at that moment. He bent over his father and whispered, "Dad?" I thought I saw some faint life in Mr. Smith's eyes, but it could have been the reflection of the flashlight's beam. "*Call 911,*" Smitty shouted at me.

I picked up the office phone, but there was no dial tone. I saw that the line had been cut.

Meanwhile, Smitty was checking his father's wrist. "I think I found a pulse," Smitty croaked, barely able to talk. "Get help, Jeff. *Go!*" As I ran out of the office I heard Smitty repeating the same words: "Stay with me, Dad. I love you. Stay with me."

I sprinted down the dark hallway, and for a few horrible moments I was lost in the maze of low-ceilinged tunnels and storerooms. I burst out through swinging doors into the basement landing, just in time to see several store employees and Smitty's mom hurrying down the stairs. I guess the way we'd acted had tipped them off that something was wrong.

Mrs. Smith was a tall woman with long red hair and kind eyes. "Jeff," she asked quickly, "is everything okay? Where are they?"

"In the office."

She took a step in that direction and then turned back to look at me. "Jeff?"

"Call the police," was all I could say. "Call an ambulance."

The next couple of hours were a nightmare of red lights and shrieking sirens, of men in uniforms rushing around and pumping on Mr. Smith's chest and barking questions at me. I couldn't seem to focus enough to separate ambulances from police cars and medics from detectives. It was horrible and it was all happening so very fast.

A crew of emergency medical technicians loaded Mr. Smith onto a stretcher and whisked him upstairs and out into a waiting ambulance. They worked on him every step of the way, and I could tell from their faces that the prognosis was not good. Smitty and Mrs. Smith climbed into the back of the ambulance with him. Mother and son held hands and watched in horror and frantic hope as a paramedic shouted "Away" and brought a paddle down on Mr. Smith's naked chest. I saw his body jump with the electrical current, and then the ambulance's back doors were slammed closed and it sped off down the block, its flasher spinning cherry red patterns on the falling snow.

A few long minutes later I found myself in the backseat of a police car, with Chief Mayweather sitting next to me firing off angry questions. The big police chief was in a terrible rush, and he kept jumping on my answers as if he could tell halfway through that they weren't going to be helpful and wanted to move on to the next one. In my muddled state of mind, I couldn't seem to explain to him how Smitty and I had known enough to burst into the store and run down to the basement office. "So you're saying you figured the whole thing out *as it was happening?*" he demanded.

"Kind of." I nodded. "We didn't know what we would find but we saw the story on the news and we feared the worst—"

"Or else you knew to run down there," he interrupted. "Troy shared some of his plans with you?"

"No, sir. He never—"

"Because that would make a lot more sense. He took off with all the money and left you holding the bag. So you came up with this nutty story . . ."

"No, sir. He never said a word about what he—"

"It's not a *what* now. It's a *where. Where's he headed?* North? South? New York? Philly?"

"I swear he never—"

"Just like you swear he never told you that he was going to rob the store? You figured that out—why don't you figure this out?"

"No. I mean, yes, I did figure that out. But I can't—"

"I don't have time for this crap." Chief Mayweather reached down and grabbed me by the shirtfront. "You and your brother cooked this up together," he growled. "I've got a body of a boy I just dug out of a hole, and I got a man I love on the way to the hospital, *and I don't need any more of your lies."* His grip tightened, and I felt myself sitting up just to breathe. "Do yourself a giant favor and start telling me the truth."

"I told you the truth," I gasped.

He glared at me for several seconds and then shoved me down so hard I bounced off the seat. As I sucked in a deep breath he said very quickly, "Know this. I've got every road and highway sealed off, and every policeman and state trooper in New Jersey is looking for your brother's car. First I'm gonna catch him and then I'm gonna deal with you." He motioned a white-haired policeman over. "Bruce, take Jeff home." To me he added, "Stay put. I may have more questions. And I don't want to have to come looking for you."

The chief got out of the back and slammed the door. The old policeman slid into the driver's seat and turned on the ignition.

"Wait one minute," I told him. I lowered the back window. "Chief Mayweather," I called.

He was already ten feet away, but he spun around. "What?"

"You're making a mistake. I don't think he's going in his car."

"The hell's that supposed to mean? I've got three witnesses who saw him haul ass away from the grocery in his car."

"Yeah, but I think he's going in a boat."

The Chief took two quick steps toward the police car and stared down at me through the half-open window, hands on his hips. "What boat? Your brother has a boat?"

"Yeah. I think so."

"And he's gonna sail off into a snowstorm?"

"I know it sounds far-fetched, but—"

"Where does he keep the boat?"

"Maybe one of the marinas—"

"Maybe? What kind of boat is it? Describe it for me?"

"I don't know," I said. "I've never seen it."

"But he told you about it?"

"No, sir. I figured it out. He had boating magazines in his apartment. And he used to watch the lights of the boats every

293

night. I understand him. He's my brother. Maybe I'm wrong but I have a strong hunch . . ."

The chief looked like he was chewing on his lower lip hard enough to draw blood. "Bruce, get this punk out of here," he said.

As the white-haired policeman pulled away from the curb, I heard Chief Mayweather say to one of his deputies, "Stan, check with the local marinas. See if they know anything about a boat."

32

Tell me he didn't do it?"

It felt like a wake. Mom was sitting in the old rocker near the window, her face a mask of sorrow and mourning. The curtains were drawn and her eyes were in shadow. Dad sat next to her, holding her hand and stroking her hair.

I sat on a couch facing them. "Mom, who knows what happened? Let's wait for the police to sort this out."

"No, I can't wait," she said, shifting her weight forward so that the rocker creaked toward me. "You know the truth, Jeff." It wasn't a question. Her right arm reached out in summons. Her fingertips grazed my knuckles and settled as lightly as a hummingbird on the back of my wrist. "Tell me now. Did Troy kill that boy?"

I looked back into her eyes, and the intensity of emotion I saw there made me shiver. All the years my mom had lived and all the things she had done had somehow shrunk to this one moment on a snowy Saturday afternoon in Pineville, and to her single whispered question. That sense of time narrowing, of years dwindling to seconds, gave her face a weight and sharpness that was almost unbearable. She knows it but she doesn't want to know it, I thought; she loves him but she'll never be able to forgive him, and she knows that, too. One question. Five whispered words from a mother about her firstborn: Did he kill another child?

Growing up, I had always thought my mom had a beautiful face, delicate and gentle, with high cheekbones and thin expressive lips. Now that lovely face seemed to quiver in a tug-of-war of opposite extremes. In that endless moment as she waited for my answer she looked both vital and haggard, almost girlish with faith and hope and at the same time tired and desolate with the hideous certainty of Troy's guilt.

I couldn't lie to her, but I also couldn't bring myself to puncture whatever life preserver she was still clinging to. I looked away and made a move to stand up. She touched a single finger to my chest and pushed me back down. Her finger moved to my chin and turned my head to face her. "Jeffrey? Did he do it?"

I had nowhere to run and nowhere else to hide. "Yes, Mom, Troy did it. He killed Tommy Fraser."

Her black eyes contracted in extreme pain. A single breath was inhaled like a dagger thrust inward. My dad reacted, too—he froze for a long second. His hand, stroking her long black hair, lay still for several heartbeats. Then it moved again, slowly and very gently. "Sweetheart, why don't we go upstairs and lie down?"

From some hidden reservoir of strength Mom managed a follow-up question. "And Walter? Did Troy do that, too?"

I glanced at my father. Go ahead and tell her, his eyes said. If you can bear it, tell her the truth. She has a right to know, and better she hear it from you than from a stranger.

"Sorry, Ma. He did that, too."

A high-pitched wail of pure sorrow trembled up through her throat, part whimper and part keening. It had no place in a living room—it belonged at a funeral, ripped from the throat of a mourner. "Why?" she asked softly. "Why?"

I had no answer to that one. I'm not sure God himself could have answered that one.

She rocked back toward the window, and covered her face with her hands.

"Sweetheart," Dad tried again, "let's go upstairs. I can bring you something to . . . ?"

"No, Frank, *damn it, no. I don't want to pill and potion my way out of this,*" she snapped.

"I just meant . . ." Dad began.

"I know and I'm sorry," she said. "But nobody deserves to escape on a day like this. Not even a sick woman with all the pills in the world in her cabinet. I want to feel what I'm feeling. We deserve to feel this."

I went into the kitchen to get her a glass of water, and my dad followed me in. "How are you holding up?" he asked in a low voice.

I shrugged. "Not great. Poor Mr. Smith. He didn't look so good. I hope . . ." I couldn't even finish.

"Me too," Dad said. And then he choked and brushed his

face with his hand, wiping away what I think was a tear. "I should have listened to you," he said. "You tried to warn me. This is my fault."

"It's nobody's fault but Troy's."

"I brought him back here," Dad insisted. "I trusted him. I'm a fool. I'll carry this around for the rest of my life."

"You're the best man I've ever known."

He bent forward and kissed me on the forehead. "Sweet boy," he whispered. He took the glass of cold water from my hand and carried it back out to my mom.

We sat there in the living room with the TV off, even though a manhunt was going on for a member of our own family. We had made lots of close friends in this town over the past five years, but not a soul came by or even called on the phone. Not a neighbor. Not a friend. No one.

A police car was parked right outside our house. The patrolman inside was sipping coffee, and we could see the back of his head move. "What's he doing out there?" my mom asked.

"Just staying close, in case they need to ask me more questions," I said as reassuringly as I could. I didn't add, they're keeping tabs on us. Making sure I don't bolt or we don't try to help Troy. Maybe they want to protect us, too, as the news gets out. And come to think of it, maybe we shouldn't be sitting in front of a window, in case a neighbor throws another rock . . .

After half an hour of sitting and waiting together, the telephone rang, splintering the terrible silence. My dad got up quickly and hurried to answer it. I could tell from the way his head sagged as he murmured a few words in a low tone that it was bad news.

My mom saw the same thing. She stood up out of the rocker. "Frank?"

Dad hung up the phone and walked back toward us. His shoulders dipped with each step and he looked ten years older.

"Is it Troy?" Mom asked quickly. "Did they catch him? Is he okay?"

Dad shook his head. "It wasn't about Troy. It was about Walter."

I stood up from the couch. For a second I flashed to Smitty. He was so close to his father. They had worked endless hours in the store together. His dad came to lots of our games, to cheer on his son the goalie. Walter Smith was a big man and he always sat in the same place, on the lowest bleacher, with his black shoes tapping on the grass as if he wanted to play himself, and his eyes on his son . . .

Dad shook his head. "Bad news," he said softly. With a great effort he added, "Walt never regained consciousness. He's gone. God bless his soul."

After that phone call there was another long period of fuzziness. I recall trying to comfort Mom. I think I remember all three of us crying at once. The police car outside became a fixed point for me. I kept staring at it, as if waiting for it to move, to do something.

They'll catch him, I assured myself. Dead or alive. He deserves to be dead. They'll pull over his car. Or if he's on a boat it will be easy to find. One way or another they'll get him.

They'll throw him into the deepest, darkest jail cell in the state of New Jersey. His hair will turn white there, and no one will ever visit him, and he'll deserve every second of that hell, just as he's condemned Smitty and his mom to hell . . .

My rage built slowly and steadily till I could barely sit there. I wanted to break the glass of the window with my fists. I wanted to shout out questions so loud that he would hear them, wherever he now was. How could you do it, Troy? How could you injure such good people in such horrible ways?

I recalled how, earlier that very morning, Smitty had said such nice things about Troy. What indescribable pain my big friend must be feeling now! Or perhaps it was just the numbness that follows sudden loss. Perhaps the truth hadn't sunk in yet. But it would, over days and weeks and months. I knew that the closest friendship of my high school years was irretrievably gone now. For Smitty, from today forward I would always be Troy's brother, flesh of the flesh and blood of the blood that had killed his father.

In my mind's eye I could still see mother and son crouched together in the back of the ambulance as the paddle came down on Mr. Smith's naked chest and his big body jumped. Smitty, who rescued birds with broken wings and loggerhead turtles with prop cuts, had looked so desperate and so pathetically helpless. And his mom! His poor, kind mother, crouched right next to him watching her husband slip away! It wasn't fair that a guy who would spend a Saturday in freezing weather helping a stupid turtle should have to endure such a moment. It wasn't just. It wasn't right.

300

And then, suddenly, I knew. I don't know how, exactly, but the certainty of it was full and complete and the only question left was what I would do with the knowledge.

I glanced out the window. The police car was still there. I was tempted for a second, but I had already tried that route, and it led nowhere. Chief Mayweather thought I had shared Troy's secrets. Not only did he not want to listen to me but he suspected me.

To hell with the police. My rage was red-hot now, and in its fiery glow key decisions seemed easy to make. This was my secret, my brother, my guilt. My father had said he would carry the responsibility for this around with him for the rest of his life, but I knew that burden truly belonged on my shoulders.

I had been onto Troy from the start. The minute my parents had talked about bringing him home, I had known in my heart where it would lead. But I hadn't warned the kids at school, or Smitty, or Smitty's dad. I should have made them hear me and believe me. I was the only one who knew. If necessary, I had a duty to climb to the highest rooftop in Pineville and shout out the truth for all to hear.

But I had kept mute. And I knew the reason I had done that as I sat there with my mother and father in our living room with the curtains drawn. Fraser had been knifed through the ribs and Mr. Smith had lost his life, all because of my desire to preserve my girlfriend and my friends and my place in this quiet town. It was pure selfishness.

Damn him for doing this. Damn me for not stopping him. But I would stop him now. I had caused this, and it fell to me to somehow resolve it. "Dad, I'm not feeling so good. I'm gonna go upstairs," I mumbled.

"Are you sick?" he asked.

"No, I'm okay. I just . . . wanna lie down for a while."

Dad nodded. "We'll be here."

I headed out of the living room and went upstairs, but only long enough to grab the collapsible brass telescope from its stand. Troy had made fun of it, but I had a feeling where I was going I might need it.

I tiptoed back downstairs to the hall closet and grabbed my winter coat off the hook. I glanced toward the living room. Mom and Dad were still seated, facing the window, silent and unmoving.

Ten quick steps took me through the kitchen to the back door. The policeman parked out front would never see me creep away through the backyards. I opened the door and then stopped.

For a long moment I stood there. I didn't know exactly what was going to happen, but I knew where I was going. I stepped back into the kitchen, to the knife set, and grabbed what I thought I might need.

Then I went out the back door and down the steps and away into the snow, staying low and moving fast.

33

The streets of Pineville were quiet and empty as the snow fell all around me and the afternoon sky darkened to a winter sunset. It had grown very cold. The swirling wind tugged at me as if trying to grab me by the shoulders and spin me around. Go back. Don't do this. Nothing good can come of it. But with each step my resolve grew stronger. This was where I needed to go and this was what I needed to do. Nothing would stop me. Not bitter wind, not blinding snow, not biting cold, nor even creeping fear.

I pumped my arms and cycled my legs and fell into a cross-country rhythm. The two inches of fresh powder cushioned my footsteps, so I ran in a dreamlike silence. Once I saw a police car cruise by half a block away. I swerved behind some trees and let it vanish from sight.

It was more than three miles to the wildlife refuge, and then another two along the rocky coast to Edwards Bay. The winding narrow road inside the refuge was slick with ice beneath the snow, so I ran with my arms out wide to either side, slipping and sliding the last half-mile to the rocky shores of Oyster Creek.

With the sun sinking and the snow falling, the visibility was poor and getting worse by the minute. I ran on, from inlet to inlet, and the water looked inky black as it beat against great blade-sharp rocks. There was no boat, no sign of Troy or any other human presence.

Finally I stopped running and stood there, chest heaving in one freezing breath after another. I had been wrong, completely wrong. My absence would have been discovered by now. The police would be utterly convinced of my guilt. My parents, already in agony over Troy, would be baffled and worried sick. I had accomplished nothing besides creating more doubt and misery.

Near me, a gargantuan bay rock sloped thirty feet above its neighbors. I ran to it and slowly scaled the rough side of the massive boulder, kicking with my feet and pulling myself up till I stood at the top. The rocky shoreline fell away beneath me in two directions, a succession of tiny bays and craggy inlets stretching as far as my eyes could see. I reached inside my coat and found the brass telescope that Troy had laughed at. I unfolded it and raised it to my right eye.

There were two sea birds, wheeling and diving through the snow, perhaps a hundred yards offshore. There was the snaking one-lane road that twisted into the distance, its contours barely visible beneath the white powder. There were five-foot waves with foaming whitecaps like teeth that bit down on the rocks of the point. And there, beyond the point, was a tiny speck of ship floating at anchor in the calm shelter of a protected cove.

I slid down the great boulder and started to run again. The

knowledge that I was right, that he was indeed here, filled me with energy rather than dread. I was still feeling the rage that had burned through me in my living room after the news had come about Mr. Smith. He was probably on his way to the town funeral home. And Tommy Fraser was probably in a body bag at the police morgue. And in a suburb of Buffalo there was a gravestone to a boy named Billy Shea.

I left the road and clambered out onto the boulders in a half-crouch, keeping low so as not to be seen. The rocks were sharp and slippery and it was hard going. I could make out the boat clearly now. It looked to be about fourteen feet long. There was nothing at all remarkable about it. No sail. No trimming or decorations. No catchy name painted onto the side that someone might notice and remember. It was the kind of boat that no one would look twice at.

A figure stepped out onto the deck, and I shrank back behind a rock outcropping. From fifty feet away I could see Troy clearly. He was wearing a heavy blue coat that looked warm and waterproof. He lit a cigarette and inhaled. A twin stream of white smoke jetted out through his nostrils. He pivoted three hundred and sixty degrees, and I crouched down and let his gaze circle over me. I held my breath and listened to my own heartbeats. When I dared to peek out again, he had vanished belowdecks.

I am not a particularly brave person. I can't tell you exactly why I emerged from behind the rock outcropping and hurried down to the water's edge. Nor can I explain where I found the strength and courage to wade out into the freezing surf with the snow falling around me and waves washing up to my hips. But I knew exactly what Troy was doing on that boat at sunset. He was waiting for darkness to sail away. He would head south, following the shore, to the Carolinas and then to Florida and then to some warm paradise. And I knew I couldn't let that happen.

There was a ladder on the side of the boat. I got one foot on a rung and grabbed a rail and scraped my face pulling myself up the side. Then I was on my knees on the empty deck as the boat pitched and rolled. I got to my feet. At the front of the boat, by the driver's chair, was an empty green plastic duffel and a smaller black gym bag. There was no sign of Troy. Steps led down to what I knew must be a very small cabin. I pictured Troy down there, making himself a hot drink, or stowing wads of stolen cash away.

I took out the cleaver I had grabbed from our knife set and clasped it tightly by its plastic handle. In our kitchen it always felt large and lethal, a sword big enough to slay a dragon but only used to chop onions. Now, on the deck of this boat, it felt smaller and much less impressive.

Minutes dragged by. I simply didn't know what to do. I had come out here with no fixed plan. Should I hide and when Troy emerged from the cabin try to stab him? Should I go down the steps after him? Should I pull up the anchor and try to run his boat onto the rocks?

I glanced down at the black gym bag, and an instinct I can't identify made me pick it up and unzip it. There was a white towel inside. A throwing knife that I suspected had once belonged to Franchise Fraser. A traveler's guide to Mexico. A small picture of my mother in a silver frame. And a dark and heavy metal pistol.

I heard footsteps climbing up the cabin stairs, and without even thinking about it I transferred the cleaver to my left hand and grabbed the pistol with my right. It fit snugly in my palm, and my index finger circled around the trigger.

Troy saw me as he reached the second-to-top step, but he made no move to jump back down. Instead he climbed up the final step and walked onto the deck. "Hello, brother," he said in a steady voice. "I wasn't expecting you."

"Why'd you do it?" I asked. I know that sounds like bad dialogue from a bad movie, but those are the words that came to me that day on the deck of the small boat when Troy and I looked into each other's eyes.

"A gun in one hand and a knife in the other," he replied. "That's not a polite way to say hello. The cleaver is useless, by the way, because it's too big and not sharp enough." He took a step toward me. "The pistol, unfortunately, has no bullets. You don't think I'd keep a loaded gun around when there's no need . . ."

He moved quickly toward me, and I raised the pistol and pointed it right at his heart. Troy must have seen my finger tighten on the trigger, because he suddenly stopped walking and stood very still.

"It's loaded or you wouldn't have stopped," I said.

"There's only one way to find out," Troy responded softly. "Pull the trigger, Jeff. Go ahead. You can't miss from this range. Even though your hand is starting to shake." The gray eyes were watching me carefully, flicking from my face to my right hand.

"That's what you came here for, isn't it? So go ahead and shoot me."

"Why'd you do it?" I asked again. "Maybe Fraser was some kind of accident, but why did you kill Mr. Smith, who only gave you good?"

I didn't know my brother's face was capable of registering guilt, but suddenly it was there, deeply and unmistakably. "He died? You're sure?"

"On the way to the hospital. With his wife and son right there in the ambulance."

"It wasn't supposed to happen that way," Troy said. "The damn fool knew I had a gun, but he still tried to stop me. I didn't shoot him. I just pushed him away. It was his own bad heart that got him."

"No, you're the one who got him," I said. "His blood is on your hands for all eternity. God damn you to hell." My gun hand was rock-steady now. I could have shot Troy at any second. He knew it, too. I could see it in his eyes.

"And my blood will be on your hands, brother," he whispered, holding my gaze. He took a half-step toward me. "Kill me and you become me. That's your greatest fear, isn't it? That's what you've been hiding from all these years." Another step. "We're not so different, brother, and we both know it. We're more alike than not alike. Born from the same mother and father. You can kill just as I can, and then we'll be identical. I love you, brother. I always have."

My hand shook wildly, and Troy suddenly jumped forward, reaching out for the pistol to turn the muzzle away.

BAM. I don't remember pulling the trigger, but the gun fired. Troy cried out and spun to the deck. He lay half on his side and half on his stomach, barely moving.

I dropped the gun and it clanged off the deck. Without thinking, I ran to him and bent over. "Troy?"

In one fast move he grabbed my arm and yanked me over so that I fell heavily against the side of the boat. When I righted myself, I saw that he had rolled to the pistol and had it in his hand. He tried to stand but clutched his leg and almost toppled. A spreading red stain was visible through his pants, just above the knee. "Damn you," he said, almost in a kind of wonderment. "My leg. You shot me in the damn leg."

"I wish I had shot you in the heart," I said. "For what you've done, you deserved it."

"But then you'd be just like me, and you just proved that you're not," Troy whispered, and it was perhaps the kindest thing he ever said in his life. "What am I to do now? You can't come with me. I can't leave you."

"We both know what you have to do. I'm a threat to all your plans. I know where you're going and how you're going, and even if I swore not to tell anyone, you couldn't take the chance. And I hate your guts."

He smiled, and then bit his lip and glanced down at his leg. "Brother, I'm going to have to ask you a favor. Take off your belt."

I took it off and passed it to him, and he quickly tied a tourniquet around his leg and pulled it very tight, all the while watching me in case I tried to make a move. Then he used his hands to haul himself up and onto the driver's chair. He sat there on the white cushion, the pistol still in his right palm. "Jeff," he said, "your logic was faultless. I can't trust you. You know all my secrets. We both know what I have to do."

"So do it. You can't damn yourself to any deeper hell than the one you're already going to."

He nodded, inhaled a deep breath, and raised the pistol so that it pointed at my temple. I looked back at him across the barrel. I thought, here is how it ends. On this boat at sunset. At the hand of your own brother. Try to see your father's eyes in his. Find the love and the kindness and die with that around you.

And then I saw Troy's hand shake. It jiggled and then it wobbled and then it shook and he finally gave up and lowered it. He seemed surprised and even, in some way, pleased. "God damn you, brother. Get the hell off my boat."

I walked to the side and swung off into the freezing water. The waves seemed to be bigger and the water seemed to be deeper and colder, and I barely made it back to shore. When I stepped out of the surf and turned, he had the anchor up and had switched on the motor.

He kept the lights of the boat off and it was getting dark, so I watched him in silhouette as he steered the little boat around the point and off into the choppy waves. It was a tiny and fragile craft heading out into a vast and angry sea, but it made headway against the wind and slowly crawled southward. As it rounded the next point, just before slipping out of sight, I saw my brother turn to look back at me and raise his right hand. I slowly raised my own. And then he was gone, into the snow and the waves and the darkness.

34

I never told anyone where I ran to that afternoon, or what had happened by the sharp rocks of Edwards Bay. The police suspected all kinds of things, but I stuck to my story that I had just flipped out and gone for a long run through the snow.

No one had seen me and no one could contradict me.

Troy was never seen or heard from again. A storm came in that evening and blew and howled for three days and nights. The police found Troy's car five days later on the beach at the wildlife refuge. They were also able to locate a marina owner in a town ten miles away who told them Troy had kept a small boat moored there under an alias, and that he had done a pretty good job of fixing it up and making it seaworthy. He had taken a few sailing lessons, and had become quite expert in a remarkably short period of time.

They searched for that small boat north to Canada and south to Florida, but they never found so much as a plank.

My mom went into a hospital a month or so later and never came home again. I visit her there as often as I can. She's taken up drawing again, and the walls of her room are covered with bright pictures of flowers. And there are often fresh flowers in vases that my dad has brought.

I have tea with her and we sit for a few hours. On good days we talk about my life and about college and I try to make her laugh by telling her about bad dates or other stupid stuff. On bad days we just hold hands and listen to music.

We never talk about Troy. She's never asked me if I think he's alive or dead. Of course, the truth is that I don't know.

I'm pretty sure Troy drowned in that wintry sea, and the little boat overturned and sank to the rocky bottom. On bad days I imagine that he bled to death from the gunshot, and that I am therefore my own brother's killer.

But, I confess, sometimes when I go to the beach with a group of college friends, I wander away onto the rocks by myself. I end up staring out at the waves, fantasizing that Troy somehow survived and escaped. I imagine that he sailed off to his own little Tahiti, some strand of silver beach in Mexico or a thatched hut in Cuba. He's fishing for his dinner and drawing pictures of a pretty girl with long hair—sexy, frightening pictures, throbbing with all the sweetness and evil of life.

I always feel terribly guilty after this fantasy. God knows Troy deserved a watery grave and a very long stay in hell. But he was my only brother, after all. And the ocean waves roll endlessly, and the gulls screech overhead, and eventually I blink away the thoughts and turn back slowly toward the beach where my friends are laughing and flirting and tossing a football around in the safe and normal world that we all so desperately crave.